Sleeping Giant

Sleeping Giant

A Novel by

Judy R. Smith

Stephen F. Austin State University Press
Nacogdoches, Texas

For information address:
Stephen F. Austin State University
1936 North Street, LAN 203
Nacogdoches, TX 75962

sfapress@sfasu.edu

Book and Cover Design by Russell K. Allen
Cover Art from Public Domain

LIBRARY OF CONGRESS CATALOGING-IN-PUBLICATION DATA

Smith, Judy R.
Sleeping Giant/Judy R. Smith—1st ed.
p.cm

ISBN 978-1-62288-097-3

I. Title

First Edition: 2015

For those buried but not silenced

There is blight on the side of the Giant, close to his belly. This Giant lay down centuries ago. Two miles long, he lies sleeping. No one knows how the Sleeping Giant came to be. Some say that a great, ancient Indian chief ate too many oysters and fell into a stuperous sleep. Others say the Sleeping Giant is Hobbomock, an evil spirit who stamped his foot into the Connecticut River, forever disrupting its course. To save the world from further mischief, Kietan, a good spirit, threw a spell over Hobbomock, a spell strong enough to last beyond time. Hobbomock sleeps, reminding us a price must always be paid. Don't believe either legend. They are not strong enough to capture Giant's truth.

The Giant's chin is nearly one hundred feet high— a cliff steep and sheer, trap rock. Many climbers have fallen to their death from his chin. Like so much spittle. On his side, near his belly, is a four-story stone lookout post, resembling a medieval fortress. The watch tower has a spider web window, facing east. Keep watch on the web. Its lines intersect, crisscross your sight. The Giant is covered with black birch, hemlock, chestnut groves. The chestnuts have blight, have always had blight. The hemlocks now are dying, in spotty patches. There's a gap in his side— a sickly, brown blotch. When you are in the center of the hemlock woods, you see only a few dead trees at the top. But when you leave the mountain, cross the road, and look back, the diseased hole hits your eyes hard. Stops you dead in your tracks.

No blight ever stopped John Dickerson, of course. Never was a Sleeping Giant to him. "Just a damned dead Indian," is what he said.

"Not dead, John. Just sleeping," is what Giant snapped into John's deaf ear.

Chief Montowese—now what would he say? He's infamous, you know. Traded Sleeping Giant to Theophilus Eaton for eleven bolts of cloth and a coat. Those are the bare facts. But don't trust bare facts; they never tell the story. Eaton got the mountain. The blight is eating away its green covering, its green coat. Records don't show what kind of cloth, what sort of coat. Somebody, somewhere must know. Things like that just don't disappear without a trace.

When you are on the Giant you can hear water underneath. Even in winter. There must be springs deep within, hidden from sight. Part of the trap rock. Water trapped underneath. Springs everywhere, running. Water trapped in rock. The sound of that—the way it trickles over your tongue at the start, the way it stops dead, tripped up on rock.

The Giant's hip is slippery. Covered with great stands of white and red oaks at its crest, in its shallows are dense stands of mountain laurel. Always evergreen. Even in coldest winter when the leaves curl in upon themselves, contract from three inches wide to a roll less than a third of that size. Even tightly curled, they shiver. But they remain, blooming every June. Rolled tight within themselves, they hang on. Not far from the laurel grove you can find Dutchman's breeches and trout lilies. Long ago you didn't even have to look for them. Now you have to go off the trail, hunt for the small patches of blooms in spring. Trout lilies join water and earth. Dutchman's breeches—well, maybe this new land ripped off the Dutch traders' breeches. Giant undressed them, left them naked, using their cloth to clothe his own side.

Some say ghosts dance on his face, others swear a ghost dance will be done on his chin. But there is blight on the side of giant, close to his belly. Legend says that if it reaches his gut, he will let forth a belch so terrible, earth will tremble. Roads will collapse, cities will fall. Rivers will change course. Some say that when this happens, this earth will become again what it once was.

Know this:

A copperhead has woven itself into the spider web window in the watch tower.

A white egret rises every morning from the pond-mist at giant's feet.

Grace Yellowbird Faith is inside the belly of the giant beast, controlling the frogs.

Two yellow birds, strong of voice and stout of heart, are inside the giant's belly, controlling the frogs.

Legend swears that his chin will dance. Legend also says that long ago the giant reached up to catch yellow bird, to crush his wing bones, to squeeze him to death, just because giant could. Yellow bird sank his beak into giant's thumb, twisted his bird body into a circular cyclone, bored a hole through giant's thumb. Giant opened his fist; out flew yellow bird. Giant held up his thumb, looked through its gaping hole. As he did so, a legion of yellow birds descended from a rent in the sky. They pecked his head with such force that he bled from a thousand holes. Emptied of blood, he fell on his back, turned to stone.

Giant sleeps, a stony shell. Gathering inside him, frogs, yellow and green, in water, rushing.

1638

Chief Montowese loves his wife Spotted Lily. He calls her Water-That-Rushes-Gently because he loves the sound of the water as it rushes over the stones in the creek bed. He often sits there, thinking, planning, deciding. Only when the sun glints around his ankles does he realize that the day is past. He rushes home to her, eager for her embrace. She is a powerful woman, powerful and kind. He feels safe with her. He finds comfort in her. Finds comfort that she does not take too much pride in her birthing magic.

They have eleven children. Three sets of triplets, one set of twins. She first bears three boys, then three girls. The third birth brings two boys and one girl; the twins are one girl and one boy. Sometimes she hopes that if she births again, it will be to one girl so the boys and girls will be in perfect balance. When her time comes, she wants to be near the top of giant so she can feel the strength of his massive neck, his great chin. He'll hold me up, she thinks. He has rock strength to give. From his head you can see the whole earth. From atop his face, her feet can plant themselves firmly on solid trap rock ledge.

She is ill, suddenly and terribly. There is no time to get her to the top of the giant sleeping; she must remain at his feet where they have made their camp. The cold seizes her with terrific force. Her whole body shakes. Her fingernails tear into Montowese's arms as he holds her. Fever high, drenched in sweat, she shivers so badly the ground beneath her shakes. He will not leave her side. She cries for more blankets though she is covered with so many that he worries she will perish under their weight. But they do not relieve the fierce cold that has taken hold of her. She begs her husband to help, begs him to warm her. The desperation in her voice shakes him.

He knows where Eaton camps. Taking the most direct path, Montowese travels, repeating the terms of the contract Eaton offers. Montowese cares little for the eleven bolts of cloth, pretty as they are. "But it is strange that there are eleven," he says aloud. "One for each of my children." An odd balance, he thinks. When he arrives, he is sweating, his muscles tense and tired, his legs aching.

He wastes no time. Eaton has a paper with many signs and symbols inscribed on its face. Eaton promises the tribe will not have to leave the sleeping giant until her birthing is well past. Montowese nods, barely able to wait for Eaton to take off the great coat made from a fur that Montowese has never seen, never touched before. Dense, deep, so dense and so deep your fingers are not long enough to reach through to the hide. The head of some great beast forms a giant hood that hangs at the back. With two hands you can bring it forward, surrounding your face with its warmth. Its eyes rest on the top of your head; your head fills the space where its mouth was. Its mouth now open, incomplete— the lower jaw has been cut away. Its teeth hang over your eyes. Around each great arm cuff runs a front foot of the beast. Its tail hangs the length of the coat, from your neck to your ankles. Eaton swears that there is no cold so fierce that the beast-coat cannot tame it.

Montowese rushes back, arrives, panting, sore, weighed down by the sheer bulk of the beast-coat he bears. He kneels at his wife's side, pulls off all the blankets that cannot keep her warm. Lifts her up, tugs beast-coat under her, pulls the giant hood over her head, lays beast-coat over her, tail crossing the middle of her belly, the tail lying between her feet. Water-That-Rushes-Gently sighs a deep, comfortable, exhausted sigh. She smiles. Her shivers cease; her body eases. Holding her belly with one hand, she reaches for her husband with the other. She needs to sleep. He starts to lie beside her. She reaches out her arm, hand extended. He leans down, kisses her. His heart wants to stay; his feet make him leave.

His brother waits outside. He wants to know about the great beast-coat in which Water-That-Rushes-Gently lies sleeping. Montowese asks his brother to walk with him, around the feet of the giant that sleeps. As they walk, Montowese reveals that their tribe will be leaving the sleeping giant soon. His brother, Bear Claw, is angry, sad, yet he understands. Knows he would have done the same thing.

"But where are the great bolts of cloth?" he wonders.

"They will be brought to us tomorrow," Montowese confides. "A driver with a long cart will bring them to the giant's feet before sun disappears tomorrow. They gave us their word."

And their word was kept. The great bolts of cloth now lie at the feet of the sleeping giant; Water-That-Rushes-Gently still lies beneath the great beast-coat.

As the week passes, she gains strength, is warm. She urges him to leave, to hunt. She is fine, she assures him. It is not time, she says. He believes; he leaves.

He is gone only a few hours, returning with many squirrels. He gives his meat to his wife's sister. She hurries off, eager.

Even before he pulls back the flap, the smell of old beast blood stops his hand. Water-That-Rushes-Gently has put herself into a kneeling position. The beast-coat eyes are on top of her head, its teeth in front of her eyes. At her wrists, its feet dance. Montowese rushes over to her, stricken with awe. She is dead and yet she kneels. He opens the front of the coat. He cannot turn his eyes from what he sees. She has given birth to four babies. He is sure three of them were already dead; they are still in their sacs. Needing to know, he rips open their sacs: two boys and one girl. He is afraid to touch the last. The cord has been bitten clean; this girl child must have been alive. Around her throat, the beast-coat's tail. Montowese runs his hands up the tail. His fingers freeze as they find the tail wound tight around his wife's neck. A tail-cord, binding, strangling mother and daughter.

Montowese yells so deeply and strongly that boulders fall from giant's sleeping feet. Small rocks rush down the mountain side, splintering as they descend. The echo of their plummeting deafens Montowese. He cannot hear his own grief as it shapes itself into growing circles of beastly roars.

When his brother rushes in, his jaw falls opens as he drops to his knees. Montowese lays prostrate before the eyes of the coat-beast. In his outstretched arms, his daughter, freed from the beast's tail. Water-That-Rushes-Gently has fallen over, on her side, with three dead children at her belly, the coat-beast's tail knotted firmly around her neck. As Bear Claw rips the knotted tail from her throat, he hears a strange roar on top of sleeping giant, shaking the earth, making the water inside the earth rush so loudly it almost deafens them.

Bear Claw saw a frog emerge from the side of Water-That-Rushes-Gently. A strange frog, yellow and green. Big eyes. Big belly. Long, sharp claws.

Montowese is inconsolable. There are so few of them left. Just ten men and their wives and children. So it does not matter that he sold the giant; they could not have defended him anyway. Yet he cannot throw off his deep sense of guilt. It can be no accident. There must have been an evil spirit living in that coat-beast. Water-That-Rushes-Gently knew how to birth safely; she could have delivered without peril. He did not think the white man had such powers but he must have been wrong. He sits, sobs, feeling his dead babies in his hands. He buries his head in his open hands. They smell of beastly death. He does not lift his face. The smell has stained the air he breathes.

Revenge is the only way. He must find Eaton, make him pay. But what keeps gnawing at Montowese is why the coat never hurt Eaton. How can it protect one person and kill another? Does it choose according to race? He looks to the sky; turns to the north, the east, the south, the west, hoping for an answer. All is silent; all is blank. He tries harder. He closes his eyes, chants, at first softly and then more loudly, trying to empty himself. He is not successful. He hears nothing; he sees nothing. No sustaining vision is his.

He begins to ascend the giant. At the top Montowese will be able to see all the land for many miles around. He can easily see the outline of Eaton's camp far in the distance. There are wood buildings there now, staked into the earth. He spends time trying to decide what to do. He cannot make up his mind; he keeps ascending, hoping it will become clear. He does not realize that he has been so slow. It is almost dusk when he reaches the top of the giant's belly. He feels no need to move west, toward the head. He sits, cross-legged, on a bed of hemlock needles, in despair, unequal to the coat-beast's magic.

"Some chief," he upbraids himself, aloud, thinking no one can hear. "You bring death to your people and don't even have the heart for revenge."

He sobs, makes a fist, pounds the earth at his side. His shoulders shrug slowly, heavily. We are too few, he thinks. "Even if we banded together with the Quinnipiac," he argues aloud, "we would only be about one hundred and fifty men." He pulls his knees to his chest. "We are too few," he yells, "we are too weak and too few." His voice has no echo. He gets up, about to make his way down the mountain. It does not matter that it is dark; he knows this rock land, knows exactly where to place his feet.

A strange peace descends. The moon is full, casting much light. Bats cross above, owls hoot in the distance. Oddly, he is not afraid of cougar, of bear. He has faith this night—they will not cross his path. They are not hungry for him this night; they have filled their bellies with other meat. He has reached the bottom of the giant's feet. He pauses, looks back upward, feeling great love for the giant sleeping man. Deeply sad that he is not strong enough to guard him, he prays that the giant can protect himself.

He turns again, looks upward for a moment. All is silent, save for the soft crackling of leaves underfoot. He is passing the pond at the giant's base. Thinking nothing, he hums softly an old song his mother sang many years ago.

> *The oysters are fat*
> *The oysters are full*
>
> *Crack open our shells they cry*
> *Pry apart our lips*
> *Set free our pearls*
>
> *So crack we will*
> *Opening wide*
> *Fat full oyster lips*
>
> *Into a pit fiery with rocks*
> *Full fat oysters steam*
> *Meat juicy and dripping*
> *Fills the air*
>
> *In a huge pile oyster shells*
> *Glow translucent in the sun*
> *Hurry child, run fast and swift*
> *Turn your eagle eye to the gleaming pile*
> *See the earth's colors shine.*

He is surprised that he remembers the words so easily. Suddenly a bright light covers everything. A wide, black, hard curling tail cuts the pond in half. He looks west where another long, black, hard thing cuts to the west of the giant's head. He hears terrible noise, sees pieces of giant explode, shatter, cascade downward. He covers his eyes. When he reopens them, the giant's face is pock marked, maimed. The noise grows greater, deafening. Sure that his head will explode, he fears for his mind. Suddenly the bright light withdraws; in its place darkness, illuminated by full moon. Montowese lets go fear, falling into a deep peace. The pond will be cut in half. The egret will not have the space to run before it lifts its great wings. It is no matter. The great white bird will just build stronger wings to lift itself vertically into the sky.

Montowese begins to ascend again, realizing with surprise that his pace is very fast, that he is not tired. He knows he must look again at the earth from the top ridge of the giant's sleeping body. He hears water deep underneath, hears the low wail of a strange beast overhead. Many springs appear and trickle down over the rock ledges. Tiny frogs have emerged. Many times he has said to himself, out loud, "Little trickle ponds, not six inches deep. Yet they house a whole little frog race. Tiny frog voices, insistent all the same." He doesn't like to think about what happens to the frogs when the little trickle streams dry up. He tries to empty himself again.

He finds himself on the highest trap rock ridge atop the giant's belly. The sun is rising. Morning dew makes giant's rock face slippery. It is no matter. Montowese is sure of foot; he knows his ground. Limber, quick, he scales the giant's sides, pauses, looks afar. Camps encircle the giant, ever closer to his feet. The birds change: night birds retire, making room for day birds, sharing sky space without quarrel. So too the forest folk. From the first time, they know who is night and who is day. Without quarrel. With perfect balance. With perfect balance, Montowese reascends the peak. Stands there, legs spread wide apart, arms outstretched, palms upward. An eagle screeches by, a red-tail hawk circles overhead. Montowese edges his feet another inch apart, stretches his hands wider, opening further the space between his fingers. He brings one hand over his face, looking out at the world through the spaces between his webbed fingers. Leaning backward, he lets his hands touch the earth behind him, his belly arched to the sky. He lifts his great legs, pulls them over himself, backward, plants his feet on the earth, stands. As he pulls himself upright, a strange rumbling can be heard deep within the giant's belly. Like two trap rock plates shifting, pulling apart, sealing back together. Just as his feet touch the earth and his legs pull him upright, he disappears from sight.

His nation heard the strange rumbling. They searched every inch of the giant. Not once, but many times. "Without a trace," they repeat, in disbelief. "No track, anywhere. No trace."

1735

They have heard many legends about grandfather Montowese, the great Chief who disappeared into the mountain. Every spring they gather near the foot of the giant and hear the story told and retold. But Red Hawk's Tail does not believe it. Just another old Indian story made up to ease the shame. It's nonsense that there's a world inside the giant. "Listen to the water inside," they urge, as if that proves anything. "Just because it's wet doesn't mean it's anything," he shoots back. He does not believe. The giant's just rock, inside and out. Just plain rock, that's all.

Because if there was something inside then it would have come out by now, that's what he thinks. Almost a hundred years since he left. Even if he was in there, it wouldn't matter because he'd have to be dead by now. Was a grown man when he disappeared. Maybe just ran off. His brother whispered something about a coat. Didn't make much sense. Most things don't make sense anymore.

Only a few Indians remain. Even fewer full bloods remain. Red Hawk's Tail is full-blood but he takes no pride in that. All he knows is that the face of the earth is changing. He does not like its new look even though he is making its new face.

They are making a trail through the west side of the giant, wide enough for horses and wagons to pass. It has taken over a year— hundreds of them, brothers, sons, grandsons. They hack slowly, deliberately, through dense stands of pine, oak, hemlock. He smells the mountain laurel, inhaling its sweet, hearty perfume. And then he cuts it off flush with the earth, tossing it aside into a growing heap of severed branches. He does not care. If it is not his hands that whack the earth there are others that will. It might as well be him. Payment, he guesses, for the mountain his grandfather traded.

If the laurel cried, he would not have heard it. He has closed his ears. Look here, Red Hawk's Tail, he tells himself. There's only a few of you, there are lots of them. They have money, power, land. Make yourself useful to them: feed your family, make no war. He shrugs his shoulders, trying hard to make this his faith.

But he wakes at night. He knows the laurel has cried out. But he closes his ears again, this time shuts them harder.

He worries about his sons and the sons they will have. He sees them looking at the English women. His people are scattered. Already there are too few Mattabeseck women for wives. He is ashamed when he catches himself looking at the English women, the way they walk. The fullness of their skirts. Their bodies dressed cannot look like their bodies undressed. This bothers him. This disturbs him. This excites him.

But he is an old man. He need not worry. These feelings will pass from him. But his sons, his grandsons. How long will they keep from those English skirts?

Then it strikes him. His daughters, his granddaughters. Do they notice the English men, with their great boots and cut jackets? Do they watch them walk? Are they disturbed by their desire?

He closes his ears to the sound of his own questioning voice. It is better not to think of these things. It is better not to see the times to come.

So he hacks away, felling trees, ripping roots from earth. It is better this way. He is helping to recreate the giant, giving him a new body, a new face.

He does not care what anyone says. Strange sounds do not come from his belly. He is dead inside, just rock. Trap rock, hard, dense. Dead, dense, dark rock.

1792

Red-Tail's grandfather warned him over and over that he carries a name on his back. He sees him looking at the white women. "Find a good Indian girl," grandfather urges, his voice unconvincing, weak. Red-Tail doesn't believe what he says. Why should he listen to an old man who doesn't even listen to himself? An old man who pretends to be so powerful, not afraid even to doubt the legends of the great grandfathers. But Red-Tail has seen him trembling, near tears, as he looks up at the giant. Crazy old man, he says to himself. What does he know anyway? He never leaves the base of the mountain. He never goes into town. He doesn't know.

Red-Tail rides into Mount Carmel, and beyond. Swift, rushing like the wind, safe from their guns. He rides; he sees; he knows.

"Red-Tail," he says, grabbing his arm. "Leave it well enough alone."

A lucky guess, he thinks. How could his grandfather have known that he plans to ride tonight?

"Red-Tail," he repeats. "No good can come of it."

He shrugs his shoulders. "Do not worry. I am not out for trouble," he assures. His voice is puny, hollow.

He sighs deeply. "Remember Chief Montowese. People say that when he was with the English, he brought back some fierce, ugly, evil thing. He didn't intend to, but he did."

"Thought you didn't believe any of those old stories," Red-Tail sneers.

His grandfather looks profoundly sad. He shakes his head, giving up. "Don't have to believe in them to worry that they have something to say."

Red-Tail wears his best beaded vest. His mother wove into its back the design of the spider, in rich reds and blues and yellows. When he walks, his legs gather the power of the sun and the moon; when he dances, his feet trace the patterns of the stars on the earth. When you look at his back, you look through the webbed bars of the stars. Look through his back and you see the design of the sky. He has told Elizabeth this before. He will tell her again tonight. As she runs her fingers over his beaded back, they will ply the spider's silky design. They will catch; he will hold tight.

They meet on the giant's hip where they can see all of Mount Carmel and beyond. Her father has built a house across from the giant. It is an English house. It does not fit the land on which it sits. Elizabeth taunts him when he says that. She says it is an American house. She says to remember that the war is over and that we have won. "We are free, silly," she laughs, "free to build American houses."

He does not know if he is included in her "we" but he does not ask.

They are together every night. She tells her father, John Dickerson, that she is going out for a walk. He has no fear. There are no Indians who would dare. Her full skirts cover her legs, keeping her safe within a wealthy fabric circle.

When she tells Red-Tail that she is pregnant she refuses his embrace. She cries, hangs her head, tells him that her father has called her the whore of Babylon. The sound of it hurling from his mouth assaults her; the sound of it curling his upper lip makes her laugh defiantly. They part. She promises to send him a sign, to let him know when the child is born. Red-Tail wonders what her father would call her if he knew that the child's father is an Indian. He wonders what will be the color of its hair, its eyes, its skin.

The child is a girl. Blonde-haired, blue eyed, fair-skinned. Her grandfather names her Grace. Elizabeth keeps her own Bible, one separate from her father's family Bible. He has written *Grace Dickerson* and the date: *October 10, 1792.* He has relented. He will not turn her out. He says it is God's design to send him a sinful child, a bastard grandchild. He will make an example of her, turning her to the Lord, raising her child as a God-fearing Christian. He forbids her to leave the house, vowing to post guards. Elizabeth makes no protest. She asks her father if she may begin to preach to the Indians who are building the road through the west side of the giant's head. Reading the note she holds in her hand, he approves her missionary impulse, believing God is working in magical ways.

The note is given to Red-Tail's grandfather. He cannot read the two words on the small page. He sends it to his grandson. Red-Tail opens the note, beams. *Have Grace* is all it says.

Her Bible has a lock on its cover. She keeps the only key. In it she has written this:

October 10, 1792. Born to me a daughter, Grace Red-Tail Dickerson.

But look closer. There is deep black line through the middle of Grace. It must have been a steady hand; the line is perfectly balanced. Over crossed-out Grace, in bold script, **Babylonia.**

Red-Tail wants to see his daughter. He decides to ride fast as the wind by their house. He knows which window is hers. He prays that she will be in her room, that she will lift Grace to the glass. He puts on his beaded vest, vowing to ride harder and faster than ever before. A candle lights her room. He sweeps by, leaning off his horse, peering into the glass. Elizabeth sees him, jumps up with the baby in her arms, holding Babylonia Grace out toward him. Red-Tail pulls the horse to a dead stop, backs up, descends. Touching his hands to the glass, he presses his lips to the thick, wavy, bubbly glass. Jumps back on his horse, rears its head around, races away.

She closes her ears to the sound. She watches, frozen, as he falls from the side of his horse. A huge blotch covers the beaded design as blood erases the design of the spider. Clutching Grace Red-Tail Dickerson to her breast, Elizabeth vows revenge. "Babylonia," she whispers, "Have Grace."

Babylonia Grace Red-Tail Dickerson loves to hear about the boy with the many-colored coats and his many dreams. Of great sheaves in the field that he and his brothers are gathering. How the one Joseph has gathered rises, stands upright. Then the sheaves his brothers have gathered bow down to his. Then he dreams that the sun, the moon, and eleven stars bow down to him. How this made his brothers very jealous, how they plotted against him, taking his coat, casting him into a great pit, dark, with no water. Then they sold him into slavery. But Great Father, God, saved him. How Joseph forgave his brothers. How before he died he told his sons that God will visit them. Babylonia always wants to know if Joseph danced. Her mother always says, "No child. Joseph did not dance." John Dickerson always nods his head in stern, loving approval.

But Babylonia Grace Red-Tail Dickerson has a favorite story. It is the one that makes her grandfather leave the room, wondering where his daughter could have heard such heathen rubbish. He has posted guards; she does not go out alone. He has lectured her, made her read the Bible at sunrise, at noon, at dusk. Made her kneel before him, head bowed. Has beaten her when she resisted. But he has failed. She will whisper it to her child anyway, so he decided just to leave them be. He is getting old; he has not the strength to fight her visions. So Elizabeth must tell her daughter's favorite story many, many times. It is about Tailfeather, a great Algonquin mother. Everyone knows the simple outline. When she and her sons were surprised by the enemy, she was quick enough to escape to the cover of the tall grass. Her sons are slow; they are murdered before her eyes. She has a great vision of a sacred drum, filled with water, with tones so deep and pure they call the spirits. In her vision, the sacred drum is made to sing a song so powerful that the enemy is frozen, helpless. If the drum sings under the first moon, the enemy falls dead to the ground.

It is the embellishments that Babylonia loves. Every day her mother weaves a new story at the center of the old one. This is Babylonia's favorite. Her mother holds her on her lap, begins:

"Long ago, before the pale people came, Tailfeather was married to

Thunderbird, the most handsome and strong and brave chief ever known. Fair, kind, unafraid, proud. He loved Tailfeather, gave her beautiful jewels he dug and crafted by hand. He scraped the inside of oyster shells, making shimmering shapes that caught all the colors of the rainbow. He opened quartz rock, picked the most deeply colored of its veins, fitted it into the outline of a great bird made of copper. Thunderbird was proud of his wife. Of the sons and daughters she bore him. Of the lustrous sheen of her hair. Of her fine, long, strong fingers. Of her strong, even, white teeth.

Every first moon meant a gathering, a communal feast. In full dress, Thunderbird would wear his long flaming red and yellow headdress, a headdress so long and full it swept the ground and created a whirlwind as he moved in circles. Tailfeather would wear her best red feathers, fresh from a red-tailed hawk. In the center of them, in the middle of her blue-beaded headband, she would fix a small circle of quartz or copper. Catching the light, it gleamed; catching Thunderbird's colors, it reflected and refracted them. Babylonia, my dear little one, you have to imagine the brightest colors in the world in a whizzing circle going round so fast they became a blurring whirl. Then you'd know how bright and strong the first moon dancers were."

As always, Elizabeth would pick up her daughter, hold her by the hands, and whirl her around and around, faster and faster. Babylonia would squeal, beg faster, faster, faster. Her mother whispers in her ear, "Joseph danced, child. Like a rainbow in a whirlwind, Joseph danced."

Breath caught, Elizabeth continues: "When the dance was done, all feasted. Oysters fat and juicy. Plenty of deer meat. Cakes, too. At the end of the festival, Thunderbird would stand, lift his palms to the sky, roaring like thunder. Then he would approach Tailfeather, kiss her quartz or copper tail-eye, take her hand, and begin the long walk home, their children at their sides.

One first moon, though, Thunderbird sent the tribe's women and children ahead, staying behind to hold an urgent council with other men. The oysters were becoming scarce; someone had sighted a large ship, with many men, taking many large baskets. They talk, deciding to keep careful watch. Every day, one of them will go to the top of the giant, look to the sea, see what shapes are on the shore. They are not afraid. Some believe the oysters can restore themselves; others say that there must be legions more oysters under the beds that are so easily dug. Down deep, whole undiscovered colonies of them, just waiting to be taken.

Tailfeather decides to take her children and leave the group of women and children making their way home. Since the children have been very good, she decides to take them toward the giant's feet, to the ponds that almost touch his toes. It is nearing dusk. She hopes they see a great egret fly from the sky back to its pond nest, hopes they hear the deep croaks coming up from under the lily pads. Perhaps even see the other great white birds that swim the pond's perimeter. The men will talk for hours. She and the children have plenty of time.

Singing, the children are skipping. Suddenly the enemy appears. Tailfeather holds her ground. They go after her son. She beats the enemy's back; he throws her off, hurling her to the ground. She gets up, screaming, growling, throws herself at the back of another. She bites his ear; he hurls her into the air. As she falls to the ground, her leg almost snaps. She pulls herself toward an enemy leg; her teeth take hold. He shakes his leg loose, breaking her teeth. The enemy kills all but one daughter. Her mother watches as her dark-eyed daughter recedes into the trail at the base of the mountain.

The men have also started home. Thunderbird hears a noise in the distance. Knowing where to go, he rushes toward the pond, toward his slain children, his battered wife. He howls; he screams. But he has no time for grief. One daughter is missing. Thunderbird is sure of the trail they have taken.

He sees the enemy ahead. He prays for the great Thunderbird spirit to direct his hand. No match for the power of his wing-arms, his talon-feet, Thunderbird Man overtakes his enemy swiftly. Beak broad and strong, he swoops down, ripping off the head of the one holding his daughter. Raising his mighty wing-arms, he knocks the whole party from its horses. His mighty talon-feet crush each enemy as he lies cowering on the ground. His mighty wing-arms scoop and cradle his daughter, carrying her back to her mother. He hopes he is in time; he fears that Tailfeather may die.

Tailfeather is weak but she is far from death. She has heard a great drum, a sacred drum filled with water. Thunderbird must carry it around his neck, must dance to the music of the water drum. Thunderbird agrees, eagerly, asking its location. Tailfeather has seen this: a frog, yellow and green with red spots, on a green pad, next to a white flower, pointing his sharp, bony claw-finger at a rock. So she tells Thunderbird that it lies at the edge of the pond. The frogs may reveal its hiding place.

He rushes to the pond edge, arriving just as the great white egret descends to its resting place. A great croak startles him. Thunderbird asks if Frog is present, if Frog will speak to him. Thunderbird fears; Frog is known for his anger. But Thunderbird need not fear. Indeed, Frog is very, very angry; it is true that Frog can be vengeful. But Frog holds no hatred for Thunderbird. Frog speaks, pointing to a rock at the edge of the pond. At its back, a sacred drum, decorated with quartz and copper cut into the shapes of the sun, the moon, the stars.

Placing the leather strap around his neck, Thunderbird begins to tap the drum. His hands seem not his own, playing a song he has never heard. He empties himself to whatever great spirit is inside the drum, letting its voice emerge, letting its sound fill the space of his dancing. A great bird flies from the pond to the top of the giant's belly. The hemlock forest bends over from the force of its wings. It stomps its foot; the giant's belly opens. The great bird disappears. Thunderbird falls into a trance. When he awakens, he is alone. Frog is gone. The drum has disappeared.

He rushes back to Tailfeather whose body has healed itself. She is sitting, cross-legged; her daughter also sits cross-legged, in Tailfeather's lap. When she sees Thunderbird, she smiles a wide and happy smile, showing teeth strong, even and white as she strokes her daughter's hair. But Tailfeather also wears a dark and heavy heart, full of empty son space.

They are silent all the way home. They sleep. She dreams his vision; he dreams hers. They confide to each other what they have seen in their dreams. Excited, afraid, they vow to tell their stories at the next first moon ceremony. At the next moon ceremony they will give their daughter another name."

Babylonia always leaps from her mother's lap, jumps up and down, begging to hear the new name. Her mother always smiles, strokes her daughter's hair, never saying it.

When Babylonia is twenty, she will tell this same story to her daughter, Grace Trap-Ridge Hitchcock. Unlike Elizabeth, however, Babylonia will tell the name. Frog Bird will have her day.

The only thing Babylonia knows about her father is that he rode like the wind. Fast, tall, proud, strong. In a vest of many colors, he rode like the wind. Like a rainbow in a whirlwind, she thinks. This, too, she will tell her daughter.

But what she will not tell her daughter is her vision: that she can see not so much her father shot, falling from his horse but that she can see her mother. Filled with both grief and grin, her mother's face was at war with itself. Babylonia never could tell which grew larger.

She will not tell her daughter that when she married she came to realize that grief and grin were equal. Seeing him seeing her, she stared back at Sanford, fascinated that, though a young man, his hair was two-thirds white. When she told him about her father, Sanford growled. Deep down he refused to believe her. He dismissed it as a foolish fantasy. Even deeper down, he was fascinated by the young Indian man kissing the window, vest flowing, then a bloody fall from his horse. Even deeper down, buried beyond his knowing, he was fascinated by the issue of Indian loins. He couldn't wait to wed it.

On their wedding night, just as he was about to ejaculate, he heard a tomahawk whiz by his head. Brain shaken, he let forth such a stream of semen it sprayed back out of her vagina, splattering his thighs, almost cementing them together in sticky, warm wet. For a split second Babylonia felt herself fill with a thousand arrows, feathers at their tips. Laughing, she moaned, digging her nails into Sanford's back. He rolled away, crying, afraid of his drawn blood.

1842

Grace Trap-Ridge Hitchcock asks her mother how it came to be that the great giant is on his back, sleeping. Her mother tells her that the giant is Hobbomock. Long ago, he stomped over all the land, doing mischief. Carved great steps into another mountain not far from where he sleeps. Some say he made the rivers change the way they run. Babylonia says "Your father's father once said that it was the great thunderbirds that put Hobbomock to sleep."

"Why? What did he do that was so bad?" Grace needs to know.

"Nobody knows," her mother replies. "Or at least nobody has said."

Grace is bothered by this. Something tells her that the story has not been told. Someday, she thinks, we'll find out what he did.

They live less than a mile from the giant's feet. Spending all the time she can on the mountain, she knows his chest, his face, his neck as well as she knows her own. She wears men's clothes: wool trousers, great heavy boots. She hunts; she climbs. She is large, almost six feet tall. Strong, muscular arms, powerful legs. Her father is outraged.

"It's that damned Indian blood in you," Sanford Hitchcock sneers.

Grace does not answer. Her mother smiles from the corner of the room.

"A damned squaw," he quips. "My own daughter, half-wild," he laments. "You don't even look like a woman," he cries. This is what he doesn't say out loud: almost thirty years old, and not married. Something's strange.

Her father works in the mill. He is ashamed of his daughter. The men taunt him. Accuse him of producing a freak. Part-man, part woman, part Indian. Damned freak. Ought to be in an exhibition or something, they holler.

He fears they are right. He curses his loins for producing such a strange and shameful being. Her eyes are so dark they are almost black. But her hair is light golden yellow, thicker than any English hair he has ever seen. The contrast unnerves him. So, too, the deep red tint of her skin. Too many colors, he thinks. Too many, he frets.

Babylonia is proud of her daughter. Proud of her strength, of her many colors. She whispers, smiling, to her daughter, "He's right. That beautiful, damned Indian blood in you. That beautiful Indian blood in you, damned it." Grace holds her mother's arm, flashes a wickedly fierce grin.

When Grace kills a deer, she uses a bow and arrow. Shoots it straight through the heart. When Sanford kills a deer, he uses a rifle. When he pulls the trigger, foul smoke envelopes him. Grace takes what meat she can eat, gives the rest away, leaving a small treat for the beasts of the mountain. Sanford kicks the dead deer, leaves its carcass whole. If it is a good male deer, with a fine rack of antlers, he takes its head, dries and stuffs it, mounts it on an oak board, hangs it high on the wall.

For years Sanford taunted his daughter. Would steal her underclothes, hang them on the deer's antlers. A severed beast head, looking straight ahead in the air, mounted on a varnished oak board, with clothes hanging from its antler tips: this is what greeted Grace every day. When she was little she'd rage, impotent, unable to reach her undergarments, even standing on a chair. Her father would laugh, a harsh, brutal sort of laugh. Her mother would try to intervene.

"Now Sanford, stop this. It is cruel."

"So what?" Sanford quipped. "She's my daughter. I'm just teaching her how to climb."

Babylonia had long ago decided that she had to choose carefully when really to fight her husband, had long ago decided that this deer head hanging was not her fight.

Grace overheard, decided she would teach herself how to climb. That's when she started going to the mountain. Day after day, no matter how cold, she'd start up the ridge. Even her mother was angry; Grace ruined a pair of gloves in two days. So Grace left off the gloves. Her hands, sometimes raw and bloody, developed strong calluses. Her mother smiled, kissed her daughter's callused palms. Whispered to her: "Climb hard, daughter. Hold tight. Giant won't let you fall." So Grace would climb. Even on the sheer, almost vertical ledges, she knew just where to plant her toe, just how to twist and heave her other leg upward. The higher she went, the stronger she became. She could hear the water from deep within, underneath her. Sometimes she imagined that she could hear strange voices, strange singing voices from deep within the giant's belly. She was not afraid. She was at home here, on the belly of the giant.

It did not take long. When she was tall enough and strong enough to climb high enough to recapture her nether garments, their war started in earnest. "Have Grace," he says out loud. He is taken aback; he thinks how strange. A curious phrase, indeed.

The next morning the deer's antlers hang no clothes. In its mouth is stuck a note, sealed in an envelope. On its cover: *To Grace, if she dares.*

Grace dares. She hops into the air from the chair. Only seven, she flies with ease toward the beheaded buck who watches over nothing at least eight feet from the floor. With graceful ease, she snaps the letter from its mouth. Lands quietly upright, turns, faces her father as she opens the envelope. In it one word: *Squaw*. In it one drawing: A woman falling off a giant.

Sanford crosses his arms, stands firm, waits for his daughter to cry. He is not prepared. Grace crosses her arms, stands firm. "Bastard," she spits.

The next morning the great beheaded buck has another envelope shoved in his dead mouth. On its cover, simply *Grace*. Once again, her small, powerful legs propel her through the air. Catching the envelope, she brings it with her to a soft landing on the floor. She turns to her father, looking him straight in the eye as she opens the envelope. In it one phrase, capitalized: *VENGEANCE IS MINE*. Sanford crosses his arms, stands firm, waits for his daughter to repent. Grace crosses her arms, stands firm. "Mine, too," she hisses.

The following morning there is yet another letter in the dead beast's mouth. Yet again, Grace sails through the air, landing with envelope in hand. Squaring off with her father, she opens the envelope. In it this: a drawing of a strange creature. Half woman, half beast. On its breast, the letter G. Sanford crosses his arms, stands firm, waits for his daughter to pray for her rescue. Grace crosses her arms, stands firm, stares. "Grace," she swears, "Goddamned Grace." To herself she whispers, "Grace, goddamned it." And again, "Goddamned it, Grace."

1852

Grace likes her middle name. Likes the hard, sharp sound of it. Trap-Ridge. It fits her. She knows her mother gave it to her but her mother will not tell her why. Her father hates it, says it has to have something to do with Indian nonsense. "What the hell kind of a name is that for a girl?" he's asked many times. Always accuses his wife. Says that she has given her daughter bad blood.

Babylonia just laughs, says probably so. Her acceptance drives him wild. He wants her to protest; he wants to fight.

Trap-Ridge. Now there's a hell of a good name, she says to herself. Giant's made of trap rock. His highest ridge is where she is set on going. "Then I'll be Trap-Ridge on trap rock ridge," she beams. Sometimes, when she dares, she reminds herself that traps open up, snap shut, hold you fast in jagged steel teeth. Or they wait for you—spring on you when you come around the blind. Today she dares. Her legs are as strong as steel.

Grace is getting dressed to go to the sleeping giant. It is a cold and snowy December day. She puts on her warm woolen coat, woolen trousers, heavy hunting boots. Thick leather gloves. She wears leather fingers these days; they do not shred against the rock the way her cloth ones did. And if they do, it is no matter. Her hands are hard with callus. If callus tears, it brings no blood. Her fingers are hard, long, strong, like steel. At her back, a pack. In it, rope, a knife, a blanket. The blanket is heavy wool, inscribed with a red and black design of a large bird with strong, outstretched wings. She needs no compass.

She sprints from the house, trots easily to the base of giant's feet. Into her pocket she has stuffed dried meat, some nuts, and an apple. Moving west, the sun rises at her back, bright, unclouded. It has little warmth. She turns north, ready to head up the giant's side. The sun falls on her right cheek, glares into her right eye. She turns her head away from the sun. She climbs slowly, easily.

Even in such cold, she hears the water from deep beneath. Rushing gently, a calming sound. Not cold, she thinks. Warm springs, she is sure. She's heard many legends about a race of beings living in the center of the mountain. She scoffs—just old myths, she laughs. The water rushes far beneath; she hears its song. Almost a lullaby, she laughs. If she listens long enough, she just might fall into a deep sleep. So she shuts her ears, climbs higher. The hemlock grows thicker; the sun reaches her now only in jagged spatters. With every step she crushes more hemlock leaves, releasing deep forest fragrance, evergreen and endless. She breathes deeply, inhaling the fragrant depth of winter-crisp, clean, pure mountain air. She sees a perfect jutting ledge, a fitting seat on which to rest. Looking over the valley beneath, she is just high enough to begin to see the shore to her southeast. She bites off a piece of dried meat, lets it slowly dissolve in her mouth, saving the nuts, the apple for later. She puts the rest of the meat back in her pocket, checks the ties on her boots, stands up, begins to ascend.

When she reaches the top of the ridge, the late afternoon sun sends only weak slants of light. The winter solstice is close. Grace thinks, suddenly, that it might be today. She smiles, certain that it's fitting that she reach the highest ledge on the giant's belly on the shortest day of the year. She eats her apple. It's the way she likes it: crisp, cold, not too sweet. Long storage has done it no harm. It has sharpened its taste. She does not hurry; she does not fear the night. Her feet can lead her down even without light. Grace sits, enjoying the rock coldness that seeps through her heavy wool trousers. After a while, the coldness seems almost warm. Long, strong, warm fingers underneath her, hold her up. Lying on her back, she gazes into the tops of the hemlock trees. There is a frog on every branch tip. Holding the hemlock tip in their front claw-hands, their back feet grasping the branch further down, the frogs sway back and forth, keeping time to some strange beat. The tallest hemlock has but one frog on it. A large frog, yellow-green, with deep red eyes, bends the tree almost to earth with each sway. Its hot breath moistens her neck. Hot and cold breezes fan her suddenly-naked breasts, her shirt, her pants now open at the seams. Between her toes, hemlock twigs, scratching, leaving fragrant blood in their tracks. A large circle of light appears overhead. As the great hemlock descends to earth, frog croaks in her ear. The circle of light closes, the hemlock returns upright into the air, frog disappears.

When Grace wakes, she is very hungry. She assumes she has fallen asleep; she is always hungry when she awakens. She reaches for the last of her meat. She devours the nuts. Satisfied, she stands. Sure-footed, she makes her way down the giant, powerful and beautiful and strong.

Grace grows large, her belly protruding bigger than a bull-frog's eyes, bigger than a bull-frog's swollen neck when he sings. Her mother wonders. Grace shakes her head no. She has not been with anyone. Babylonia believes her. When Grace leaves the room, Babylonia takes her Bible from the chest, takes the key from its secret place, opens it. It is the Bible her mother gave her. It is the Bible in which her mother renames her Babylonia. She now wonders what names she will write in this Bible. She wonders now if she will write any name at all in this book. She closes it, locks it, returns first the key to its place and then the Bible to its. It strikes her. "A goddamned virgin birth," she cackles, deliciously, irreverently.

Grace's labor is long, torturous. For days she struggles, pushes, writhes, falls exhausted on her pillow. She can stand it no more. She rises painfully from her bed, positions her strong legs wide apart, squats. She gives a great heave. Just as the head of her child begins to emerge, a thunderbolt lights the sky. A second thunderbolt, larger than the first, hits the house; a light brighter than any earthly light forms a halo around it. The house shakes. Sanford runs screaming from his open front door, asking for salvation, begging for grace. Babylonia stands amazed but unafraid. Grace holds her daughter in her arms, then sets her into the perfect cradle of her strong, squatted thighs. The baby cries out. She must have the lungs of a full-grown man, her cry is so loud, so long, so deep. This girl child is large, nearly ten pounds. This child is dark. Deep coal black eyes. Hair thick and long, like a new-born wolf. Skin so dark red it seems black.

Sanford rushes back in, declaring it a miracle that the house has not been set ablaze. He looks down at his still-squatting daughter, cradling her daughter on her knees. He sighs. He cannot be happy. But he is relieved. "At least it looks all one color," he whispers to himself. "Even if it be black, it is just one color."

Grace returns to bed, her suckling daughter at her side. Her mother sits, rocking, in the corner, humming an old lullaby. Her father goes to the front room. Yelling, he comes running into the room, an envelope in his hand.

"It was in the buck's mouth," he cries, amazed. "Out of nowhere, it just appeared," he marvels.

It is not an ordinary envelope. It is a leather pouch. Engraved on its front and back are flowers, trees, a running deer. In the lower right hand corner both front and back a tiny frog with red eyes. He gives it to Grace. She opens it, slowly, carefully, unafraid.

In it two words: *Frog Bird.*

So the child born the night of thunderbolts is known as Frog Bird. Her mother and her grandmother do not question the name. It seems fitting, that's all. What they do not know is that Sanford also keeps a hidden Bible, a hidden key. In it he writes:

September 25, 1853. Born, a girl child, Frog Bird.

But look closely, very closely. "*The chosen one, I fear. But chosen for what?*" has been blotted out, leaving a dark blue smudge on the page.

Grace leaves Frog Bird safely in her grandmother's arms. The giant is calling Grace. She cannot resist.

"Mother, it is very, very strange," she confides. "I keep hearing something deep inside me telling me to climb the giant's belly."

"Has this happened before?" her mother wonders.

"Not really," Grace says. "Sometimes I have had a great urge, a great desire to go to the mountain. But it was not like this."

"How is it different?" Babylonia wants to know.

"Because I really don't want to go," Grace confesses.

The truth is that after Frog Bird's birth, Grace has abandoned the mountain. She does not know why. She is not even aware that she abandoned him. She has dreams—strange, unsettling dreams. She hears frogs. She smells hemlock. Scoffing, she tells herself she's just crazy. But the dreams persist. So, too, does her unease. The whole community talks about them. The thunderbolt. The bastard child. Some call her a miracle. Others proof of her mother's sin. This does not stop Babylonia and Grace from dressing Frog Bird in the richest, most colorful fabrics they can find, putting her in her carriage, and walking her through town. Women whisper to each other when the three generations are safely past. One day an old Indian woman approaches them. She asks if she can give the child a gift. Grace nods yes, please. The woman draws from under her shawl a pair of tiny moccasins. The bead work on them is intricate, beautiful. They are a perfect fit. Frog Bird wears them whenever she is outside. Grace cannot forget the woman's face. Sad, serene. She had made these moccasins, sure that someday her own child would wear them. Her belly stayed empty, the moccasins unused, the bead work shut away from sight. When Frog Bird kicks her little feet in the air, tiny deer prance across the leaves. In the center of each has been sewn a diamond-shaped piece of mother-of-pearl. Grace is grateful for this old woman's generosity. Grace has been touched by it. Haunted by it.

"Well, then, don't go," her mother snaps.

The truth is that Babylonia wishes Grace would go. She wants to be alone with her granddaughter. She loves to carry her in her arms, dance around the room, whisper old stories, say her name over and over again:

> *Frog Bird, Frog Bird, what do you know?*
> *Frog Bird, Frog Bird, where will you go?*
> *Frog Bird, Frog Bird, from where did you come?*
> *Frog Bird, Frog Bird, who gave you your name?*

"I know it's crazy, but it's just something I have to do," Grace shrugs.

"Well then go do it. The sooner you start, the sooner you'll be finished," her mother urges flatly.

Grace dresses, wearing heavy trousers, heavy boots, thick leather gloves. It is cold. Christmas is near. She thinks that she will gather some hemlock, some pine boughs and cones to decorate the house. She has a secret present for Frog Bird. Grace had met again the strange, sad, serene old woman who gave Frog Bird the moccasins. The old woman held Grace's hands. From under her shawl the old woman took a package wrapped in plain, coarse paper. It is tied with string; under the string, a bright red feather. Fresh from a red-tailed hawk, the old woman said. They sat and talked a long time. The old woman knows much English; Grace knows a little of the old woman's language. The old woman is one of the last of her tribe, the ones the English have named Quinnipiac, or long water. She laments how her people have been scattered. She fears the number of houses being built near the giant, trembling that soon there will be one built on the giant's side. She shivered, saying it will hurt giant to have his skin pierced so. Grace did not try to comfort her. She asked Grace about her daughter's name, wondering how she came to bear it. Grace laughed, admitted that it is a mystery. The old woman nodded, reminding Grace that names are powerful things. Grace asked the old woman her name. The old woman nodded, winked, smiled. "Just call me Frog Queen," she beamed. Grace laughed, liking the old woman's humor. The old woman rose, asked Grace to give the child the package for Christmas. When she hugged the old woman, Grace smelled hemlock.

When Grace got home she carefully unwrapped the package, making sure the feather was safe. Inside, a vest of deep, rich blue, filled with beads of red and green and yellow and white. Grace found no pattern. Just colors at random, she told herself. No need to be afraid. She carefully retied the package, putting the feather back in place.

Dressed, she starts her journey. She has not run or climbed much since her daughter's birth; the going is slow. She labors to ascend. Her hands slip; her toes do not find their niche easily. Out of breath, she decides she will stop, turn around, go home. But something urges her on. A little more than half way up the giant's side her strength returns. Her toes find their hold, her fingers grasp tightly, her legs push her upward. She hears the water deep beneath. Thinking she hears voices, she scoffs again at the old stories of a strange race in giant's belly. Ascends higher, almost flies to the top of the ridge. "Trap-Ridge, old girl," she says aloud, "you've still got it in you."

Stretching, she turns her face to the sun, disappointed it gives no warmth. Leaning against the trunk of the largest hemlock, its sharply-incised bark pricks through her heavy trousers. She hears a strange rumbling noise, then a loud, rasping, breaking sound, like trap rocks split apart, rubbing together. Then a shriek so loud it seems to pierce her heart. A bird, huge, black and green, with enormous wings emerges from the earth. A thunderbird with a frog's head, its eyes red, its wings tipped with yellow, glares. Grace crosses her arms, stands firm, stares. Hot breath moistens her neck as strong wing-bones wrap around her. As a feathery darkness enfolds her, she lays her head on the beast's breast, heart beat steady, strong. If she listens to it long, she will fall into a deep sleep. She closes her ears; she still hears the steady beat. Like a drum, she thinks. Like a water drum.

The trap rock of giant's belly opens up wider. Great bird, with his treasure safely wrapped inside him, flies upward, turns, and with head first, swiftly descends, straight as an arrow. The rocky arms of the giant close over them both. At the top of the hemlocks, tiny frogs, sway with the wind.

The mill men search every inch of the giant. For days on end, parties of ten, twelve men go out in separate directions, fanning the landscape, looking for any clue. There has been frequent snow, making their task difficult, if not impossible. After seven days of searching, even Sanford agrees it is useless. If there were tracks, the snow has buried them, erased them from their sight. Sanford had a moment of hope. He had gone about a quarter mile to the east of the search party he was with, still within earshot if not eyesight. He was in a dense stand of hemlocks; for some reason he found himself looking upward. For the briefest moment he could have sworn he heard her voice, from somewhere deep beneath. Faint, insistent. He was about to call out Grace but at that moment he thought he saw a large green frog swaying in the top of the hemlock. "Stupid bastard," he chides himself. "And you used to call her crazy."

Sanford misses her terribly, cannot believe how terribly he misses his six-foot, dressed-like-a-man, part-Indian daughter. He has no purpose. His spirit is puny, weak. He will move the family over to Dragon Town; he can't stand the sight of the giant. Can't live any longer at the giant's feet. As he walks back to his search party, he thinks of Frog Bird. She is very tiny. Small, sinewy, strong. She has her mother's blood. He has been afraid to know her father's blood. He thinks he may hold Frog Bird tonight, that he may love her, after a fashion. As he descends the giant's side, he is comforted by the sound of water rushing deep beneath. Never gets too cold in there, he assures himself. Water's never frozen.

At home, Babylonia sings to Frog Bird. It is Christmas Eve. At midnight, Babylonia will open the package. She will untie it very carefully, making sure to keep the red feather strong and straight. She will marvel at the vest, at the intricate, layered colors that are beaded over its front and back. She will be a little disappointed; the vest is far too big for Frog Bird to wear. Babylonia runs her fingers over the intricate beading, wondering if some of the beads are old, maybe even ancient. They do not resemble the ones that are common now, freely traded, for sale in the stores. They are rougher, more uneven, the colors more pure, more natural. Just beautiful random whorls of beads, free from pattern. She will pick up the vest, show it to Frog Bird; Frog Bird will reach for it, as if she knows it is for her. Frog Bird will giggle, raise up her tiny legs and feet, take her tiny fingers and wrap them around her tiny feet, squealing with delight. If she misses her mother, she has not given a sign. The wet-nurse provides her milk. Her grandmother holds her day and night, rocking her, singing to her, holding her up by the arms, letting her little toes touch the flowered carpet. Babylonia will laugh with delight too. Babylonia will also feel an empty hole in her heart, an empty daughter space. Babylonia will put the vest back in its package, and without knowing why, will retie it, putting the red feather carefully in place, still curious why there is no pattern. When Frog Bird is old enough to walk, she will wear this vest. When she walks just right, dances almost, the pattern will emerge: tiny frogs will seem to fly, front and back.

Mother Thunderbird sits in her nest. Father Thunderbird stands nearby, scanning with sharp eye the earth below, guarding their golden treasure. Many months ago, Mother and Father Thunderbird were going about their usual Thunderbird business: gathering food, having fun flying in the wind, caring for Thunderbird babies, warning the world against thoughtless war, preparing it for just war. Suddenly they heard a little cry, so tiny that they had to stop flapping their wings but the wind through them made it almost impossible to hear where the little cries were coming from. As their sharp ears located the site of origin, with sure and steady wings they descend to the spot. At first they cannot see it, but then it comes into focus: a tiny frog trapped in a fissure in a rock. Father Thunderbird gives the rock one sharp tap. As the fissure opens wider, tiny frog jumps free. As it scampers down the face of the rock it turns, croaks out a tiny thanks, raises its right front leg, waves. Mother and Father Thunderbird smile, then return to their everyday Thunderbird business, soon forgetting the tiny frog.

One day, many months later, they are having their lunch, resting after a long morning of hunting. Suddenly they hear a rumbling so strong the mountain shakes. They are almost blinded by a huge fireball of light that bursts open above their heads. From it emerges a huge and wondrous creature. It has a frog's face, a bird's body, a man's feet. Mother and Father Thunderbird welcome this strange creature, inviting it to share their meal. This great and strange creature nods, shares their meal, then rises, speaks:

"To you it is given the sacred privilege of bringing into this world a great treasure. You will find in your nest a pair of yellow birds. You must do whatever you must do to protect them. The world depends on these birds. You have been chosen because of your diligence, because of your kindness, because of your strength. You will need all of these; you will be challenged by enemies, enemies strong and devious. You must be equal to them. You must protect the yellow birds. No matter what you have to do, no matter how strange or risky, you must protect the yellow birds."

Mother and Father Thunderbird nod solemnly, accepting their duty, grateful to have been chosen. Mindful of the seriousness and difficulty of their charge, they determine to meet whatever challenge with strength and grace.

The grand creature prepares for departure. Once again a huge fireball of light appears. The great being with a frog's face, a bird's body, and a man's feet is swallowed gently into the center of the fireball. The fireball disappears, leaving no trace.

Mother Thunderbird flies swiftly to her nest. In its center, two birds, dazzling yellow. Brighter and deeper than the corn, brighter and clearer than the sun. Taking her massive wing, she lovingly touches the downy heads of the yellow birds. They coo, arching their backs to meet her loving wing. She bends over them, her beak softly preening their feathers. The yellow birds arch their necks to meet her beak. Nearby, Father Thunderbird looks on. Mother Thunderbird beckons to him; she rises, flies to a nearby branch. Father Thunderbird lands gently on the perimeter of the nest. As his beak reaches down, the yellow birds meet it with their own. They kiss, gently. Father Thunderbird moves into the nest, very gently and lightly. Yellow birds hurriedly scuttle underneath, peeping with glee. They nestle, warm and happy under his feathered breast. Father Thunderbird holds his children for a long time. He beckons Mother Thunderbird. They change their places so quickly, so quietly, so softly, the nestlings do not awaken. Her feathered breast warms them, protects them; his strong wings take to the sky to find them food.

They meet challenges, just as Frog Bird Man predicted. They have saved the birds from an eagle. They have saved the birds from a sudden wind current which swept them, almost breaking their wings. They have saved them from a sudden storm of pine cones hurling to the earth when the earth beneath them violently shook. Mother and Father Thunderbird do not become complacent; they remember the warning and are always on guard.

They have heard about a great giant who lives on the other side of the bay. His feet stomp; the earth shakes. But he has always stayed on his own mountain, never venturing to where Mother and Father Thunderbird play. This giant is not slow. When he moves, it is with swift rapidity. They keep guard, always watchful, always waiting.

This giant is smart, devious. They do not hear him come as they always expected they would. Perhaps he rode the clouds, perhaps he flew, perhaps he silenced his feet. All they know is that suddenly the great giant Hobbomock appears, swift and strong as a thunderbolt, holding the yellow birds. Instinctively, Mother Thunderbird calls upon the frogs. Thousands of them emerge from the ground, fall from trees, spring from streams. Tens of thousands of them circle giant's feet, spring up his legs. Driven mad, he loosens his grip; yellow birds escape his giant fist. Swift and strong as a thunderbolt, Father Thunderbird spins, twisting his bird body into a circular cyclone, drilling a huge gaping hole through Giant's thumb. The frogs continue their frenzied climb, their claw-fingers driving the Giant mad. His arms, his bleeding hands flail the sky. Father Thunderbird skillfully dodges his blows. Father Thunderbird spins again, twisting once more his bird body into a circular cyclone, drilling a large, gaping hole through giant's belly. The frogs continue their attack. From the sky come a thousand yellow birds, each pecking another hole in the giant. Covered with yellow and green and red, giant empties of blood. He falls on his back, turns to stone, still covered with a blanket of yellow, green and red.

Mother and Father Thunderbird are still not satisfied. They must protect their golden treasure, the world's golden treasure. If this giant could come so quickly, so quietly, then so could another could, they reason. The frogs agree, wondering what would happen if they could not emerge and converge quickly enough. The yellow birds that came from the sky cannot stay; they cannot be sure sky can open up quickly enough to let them return in time to vanquish another enemy. Mother and Father Thunderbird keep thinking, pondering, wondering. Suddenly Frog Leader asks to be lifted up to Mother Thunderbird's ear. Stretching out one of her wings, she lays it on the earth. Frog Leader hops on, holds tightly for his ride high into the air. He whispers something into Mother Thunderbird's ear; she grins, nods. Turning to Father Thunderbird, she whispers into his ear. He beams. They all bend down to their golden treasure, whispering into their ears. The yellow birds of earth agree.

Frog Leader asks a favor. "Mother Thunderbird, may I please ask of you a great thing?"

Mother Thunderbird nods.

"I want to know what it feels like to live in a nest high in the sky. Even for a moment, I would like to know what that is like," Frog Leader begs.

"It is done my son," Mother Thunderbird says.

Gently cupping Frog Leader in her strong beak, she lifts him to the tallest hemlock tree she can find. Frog sways there, mesmerized by the beauty of the world below. He is satisfied. She gently lifts him to the earth below.

Frog Leader sends the word through his troops. The legions of yellow birds from the sky prepare to return home. Father Thunderbird calls upon Frog Bird Man to make his wings as strong as stone. Father Thunderbird flies to the highest point of the sky. Turning, one wing extended downward, with precision and balance he cuts a vertical slit through the belly of the sleeping giant. The frogs descend. A long column of frogs, led by Frog leader, carry the yellow birds of earth to safety. As they carry the yellow birds of earth to safety, the frogs chant a sacred chorus, celebrating the power and the kindness of Frog Bird Man and the yellow birds of earth.

Inside the mountain is clear, fresh, rushing water, evergreen glades, an abundance of berries and roots and seeds. Many creatures live here, among them a man and a woman. Everyone and everything in this inner world is young, unchanging. Earth time has no place deep within the rock. Chief Montowese, strong and powerful, holds the hand of Grace Trap-Ridge Hitchcock.

A few months later, they hear a great and strange noise, almost like trap rock plates rubbing against each other. They see a slim shaft of light high above. In a narrow halo of light, Frog Bird Man descends. All greet him with great joy, knowing the wondrous story of Mother and Father Thunderbird and the giant beast-man. All have faith that Frog Bird Man's power is good. He walks and flies around the underground world, holding the yellow birds of earth in his great wings. Mother and Father Thunderbird have done well, done well indeed. He opens his frog lips, blowing up his neck so that he may speak.

"Chief Montowese and Grace Trap-Ridge Hitchcock" he begins. "To you this mountain of sleeping giant is now sacred land. You did not always think that. In fact, you betrayed mountain, each in your own way."

They nod, solemnly, slowly, knowing they have betrayed the mountain, but also knowing they will never betray him again.

"You have been given a sacred vision."

"Yes," they sigh, a sigh deep, peaceful, thankful. "Yes, we have been given a strange and great vision."

Frog Bird Man nods. "Great visions need protecting, my children," he warns. "They are precious things. Beware. Take good care of what issues from your great vision."

They nod, eagerly agreeing.

Frog Bird Man balances his man's feet on the earth. With wings more powerful than any, he lifts himself straight upward, a vertical line ascending rapidly. A small shaft of light appears high above. Through it flies Frog Bird Man, the shaft of light closing tightly.

The yellow birds of earth approach. Into the Chief's hand, the female yellow bird places a seed; into Grace's hand, the male yellow bird places another. Chief Montowese and Grace Trap-Ridge Hitchcock join hands. Before them appears a wondrous female being. They immediately feel love for her, calling her their child. Her hair is parted down the middle, drawn into thick braids. The left half is golden yellow; the right half jet black. Her left eye is blue; her right eye deep hazel. Her fingernails are bright red. In the middle of each, a green circle; in the middle of the circle, a red diamond; in the middle of the diamond a yellow square. Light of foot, powerful of arm, Grace Yellowbird Faith makes the middle of the mountain her home. As the yellow birds fly above her braided hair, the frogs follow her feet. Chief Montowese and Grace Trap-Ridge Hitchcock hold her many-colored, cold, gentle hands.

Grace Yellowbird Faith is weaving a huge blanket, large enough to cover the mountain. A blanket rich with reds, and greens, and yellows. On it appear a frog with a great gold headdress, a thunderbird, and a yellow bird with a red tail. It will take many years, maybe many hundreds of years, to finish this blanket.

Grace Yellowbird Faith has been weaving this blanket for a long time. She is still weaving this blanket. She will still be weaving this blanket for many years to come. If the time is right, and the blanket is finished, Grace Yellowbird Faith will restore the earth to itself.

Sanford and Babylonia argue. Sanford wants to move but Babylonia does not. She finds great comfort to be able to look out the window and see the sleeping giant that holds her Grace. She sees her baby in the giant's belly, living among the strange race the legends warn about. Her mother once spoke of these strange beings, said that there had to be something to it. Otherwise there wouldn't be so many people hearing those voices. Babylonia wonders, not sure she believes. But she doesn't disbelieve. So she likes to be near the giant mountain man that stole her child, dead or alive.

Sanford cannot stand to look at the mountain. Every time he sees the sleeping giant, he makes a fist, barely able to control his rage. He feels small, useless. The sleeping mountain giant left him nothing, not even a trace. All he can think about is how he has lost his daughter—his only daughter—to the sleeping giant man. Sanford is in danger of losing his job at the mill. He daydreams, he mismeasures, costing the company money. The other men avoid him now, afraid he is becoming deranged. He looks so: he has let his hair grow long, almost to his waist, gathering it in back with a strip of leather into which has been beaded a large bird. They say he spent his last money on that beaded leather strip, money that should have bought food for his wife and granddaughter.

At night, he sits, staring at the beheaded buck. He says it is trying to say something to him. Babylonia fears for her husband's life. If he keeps acting so, something terrible will happen. But she does not want to leave the mountain; she needs it for her own life.

Frog Bird has become a little person, having started to walk, to talk. She loves her grandfather's long hair. He gets on all fours, unties his hair, throws it forward over his face. She grabs on, laughing, squealing, pulling, pushing her tiny face into his hair. In these moments Babylonia thinks they will be saved. Sanford seems at peace, balanced. It is right after one of these moments that Babylonia goes to the old wooden chest in the far corner of the room. In its bottom drawer, still tied with the red feather, the vest of many beads. She removes the package, carefully unties it, making sure not to bend or break the feather. She holds it out for Frog Bird to see. Frog Bird dances with delight, picking up each leg, setting down each foot to a child's imagined beat. Babylonia slips it over Frog Bird, pulling her arms through. Frog Bird squeals, begins to dance again. Sanford has drawn back his hair, tied it, is sitting cross-legged, smiling as he has not smiled in months. He claps his hands, hums a tune, delighting in his granddaughter's impish steps. Frog Bird picks up her pace. Moving beyond the perimeter of the flowered carpet, she twirls and swirls across the great oak boards of the floor. Faster and faster she swirls. Faster and faster she twirls. Suddenly her grandmother cries out, "Sanford, look, flogs are flying all over her."

Sanford grabs Frog Bird, stopping her feet. Despite her howls of protest and fear, Sanford rips the vest from her, throws it across the room. Babylonia runs, scoops up the vest, and holds it to her breast.

"Enough of this craziness," he roars. "I will have no more of this in MY house," he bellows.

Babylonia still holds the vest to her breast. Pressing her back against the vest in Babylonia's arms is Frog Bird, face stained with tears, pouting. She picks up her tiny right foot, stomps it as hard as she can, having to hold onto her grandmother's leg in order to keep her balance. "No," she says as loud as she can, her voice still hoarse from crying. "No," she repeats.

Sanford has turned his back to them, staring at the beheaded buck on the wall. He moves toward it, looks at it with what Babylonia can only imagine is rage, or fear, or maybe some strange combination of the two. He wraps his hands around the buck's truncated neck. With a grunting roar, Sanford rips the beheaded buck from its place high upon the wall. Holding it to his chest, antlers going forward as he lunges toward the door, he flings open the door, heaves the buck out into the yard, toward the sleeping man mountain. "There, goddamned you, go back where you belong. Go back to the goddamned mountain." Sanford slams shut the door. With his back touching it, he slides to the floor, knees bent. Exhausted, he cries, quietly. In his eyes, a vacuum.

Babylonia knows they must move. She strokes Frog Bird's hair, hoping they will be all right. She stops, taken aback by something she thinks she hears. No, she reasons, it cannot be. Not from the mouth of a baby not even two years old. No, she shakes her head, just imagined it. Frog Bird did not say "yes, god-damned, you, go." No, Frog Bird did not say "Bastard, Grace."

In a few weeks they leave their little house at the foot of the sleeping giant and move to New Haven. They buy a small house on Quinnipiac Avenue where there are rows of cottages lining the shores of the Quinnipiac River. Sanford has found work in the fish and oyster business. Cold, smelly work, but steady work. Part of the pay is the rental of a house on the riverbank. All the fronts of these houses are on stilts, extending over the water. Their backsides are built into the hill that rises on each side of the river bank. Frog Bird loves the front room, begs Babylonia to let her sleep there so she can feel cradled by the lapping waves beneath. Babylonia easily gives in.

Sanford avoids the front room, not comforted by the sound of the water underneath. The kitchen and the bedroom are at the back of the house, in the hill. He spends most of his time there. Babylonia divides herself front and back, between her husband and her granddaughter who now seem not to be part of the same house, the same family. There is a small, cramped attic in this house. A small hole has been cut into the kitchen ceiling. You slide the moveable board away, hoist yourself through the hole into a small, dry storage space. It is here, in a wooden box, that Babylonia stores the package, tied, feather in place. In it, lovingly folded, the child's beaded vest. As she slides back the moveable board, Babylonia assures herself that this vest will never be unworn for long. "After all," she whispers aloud, "I have as much right as he does." A moment later: "After all, this is MY house, too" she growls.

Sanford has cut his hair. He no longer wears the leather strap with the beaded bird upon its back. Babylonia does not know where it is. It is not in the drawers of the wooden chest. It is not anywhere easily seen, as far as she knows. She has looked for it. There is only one place it could be. Ever since they were married, Sanford has always kept a locked wooden box. Handmade by his grandfather, painted black, over which, in reds and blues and yellows, hearts, flowers, ribbons. Before they were married, he showed it to her. He said, simply, "This is mine. Only mine. For all time." She agreed. Never once, in all these years, has she tried to open it. After all, she showed him her plain wooden box, locked as well. Her Bible box. All hers, only hers. A fit balance. Without grudge, almost with loving ease, she imagines the beaded leather bird at rest in the painted chest.

Frog Bird, however, has little ease. For years, the neighborhood children tease her terribly. They taunt her about her name, about her strange eyes and hair, about her being too many colors. "What are you, anyway?" they jeer. She keeps shrugging her shoulders, always responding the same way. "I'm Frog Bird, that's all." But they will not leave her alone. They continue to taunt, excluding her from games. No one will be her friend. Steeling herself, she crosses her arms, glares. Sneers. She doesn't care, she yells. But at night, in the front room, sleeping on a thick blanket on the warm wooden floor, she cares. As the waves lap beneath her, she cries. She wants to hold hands with the children, wants to feel the hugs they give to each other. Would like to be pushed by one of the boys. Just to be touched. Now they simply leave her alone. She doesn't remember just when, but they stopped taunting her. Frog Bird listens to the waves below, imagining they are singing a song. A sacred song. A song of grace. She has heard the children talking when they returned from Sunday school. One of the last things they said was that she would never receive grace. When she asked her grandmother if she would have grace, her grandmother smiled, held her and said. "You have already had Grace. You are a part of Grace. She is your mother." Next time she saw the children she gloated, "Hah! I do so have grace. Grace is my mother. I'm Grace's daughter." When the children told their mothers what Frog Bird said, they were convinced Satan spoke from the mouth of the strangely- colored young girl.

Frog Bird doesn't care. She goes to the river for hours, digging hermit crabs. Fascinated by them, she learns from them. They pull themselves into their shells, living alone, trying to be safe. She may tickle them to come out for a moment, but she lets them go home unharmed. She digs a little trench in the sand, puts them back, watching the water creep back in, covering them, keeping them safe. Hard, empty shell, she thinks. But she also knows that others dig the hermit crabs. Pull off their little arms, their tiny little feet. Shell, no matter how hard, did not keep them safe. Frog Bird watches the hermit crabs, studies them, gives them names.

Frog Bird is thirteen, an awkward age. She has fallen in love with one of the neighborhood boys. A boy with a surly lip, prideful stride. Dark, curly hair, brown eyes. He looks right past her, his eyes always on another neighborhood girl. Long blonde hair, crystal clear blue eyes, pretty clothes: that is who he wants. Frog Bird is first very sad, then Frog Bird is very mad. Thirteen years of rage, thirteen years of sorrow coalesce. Frog Bird is very small, sinewy and strong. She literally flies with rage, propelling herself not against the blond-haired blue-eyed maiden, but against the dark and prideful boy. Blonde maiden screams for help; all the neighborhood gathers around or looks from their windows. Frog Bird, bloody of lip, panting, stands over dark and prideful boy. Hands still in fists, she stands there. Bleeding, his nose is broken; mouth open, he sobs, crying for his mother. No one intervenes, no one speaks. Before she turns, Frog Bird kicks him in the side, sneers. Babylonia has watched from her front window. As Frog Bird mounts the back stairs, Babylonia imagines yellow and green frogs racing alongside. When Frog Bird opens the back door, steps into the kitchen, her grandmother throws her arms around her, grinning from ear to ear. When Sanford comes home they know he has heard all about it. He sits at the table, eating his stew. He seems calm, relaxed, almost happy. As he finishes, he wipes his mouth. Then he says "That'll show them not to mess with Frog Bird Hitchcock."

That night, almost despite himself, he goes into the front room, kisses his granddaughter goodnight. She dreams that night of a great hermit frog. His shell is the stone of a mountain. Buried deep beneath the rocky sand, he is very, very safe.

When the young men and women of the neighborhood see Frog bird the next day they say hello. Ask her to play. The blonde maiden wants to hold her hand. The dark and prideful boy wants to hold her hand. Frog Bird invites their touch, lets her body be one of them. But her heart is safely hidden, locked up deep inside a stony box.

1875

The dark and prideful boy is dark still, but not so prideful. Seven years after he met with Frog bird's pent-up wrath, he finds he has fallen in love with her. He was afraid of her at first, but her hands were soft, strong. At times he found them cold, but always gentle. When she was seventeen he thought he had fallen in love; now that she is twenty he is sure he is in love. He can tell her anything. Even things he has never told anyone before. He hopes she trusts him enough to love him.

Sitting down by the river, she notices the water become increasingly murky, with a brown underside to the blue.

"The water doesn't look right," she says, her voice betraying her fear.

"I know," he agrees. "My father says the fish are dying in parts of the river."

"I know," she repeats. "My grandfather says the same thing."

"It's not just the fish," he continues. "The bay has almost no oysters. Many have just died. Others are puny, strange. Many of the shells are cracked."

Frog bird shivers. Her grandfather has talked of this too.

"You know that New Haven used to be called Dragon Town?" he asks.

"Yes," she laughs, "my grandfather still calls it that."

"Do you know why?"

"I guess it's because some think the devil is here?"

He laughs, shakes his head. "It was a long time ago. Nobody living can remember seeing them. But the bay used to be full of seals. English folks called them sea dragons. So when they settled here, they called it Dragon Town."

"Too bad they still don't. I like it a lot better than New Haven. Makes me imagine great and strange things could go on in a town named Dragon."

They laugh, playfully shoving each other, knowing the importance of names. She still remembers how he blushed when he first told her his name was Earnest Hightower. She's sure she never blushed when she told him hers.

He starts talking about the sleeping giant just to the west of New Haven. Says he wants to go. He knows someone who is going there to make a delivery and they could ride in the back of the wagon. They'd have a few hours. After making the delivery, his friend would be visiting someone nearby. He'd pick them up on his way home. She's excited. She cannot remember, but she knows she was born across from the giant's feet. That night, at supper, she tells them. She notices that her grandmother smiles, eagerly, urging her to go, have a great time. She notices, too, that her grandfather says nothing. Purses his lips shut, shakes his head no. Frog Bird Hitchcock almost asks for the thousandth time to tell her more about her mother and being lost on the mountain but she knows it is useless. He will not talk about it. Her grandmother respects his silence. So Frog Bird plays over in her head the little she does know. How her mother went to the mountain. How she never came back. How many men searched for many days and found no trace.

Frog Bird Hitchcock also remembers the only thing her grandmother will say when asked who is Frog Bird's father. "Grace, child," Babylonia says. Frog Bird Hitchcock always protests. "But that is my mother's name. What is my father's name?" she persists. "Grace, child. Have Grace," is all her grandmother says. Frog Bird dreamed once that her mother and her father were one strange beast, living in a deep hole somewhere, under hard, black rock.

Earnest Hightower and Frog Bird Hitchcock start out a few hours before dawn. They will not be back until midnight. They bring lunch, snacks, stuffing their pockets full of nuts, apples, dried meat, cookies. Holding hands in the back of the wagon, they do not yet know that when they return they will be engaged, that they will have already named their future son. Holding hands, they laugh the laugh of the young who are very much in love. When she was seventeen, her heart was locked in stone. When she was eighteen, the lock had opened a bit. At nineteen, the lock fell away. At twenty, her heart is ready to be an open box to the strong and gentle hands of Earnest Hightower.

They jump from the back of the wagon, waving as they prance through the fields that lead up to the giant's base. As they pass the ponds that lie at his feet they see great white wings ascend, feeling the wind rush as a large egret lifts itself to the sky. Trailing it is a mist that catches the golden rays of the emerging sun. Both of them stand perfectly still, breathing the golden mist that almost forms a halo around them. As the bird disappears from their sight, frogs croak. They catch quick glimpses of many frogs, on water lily leaves. Following alongside the pond, Frog Bird notices beautiful flowers a little way from the pond's edge. She reaches down to pick them when she suddenly has the urge not to touch them at all. They reach the beginning of their ascent. There is a clear trail there now. So many people have come to the mountain, it is now a popular picnic area. Starting up the trail, they are not surprised it stops less than half-way up the giant. They will make their own path the rest of the way up.

They stop, eat, before going further up. When they reach the ridge, a panoramic vision—they can see clear to New Haven harbor to the east and to the west, far out into fields and valleys. From the giant's breast, the houses at the base look like silly little sticks.

"Froggie," Earnest Hightower says, "can you believe how beautiful this is?"

"You bet, Ernie boy."

When they are alone, they love calling each other nicknames. "So, Birdie, can you remember which of those little houses was yours?"

"No. I was way too young. I can't remember anything about that house except one thing. A big deer's head, stuck on a wall And one night my grandfather opened the door and threw it out. Next morning my grandmother started laughing so hard she could hardly breathe. The deer's antlers got hooked into her clothes pole. There it hung, in mid-air, staring at the door. Poor thing. She cut it down, made my grandfather haul it off to the woods."

"How did you get your name?" he finally asks. For seven years he has wanted to know. The sheer space at the top of the giant gives him strength.

"I wish I knew. I just live with it, ugly as it is," she confides.

"I have another name," he confesses. "My grandfather always called me Yellow Tail. Said that was my real name. But my parents wouldn't listen. Something to do with an old Indian legend about a Chief who sold the sleeping giant to an English man. Grandfather said I am related to him, from way back. Chief Montowese, I think. So nobody but my grandfather ever called me that, and not inside the house. So my grandfather would take me for walks, call me Yellow Tail, tell me old and fantastic stories."

Frog Bird's heart opens fully. "Earnest," she says seriously, "my mother disappeared on this mountain. Maybe even right where we are sitting. Shortly after I was born. People searched. Never found a trace." She shivers, pulling herself close to Earnest.

He holds her, firmly, gently. Then he braces his arms in the earth at his side; she cups herself into his bent breast. They gaze at the sky, watching birds soar overhead, hearing the sound of water rushing beneath. A red-tail hawk glides by. Soon after, a bright yellow bird darts in front of the hawk, seeming to turn its red tail into a golden yellow. Frog Bird sits up quickly, exclaiming loudly: "I just saw Yellow Tail born."

Their silence breaks into uneasy laughter. Neither understands what she has just said. Neither wants to talk about it. So they lie together, holding each other, safe on the top of the giant's belly.

On the way down they have already forgotten what they think they have seen. They stop and rest on a ledge that juts from the giant's side. They thrill to the sound of pieces of rock breaking off, tumbling down the cliff. When he asks her to marry him, her feet dig into the edge with such force that she sends a sheet of rock tumbling, fragmenting into a hundred tiny stones, pelting the clinging roots that hold onto the rocky sides of the giant man. They giggle, so much in love that they do not notice the tiny frog crushed underneath.

Swinging arm in arm, they descend, laughing. They call each other by their old nicknames. Frog Bird, on a whim, calls him Yellow Tail; he laughs, likes it, decides to keep it for his name.

"What else do you know about the old Chief, the one who has something to do with your name?" Frog Bird needs to know.

"Not much. Only that he disappeared on the giant's mountain too. As far as I know, nobody has ever found a trace."

Excited beyond words, they turn to look up at the sleeping man-beast. Each wondering if the stories are true, each hopes that the mountain someday may leave a trace. But each is also pretty sure that this old Indian nonsense has nothing really to do with them. Just old stories. Just fun old stories. Like the Bible, Frog Bird thinks.

They near the pond's edge. Frog Bird gets on her belly, putting her face close to the water. She sees the intricate web of a small spider at the edge of a lily pad. In it she sees trapped a tiny little frog with tiny red-bead eyes. She tells Yellow Tail to lie down, to look, to help. Quickly he is on his belly but it is too late. When they turn to look again, the web and the frog are gone. Frog Bird quickly forgets it.

As they are talking in the back of the wagon on their way home, Yellow Tail has an inspiration.

"Hey Frog Bird, I have a great idea" he says, tickling her. "Let's name our first child Yellow Tail Frog Bird."

"Hey Yellow Tail, I have a great idea," she says, tickling him. "Let's name our first child Frog Bird Yellow Tail."

They do not know it yet but their first child has just been conceived on top of the giant's belly. Right after yellow bird crossed in front of hawk's tail, a boy child began to be born.

Nine months later they are the proud parents of their son. He has two names. Charles Sanford Hightower is his official name. It is entered into the family Bibles. Charles after Earnest's father, Sanford after Frog Bird's grandfather. Both sides of the family represented—a good balance. They also know his other names. His parents joke about it all the time. He is large-boned, tall, hefty. At three months he can pull himself up. He is crawling at seven months, beginning to walk by nine. When he is walking well, Babylonia proudly brings to him the beaded vest that his mother wore when she began to walk. Earnest puts it on his son, lovingly pulling his arms through the sleeves. He holds his son's hands, holding him just off the floor, letting his feet dance. Charles Sanford starts to twirl, to whirl and to swirl all about the room, faster and faster, twisting himself into a little circular cyclone. Faster and faster and his parents shout— "Look. Look there! Little frogs dancing, everywhere!" If Sanford were here, Babylonia thinks, he would want nothing to do with these reappearing frogs.

Charles Sanford exhausts himself, falls asleep. When they put him to bed, Frog Bird takes off his little vest, putting it back in its package, meaning to put the feather back in its place. She forgets. The cat gets hold of the feather, chews it, spits out undigested fragments. Frog Bird admonishes kitty but is not really upset. Just an old feather, she thinks. Very old, very brittle, ready to break apart anyway. The paper gets rumpled, thrown away. The beaded vest finds itself in the bottom of the trunk, covered by more useful things.

A month later, Babylonia is found dead. Peacefully, in her sleep, her hands open at her sides. Sanford never recovers. A month after that, he too, is found dead, also in his sleep, his hands clenched hard, crossed over his chest.

Frog Bird takes her grandmother's plain wooden box and her grandfather's painted wooden box: only these things does she keep. She knows she will open them, reasoning that they would not have kept them if they did not want her to know what is inside. She opens Babylonia's Bible box first. Frog Bird smiles as she sees the names, even those crossed-out. She is proud of her grandmother's secret strength. Suddenly she feels sad: generations of people, stuffed in a book, held neatly in a hand. She opens Sanford's Bible box next. Here, too, the list of names. Births. Deaths. The blotch on the page. She wonders what had been there, what has been erased. Or maybe just an accident. Just a blotch of ink dropped on the page. She turns the page, stops, hardly able to believe what she sees:

Yellow Tail Frog Bird
Frog Bird Yellow Tail

From left to right, corner to corner, the same. The perfect balance. I believe, she whispers. I must believe, she chants.

At the end of this entry, in bold script, **SH**. Tucked between the pages, a leather strap, beaded with a large yellow bird. Frog Bird looks again. Tucked in the corner, a tiny frog, with open mouth, singing.

1935

Frog Bird has been a grandmother many times over, a great-grandmother more than a half dozen times—a rich, full, good life. Her son, Yellow Tail Frog Bird Charles Sanford Hightower, is a good son. He, too, has been a father three times over, a grandfather six times. Earnest has been dead for twenty years. Suddenly, keeled over, dropped dead. His heart, they think. Frog Bird is desperately lonely. She and her husband were friends. She could tell him almost anything. Missing now the chance to voice her deepest fears, she can tell them to no one, not even her loving son.

She keeps having a terrible dream. She has been having it for many years but it is getting worse. A dream that shakes her awake, leaves her trembling, soaked with sweat. She cannot get back to sleep; she tosses, turns. If she closes her eyes, the dream starts all over again. For a while, the dream came only at night. Then it started coming during the day, if she closed her eyes even for a moment. Now it comes eyes open or closed. Now it is with her night and day, appearing and reappearing, always the same.

When it started, Frog Bird started a scrapbook. Articles about the Sleeping Giant. He's been given this formal name. She would not paste them in; she left them free, so she could rearrange them if necessary.

1890. Cedarhurst built on the Sleeping Giant. A great house, "fastened to the ground with iron ring bolts."

Later: a notice that Cedarhurst has been sold to a man named Heaton. He has 350 stone steps carved in Giant's side, leading up to this house.

1900. Reports that a Black woman, Miss Demaroy, lives in a cabin to the south of Giant's neck. She is reported to have "gathered herbs and ground up small creatures into a salve."

1888. Article in the paper about Blue Hills Park opening. The name before it was officially named Sleeping Giant.

1912. Article reporting that blasting has begun on Giant's face, on Giant's neck. Mt. Carmel Trap Rock Company is mining the trap rock for building roads. They swore they would not blast any part of his face that could be seen from Mt. Carmel Avenue. They lied.

1924. The Sleeping Giant Park Association has been formed.

1923: A poem, in *The New Haven Register*, attributed to William Avis:

> "Hark! Comes that rumble from the throat
> Of the Sleeping Giant in his dreams.
> From Hill to Hill its echoes float
> Crashing-smashing o'er field and streams.
> Again, again, that crashing sound
> It comes from the Giant's gashed brow!
> Through all the country 'round and 'round
> Man, woman, child, all hear it now!
> Up! Up! Remember Paul Revere!
> George Washington at Valley Forge!
> No task to us should seem severe,
> To save our Giant from the Scourge!"

1930. A group of citizens has bought the land, swearing they will save the Giant from any future disfigurement. Already his face is pocked.

1930. Report in *The New Haven Register* that "The Giant's chin is now as thoroughly battered as the Sphinx's."

1933. From the Hamden annual minutes: "From now on may his repose be unbroken, whether by forest fires or by forest blight. May Nature speedily restore his fallen locks. May the rips and holes in his raiment be speedily repaired through gifts of land and money, and may all succeeding generations feel for him the same keen love that we feel whose efforts have bought his freedom."

1933. Under the WPA, a grand watch-tower has been begun on the Giant's summit. It resembles a medieval castle. It will have a spider web window. It will have a parapet. It will have a grand, winding inside ramp. It will have windows on every side. It will have a spider web window on one side, facing east.

1935. Report in *The New Haven Journal Courier*: "The Giant's dandruff has been completely and finally cured. His bald spot will grow no larger, and in time his mother, nature, may re-equip him with a magnificent head of trees."

Frog Bird hears the Giant call. The more she closes her ears, the more insistent his voice becomes. She cannot erase from her mind what happened sixty years ago.

At the very moment Earnest asked her to marry him, she heard her mother's voice from deep below. She dug her feet into the ledge to keep from falling into fear, her giggle a blotch upon her fear. At the very moment she conceived her son atop the Giant's belly, she heard her mother singing a lullaby, from deep within the man-beast's belly. Her mother's face which she could not remember ever having seen, she now saw. Her mother, singing a lullaby, holding in her arms a child with the head of a great frog, with deep red eyes.

This dream has been with her all these years. At first only an occasional guest, it is now a constant companion. It was the one thing she never told Earnest—the one secret between them. With each replaying of it, her mother's face is clearer. Her mother is large, strong. Her frog baby holds up a hand-claw; it is crooked, seems broken. It bleeds. It cries. Grace Trap-Ridge Hitchcock bends to kiss her frog child, sucking its blood to ease its pain. Frog Bird jolts, hearing a tiny crunch as her foot held tight the rock ledge that stopped her fall.

Over and over, the face, the crooked, broken hand-claw, the blood. Every time a little more distinct, every time a little more difficult to forget. Frog Bird knows what she must do. She must return to Giant. He is calling her. She does not know why. All she knows is that she must go.

But how? She is eighty. Bent, stooped, twisted. But she has faith. She asks her son Yellow Tail Frog Bird Charles Sanford Hightower to take her, help her up the trail. He is her baby, always her baby; she forgets that he is no young man. At sixty, he is bent and twisted himself. But mother and son set out on the summer solstice of 1935, taking the trolley to the base of the Giant's feet. Frog Bird carries a massive cane, carved of black forest wood. On its top, the carved head of a lion, with ruby glass eyes; around its neck, a band of gold, and another band of mother-of-pearl. A great brass tip at its end. It catches and reflects the light as she taps the earth.

She walks very slowly. Holding her by the elbow, letting her bone settle into the palm of his hand, they cross by the pools at noon. No egret ascends; the frogs are silent. It is no matter. Frog Bird can still see them, remembers them, knows they are there, somewhere. Mother and son are at the base of the Giant, stopping to rest on the benches that now line the bottom of his great base. She is exhausted already, thinking this a foolhardy venture, indeed. The SGPA is meeting there today. They carry a paper brochure: Sleeping Giant Park Association. She has read about them and tells them so. They are interested in why she is here. She tells them of her journey up the Giant as a young girl, of her journey down as an engaged young woman. Of her deep desire to reach the Giant's summit once more before she dies. They devise a plan. They will tie a great rope about her waist, forming a human cable, pulling her and her son to the summit, inch by inch. She beams. Thinks to herself that it is crazy, that it will never work, but she beams. And then she has more faith.

It will not be dark for hours. They ascend, slowly, surely. She finds herself almost propelled up the ridge, gliding, flying over the rock. They ascend higher, to the great hemlock groves where she opened her heart and her legs. She hears the water rushing underneath, imagining her mother sitting by a spring, drinking. As they make the summit, she is startled by the watch-tower-in-progress. The spider web window is in. She looks down, out over Giant's belly, and then she goes down the ramp and looks up. Its web dissects the world into fragments, inscribing itself on all she sees. She and her son have been untied. They walk slowly over the summit. Frog Bird plants herself near a protruding ledge, sure that her feet are strong enough to hold her there. Memories fill her. Sounds, smells, the touch of fingers. She can even taste the dried meat they shared, the nuts. The cookies, baked fresh, frosted with coconut. Their feet dangling from the wagon, the dust as the wagon wheels ground into the road. The mist the egret left when he ascended to the sky. The throaty croak of the frogs, diving into the water, safe. She breathes deeply, feeling old. Well, hell, she reminds herself, you are old. "More than old," she mutters. "Damned ancient."

She wonders what the Giant wants with her. He has asked her to come—no, he has insisted that she come. She tries to empty her mind. She holds her son's hand. A good hand, warm, strong. A sudden ball of light appears. Exploding, it envelopes them. Then a great noise, as if huge trap rock plates are scraping together. A fissure expands beneath her, the light intensifies, water rushes, loudly, rapidly, forcefully. A great slit of light closes over her. Flying downward, she hears her mother speak.

The newspaper report may have read:

Tragedy at Sleeping Giant

The Sleeping Giant Park Association regrets to announce the tragic disappearance of a woman and her son. Both elderly, they had been helped to the unfinished watchtower by the members of the Association who had gathered there for a picnic and a meeting. They made it to the top of the ridge without incident. The elderly woman and her son were just walking around, looking at the tower, taking in the sights. The Association members sat in a circle, discussing business matters. They heard a strange sound; when they looked up to see what it was, they realized that the elderly woman and her son were nowhere in sight. They immediately formed a search party. One of the Association members is a detective, well-trained in search techniques. The search was conducted according to scientific principle. No traces of either the elderly woman or her son have yet been found. The detective is not hopeful; he says that the brush on the Giant's side is so thick, they could search for a thousand years and still not find them. "Ironically, they could be right under our noses," he said, "and we wouldn't be able to see them." The Association expresses deep regret and deepest sympathies for the victims' families. The Association also reminds people to be very careful when hiking on the Giant; the hills are steep, the rock ledges slippery and most dangerous of all, the plant thickets are dense and impenetrable. Since it can be dangerous, they advise extreme caution.

In the family Bible, this:

Frog Bird Hitchcock
1855-1875
Yellow Tail Frog Bird Charles Sanford Hightower
1875-1935
Buried, somewhere, on the giant mountain man

Two old men sit on a bench at the base of the sleeping giant. They scan the newspaper headlines, chuckle ironically.

"Looks to me like old Hobbomock is hungry again," the first old man says. He chews tobacco, spits.

"That strange race in his belly got lonely. Needed company," growls the second old man. He chews tobacco, spits.

Together, in unison: "Strange nation in his belly. Damned strange."

1942

They are living in a two-story house flat-roof house on Montowese Avenue. In the upstairs kitchen pantry is a skylight. The glass is opaque, rippled. It lets in filtered light but does not allow you to see the sky except as a bluish-white blur. On hot summer nights, they open the skylight, pull themselves through, sit on the roof, feeling the wind and watching the stars. Tonight, though, it is early spring, cool; the skylight is closed. Their old dog, usually calm, sleepy, runs to the kitchen pantry, the hair on his back bristled. He growls, bares his teeth, paws furiously at the air. They gather, yelling at the dog to stop. The dog's frenzy grows. George Star Smith opens the skylight, pulling himself through. Strong, his wife easily pushes herself into the opening, pulling herself through. After all, whoever is up there will have to contend with her too. They have just stood upright, scanning the roof, trying to discover the thief. As the house begins to shake, they fall to their knees, hands gripping the roof tar to balance themselves. They stare, in awe, in fear as a great ball of fire streaks through the sky. Riding it, a great bird, with a frog's face. A massive frog-faced bird, with red eyes, a deep yellow tail.

Rushing, they descend into the house. Safe inside, they try to make themselves believe that there must be some explanation for this. They did not see what they just saw.

Doll Red Feather Bird Smith emerges from her bedroom. She couldn't be bothered to interrupt her dressing because the old dog was having a fit. They tell her what they have seen. Scoffing, she tells them that they have been deceived. "Hogwash," she spits. "Just blamed nonsense, that's all." Waving her hand, she struts into the kitchen. She is wearing her favorite outfit. A large yellow hat. On its brim, a red bird. A long tail feather runs down her back. A green velvet cape, embroidered with flowers and little green shapes that look like frogs. A yellow dress, of a material resembling silk. Red shoes, with high heels, open toes. Silk stockings, with a black seam running up the back of her leg. She carries a cigarette holder, of tortoiseshell. "Damn family," she sneers, "all that old Indian shit. All because of that stupid Red Man's Lodge down the street. Got them seeing things."

It is true that her father, George Star Smith, has started attending meetings at the Red Man's Lodge. It opened about a year ago in an empty storefront, on the corner. He and his wife, June Bug, go every Wednesday evening and Sunday afternoon. George Star is half Mohican, half English. June Bug is not sure but knows she is at least part Mohican, part Irish, part English, and part who knows what. Remembers her grandmother talking about some other Indian tribe she belonged to but can't remember the name. Though none of them ever before really thought about themselves as Indian, the Red Man's Lodge has made them more conscious of their many races. At the Red Man's Lodge they talk about the old ways. Not just old Indian ways. But old Irish ways. Old English ways. Swap stories from different tribes, different races. Mixed bloods, all of them. A motley crew, gathering together, to complain about how much is being lost, about the prejudice. Confess to each other they have tried to pass—sometimes for just white, sometimes for just Indian. Just hang out, trying to feel a community even if there isn't one. The man who started it has been out West a lot. He says it's different there. Better off and worse off at the same time. More full bloods there than here, but all in all, a lot poorer, sicker. George Star and June Bug complain about the children these days. How they have no interest in any of the old ways. Everyone agrees. It's a shame; they wonder what will happen by the next generation. June Bug says she isn't sure what will happen to Doll Red Feather Bird Smith who hates her name, says she got it because of some foolish whim of some old fool. Won't listen to the old stories from the family—not the Mohican, not the Irish, not the English, not any of them. But especially the old Indian stories, Mohican or any other. Just gets up, stomping her feet on the linoleum floor as she leaves the kitchen. June Bug shakes her head, catches her breath. Frowns. One night her daughter went so far as to yell, "I'm not listening to this Old Indian crap. Who'd want to be Indian anyway? It's worse than being nothing."

Doll Red Feather Bird Smith is thinking exactly this as she opens the kitchen door, walks down the back stairs. As she shuts the door, she leaves them still talking, sure that they never even bothered to notice her leaving. Doll Red Feather Bird Smith closes the back door on the bottom floor, walks down the long, narrow alley on the side of the house. As she emerges onto the sidewalk in front of her house, she smacks her gum loudly, in perfectly metrical time, like the beating of a drum. As she struts, her calf muscles knot. Strong, hard muscle, killer legs. Dark, long, thick hair. Hanging loose, halfway down her back. On the corner, waiting, a young man. Montowese Frog Jones, Frog Bird's son's grandson, Yellow Tail Frog Bird's son's boy. He scoops her hair into his hands, holding it at the back of her neck. Long, dark, thick hair. His fingers make tracks on her skull, webbed trails that close in on themselves. Hand in hand, they walk the city streets, avoiding the glare from the streetlights. Sometimes, when they have enough money, they go to the movies. Sometimes, if they have a little money, they go to the drugstore, sit at the counter, have sodas. Doll Red Feather Bird Smith loves the great deep blue cobalt jars on the drugstore shelves. If the light hits them just right, the blue seems streaked with deep red. She is very disappointed to find that inside those deep blue glass walls is nothing more than medicine for belly gas. Most times, though, like tonight, they will be walking the streets for a while, looking in shop windows, finding a quiet, dark alley, making love.

It is no surprise that Doll Red Feather Bird Smith and Montowese Frog Jones get married. It is no surprise that they refuse to have the ceremony at the Red Man's Lodge. They also refuse to have it in church, any church. They are wed at City Hall, have a small reception in her parent's postage-stamp back yard. She wears a plain brown and blue plaid jumper over a cream-colored sweater. On her feet, low black heels. Her stomach is so big she can see only the pointed tips of her black feet. As she stands there at City Hall she thinks that not too long ago she was fetching. Long, dark hair. Deep, black eyes. A red-tinge to her skin. Black leather high-heeled shoes, laced up to her ankles. How she could strut. Oh hell, she scoffs. That seems a million years ago. Look at me now. Hair getting thin, a big belly. Have to pee all the time. She snaps her attention back to City Hall, hearing herself say I do. Feels a ring slipped on her fingers. She smiles, kisses him back. She is not unhappy. She really loves her husband. It's just that her mind wanders so these days.

She slips away from the ceremony again, back to the night when she told him she was pregnant. She waited as long as she could. She was sure he would take off, leave her. That's what all the boys in the neighborhood seemed to do. But she was dead wrong. He didn't take off. He actually wanted to stay. In fact, he already knew. Was just waiting for her to be ready.

"Hey, Monty, I have something I need to tell you," she says, voice wavering.

He took her hand. Squeezed it, hard and gently. "I know."

"You know?" she says, surprised.

"Sure. Of course. It's my baby too. How could I not know?"

She lays her head on his shoulder, grateful. He slips his arm around her growing waist, eager, waiting to feel his child.

She returns to the ceremony. They are outside, their families kissing them. Doll Red Feather Bird Smith Jones grabs her husband's hand, puts it on the center of her belly. His hand jumps to the baby's hard kick.

They move into the downstairs flat in her parents' rental home. Her grandfather, the one on her father's side, hates Indians. He says it with pride. Her grandmother is always horrified. Always says, "Now, grandfather, you do not mean that." "Like hell I don't" he always replies. Usually Doll Red Feather Bird Smith Jones just ignores him. She's not exactly proud about being part Indian herself but she is proud of her black hair, her dark eyes, the red tinge in her skin. Colors just as good as white, what she always said secretly to herself. But never to her grandmother. A pale woman. Irish, maybe Scottish. Always made Doll Red Feather Bird Smith Jones think of hillsides shrouded in fog. Just shut her ears when her grandfather would insist that the Indian blood was not on his side of the family; no sir, no matter how it looked. But she is nearly full-term; she is very large, uncomfortable these last few days. And alone. Montowese Frog Jones was drafted the week before they got married. He is still in America, in training. She prays he will be able to get a leave when the baby comes. Because if he doesn't, he told her, he'll come anyway. AWOL, if he has to.

Quick, easy labor begins. The boy child comes screaming into the world just four hours after her first pains begin; he is hale, hearty, lungs like a full-grown man. Swears her Indian-hating grandfather has pride in his eye. She thinks about taunting him, reminding him that his great-grandson has bad blood too, but decides it's not the time. She dozes. When she wakes, Montowese Frog Jones is there, beaming. Right behind him, two Military Police Officers. Arms crossed, sullen. The baby wakes, cries. Out of the corner of her eye, she sees the military police men smile too. She's thankful that her husband won't be shot as a deserter. It's war time—anything can happen to a deserter. Within an hour Montowese Frog Jones must go. That's all they can give him; they have to take him back. Seems he jumped out of the bathroom window of the train as it was taking them to training. Montowese Frog Jones said they shouldn't have been surprised. Told them he would. When they said he couldn't have a pass, he told them straight up that he'd go anyway. A man of his word he is, he reminds them.

Before they take him they must decide on a name for the boy. They have thought about many, narrowed it to two or three. But June Bug begs them to please, please, please give the boy a special name. A name of power. Montowese Frog Jones doesn't much care. All he cares is that his son is strong, healthy. Doll Red Feather Bird Smith Jones is dead set against it, shakes her head, holds her son tightly to her breast as though to protect him from the name. But her mother begs again, this time joined by her father. A year ago, even a month ago, she probably wouldn't have seen in their eyes a world of faith, a world of despair. She realizes it is in her power to help them. She agrees. Silently she snaps, what the hell's in a name anyway?

Into the family Bibles this:

Red Man Jones
Born October 13, 1942

Montowese Frog Jones kisses her, kisses his son. He is led away by the two Military Police Officers. They have each pressed a dollar bill into her hand.

December is unusually warm. She dresses Red Man and takes him for a stroll in the carriage. As she passes the Red Man's Lodge on the corner, she is struck for the first time by the image of an Indian Chief in profile. Great headdress, long feathers at his neck, down his back. Strong chin, strong, square forehead, almost like a trap rock ledge. Long, dark lashes. Rugged, rough, deep red skin. She wonders what he sees. The irony of it all hits her. A great Indian Chief but only a head. Beheaded Indian Chief. Plastered on the side of a corner building, looking over nothing. She hastens, quickly putting it all behind her.

The spring is slow in coming. A blizzard in March. Many light snows in April. Doll Red Feather Bird Smith Jones begins to despair spring will ever arrive. The crocus has been frozen; the forsythia blooms turned black with the frost. The daffodils are in danger. Their little heads hang on the earth, their stems frozen to slush. She fears they will never have the strength to hold their heads up in the air. Too cold to walk outside or go to the neighborhood park, she has been playing inside with her son. She has borrowed from the library and a volume titled *World Myths*. She begins with a Penobscot legend:

"A shaman was once pursuing a man whom he wanted to kill. When the chase started the man was given a whetstone, some soap, some punk fungus, and an awl to help him in his flight. When the shaman gained on the man he threw down his soap and it became a bed of quaking mud. The shaman could hardly get through this but at last succeeded and began gaining on the victim again. This time the man threw down his whetstone and this became a wall of rock which stopped the shaman until he got an army of woodpeckers to peck it to pieces for him. Then he went on again, and soon gained on the man. Then the man threw down his punk. This turned into a burning tract. The shaman could hardly survive, trying to get through this place but at last he succeeded, and began gaining on the man again. Lastly the man threw down his awl. This became a thicket of thorns which entangled the shaman. In spite of his efforts he could not free himself and there he stuck. The man then escaped and got home."

She skips pages. Comes upon this, from *The Bible*:

"And God said, 'This is the sign of the covenant which I make between me and you and every living creature that is with you, for all future generations. I set my bow in the cloud, and it shall be a sign of the covenant between me and the earth. When I bring clouds over the earth and the bow is seen in the clouds, I will remember my covenant which is between me and you and every living creature of all flesh; and the waters shall never again become a flood to destroy all flesh. When the bow is in the clouds, I will look upon it and remember. . . .'"

There is a knock at the door. A man in uniform stands there, holding a telegram in his hand. She watches herself reach out her hand, take the telegram.

She hears herself thank him; she hears the door close. She does not open it. She does not need to. She knows what it says, what it must always say. She holds her son to her breast; lets her tears wet his thick black hair. "We regret to inform you that your husband. . . ." Will he be given military honors? Will he receive a purple heart? A commendation? It does not matter. She does not care. She sees him standing at the side of the bed, beaming, the military police trying to be stern. Dead. In the army. Somewhere overseas. Europe? The Pacific? Her baby screams, frightened by his mother's tightening grip, the beginnings of her howls.

His body is never recovered. There are many possible versions about how it happened. In France, he steps on a grenade, is blown into a million tiny bits of flesh. In the Pacific, he falls off the boat, is devoured by sharks. In Germany, he mistakes friend for foe, is shot, dismembered, fed to the animals at a zoo. Or maybe even he never shipped out, still in training somewhere. Maybe he met another kind of enemy. The one that, at the bar that fateful night as Montowese bragged about his little Red Man, called him a goddamned good-for-nothing Indian. Didn't deserve to wear the uniform. That Montowese, a little drunk, celebrating still the birth of his son, lunged at the swearing man, got caught in the deadly embrace of a thousand white arms that tore him to shreds, scattering his shredded flesh over the mountainside.

His body is never recovered. But he is very, very dead.

They hold a ceremony at the Red Man's Lodge. A box, carved heavily with ornate flowers, leaves, draped with an American flag. They gather. Her father-in-law wears a full headdress. He dances. Slow, somber to start, then faster. Another man, wearing a beaded shirt, beats a drum. The drum is decorated with arrows, a thunderbird, snakes. Her father joins them. She closes her eyes, shutting her ears. This is silly, she thinks. Stupid. He never believed any of this. But she thinks, oh well, what will it hurt? Can't be worse than a church service, she guesses. Red Man begins to bounce up and down on his mother's lap, dancing. Before they left the house, her mother-in-law said she wanted to give her son something, something that had been handed down through generations, at least as far back as his great-grandmother. A little vest, a beaded vest. Thought that he should wear it today, even if it is too big for him. Doll Red Feather Bird Smith Jones agrees, even if it's a little musty, creased, as if it's been shoved into the bottom of a trunk or something.

She lifts her son from her lap, holds his arms, lets his feet tap the floor. He giggles, squeals. She picks him up, twirls him around. Twirls faster and faster, twirling and swirling across the floor, to the beating of the drum, the chanting of voices all around her. She opens her ears, her heart, emptying herself, swirling to the sacred chants of many drums. Under her feet, vibrating through the soles of her shoes, drums, songs, voices, buried, deep, dead, insistent. Red Men dancing, singing, chanting, birthing, dying, grieving, rejoicing. Telling stories, burying their dead. Red Women, Red Men, White Men, White Women, Black Men, Black Women, Yellow Women, Yellow Men, forming a million circular cyclones, dancing to the beat of the earth.

Suddenly she hears all her parents say, in unison: "Look, look, a hundred tiny frogs, dancing." They clap, they sing praises, they take off the little boy's vest, examine it closely. They see nothing. They pass it around again, each looking with magnifying eyes. Red Man Jones bounces up and down. He wants to dance again. They put back on his vest. One by one they hold him, twirling him as his mother did. Faster and faster, twirling and swirling and whirling across the floor. All eyes intent on the vest, both front and back, but no frogs dance. Red Man Jones is swirled once more, twirled and whirled, trying to make the pattern emerge. But the beads make no pattern. The frogs have left.

When Doll Red Feather Bird Smith Jones goes to bed that night, she believes she has heard voices from deep within the earth. They came right up through the dancing floor, making their way into her feet. Tiny, green little things, scratching at her ankles.

1960

Red Man Jones has avoided the Giant. The more he has heard about it, the more sure he is that the legends are just crazy old stories. He hasn't been there. Figures it can't be much different than East Rock. He goes there all the time. A good climber, he can handle the steep rock ledges with ease. He bought climbing gear for a song at a local auction. His high school sits right on the base of East Rock. He remembers sophomore year, looking out the window, watching someone jump from the top, bounce off the rock ledges on her way down. He couldn't move away from the window, paralyzed, fascinated with fear. Wondered how if felt to be falling through the air, then having a rock ledge hit you in the back, crush your spine, tear off your leg. What that did to alter the course of your body mass falling through space. There must be some way to calculate that. Maybe he'll ask in physics class next week. There must be a formula somewhere. All physical things are governed by natural laws. He has faith in this. He plans a career in science if he can get into college, if he can afford to go.

He is very popular at school. Very tall, strong, handsome, he has thick, wavy dark hair, a mix of dark brown, black and red. A killer smile— strong, even white teeth, full, shapely lips. A gentle sneer. The girls adore him. So, too, do some of the boys. He crosses over between groups with ease. He's friends with the college prep kids, he hangs out with the kids studying business, and he has close ties with many of the kids taking the shop program, studying woodworking or automobile mechanics. Just about everyone stays in one group. Red Man Jones belongs to no group. He's part of all three. That makes him very popular, and very mysterious.

The one group he does not belong to is the Red Men's Lodge. His grandparents have begged him to attend at least some of the time. Tells him it's not just for Indians. History needs noticing. Valued. Preserved. His mother urged him once or twice. After that, she figured it was up to him. Since she didn't go herself very often, she thought she couldn't say too much about it. Besides, he's a good kid. Never into any trouble. So she doesn't want to be on his back about anything. Except his name, that is. He hates it. Says when he is twenty-one he is going to the courts to have it changed. She hopes it's a phase that will soon pass. But she fears otherwise; she fears what he said when she asked him why.

"But why do you hate your name so much?" she needed to know.

"Because I just do, that's all," is his first reply.

She knows better. "You know better," she challenges.

"You really want to know?" he challenges back.

She thinks she probably really does not want to know, but must say that she does. "Yes, I really do want to know."

"O.K., but don't say I didn't warn you," he snaps. "It's because it's all hypocrisy, that's why. Red Bird Jones is just a stupid name. It's like it's staring you in the face. Trying to put a red face on me when I've got as much or more white blood in me. Way more white blood, probably. Who the hell wants to be an Indian anyway? All you get is trouble. People look at you differently. Think you're stupid, shiftless. This name, it's like playing Indian. It not like I care about being Indian. I don't care. Stupid old stories, dumb costumes with feathers all over the place, crazy dance. I don't care about all that stuff. Why aren't the Indians interested in science? Why doesn't the Red Men's Lodge hold a science fair? Hell no, all they hold is some stupid ceremony where people dress up, dance, run around, complain, maybe chant. Want me to come and dress up in those stupid costumes, grunt some stupid song, stomp around like an idiot. Give me one good reason for wanting a name that pretends I'm an Indian."

His mother says nothing for a moment. "But you are so popular at school. Your name has not turned anyone against you."

He blushes. "It's because I told them it was a mistake," he admits. "And that someday, when we have enough money, you're going to get it fixed."

"A mistake?" she asks, incredulously.

"Yah," he admits. "Remember how you told me how Daddy jumped out the toilet window to come see me after I was born? How the military police took him back? How he died shortly after that?"

She nods. Of course she remembers telling him this, many times.

"Well, I sort of told the kids that Red Man was the name of the train car he was on. That the police had to write that down on their report. That he left Red Man to go see his son. Somehow, the person transcribing the report, said that Daddy went to see Red Man, his son. They sent a copy of the report to you, you never really read it, just showed it to the people at school for some reason that even you couldn't remember. So I got stuck with the name of Red Man."

She does not know what to say. Doll Red Feather Bird Smith Jones knows something about having strange names. Knows something about how heavy a name can be to carry around. But she doesn't know anything about being ashamed of a name.

"What would you like your name to be?" she asks, calmly.

"Robert M. F. Jones. Bobby for short."

"Why the M. F.?"

"For Daddy. But just the initials. Not the names."

"I will find you the money to change your name," she promises.

His victory is too swift, too easy, leaving him guilty, ashamed. Almost decides that he doesn't want to change his name. Almost wants to pretend he doesn't mind being part of an Indian.

But he minds. Every day in American History he minds. Every time he reads another history about America, he is terribly mindful that he minds. Always stupid, always trusting, always deserving what they get. Paraded around Wild West shows: how could they be so stupid? Didn't they know they were fools? Just helping the very men who took their land to get richer? The more he thinks about it, the angrier he gets.

One of his favorite classes is Geology. Every spring the class goes on a field trip. Red Man Jones is anxious for the trip, eager to find out where they are going. His face freezes when the teacher announces that they will be going to Sleeping Giant State Park. New trails, designated by colors, have just been opened. One trail, an easy one, takes them to the watchtower. Another steeper, longer trail also leads to the watchtower, to the summit at the Giant's left hip. Says they will be able to see literally layers of years, layers of history written upon the Giant's body. Says they'll use the first trail. The other one, marked blue, is part of the Quinnipiac trail system. It is one of the most difficult trails on the mountain. Very steep. Only for the experienced climber.

Red Man Jones has stopped listening. He sees the passage from his history book, the words incised on his brain. It is 1839. The canal from New Haven to Northampton, Massachusetts runs through Mount Carmel, along the base of the sleeping giant. A load of cargo drew spectators for miles. A band of African mutineers from a slave ship were being taken to the Hartford Court. Hundreds of people lined the banks, watching, gazing at the black bodies shackled in the boat. The reporter notes that among the crowd was a band of Indians, in full dress. The reporter notes the Indians laughed the loudest laugh, pointed the longest fingers.

When the bell rings, Red Man Jones does not move from his seat. He sits, staring at East Rock, at the faces of the cliffs. Long, sharp ledges—impossible to hold your footing without the proper gear. Suddenly he thinks about the old legend that says the Sleeping Giant came from East Rock. After he built his giant steps. Big crushing feet, building giant steps, changing the face of the earth. Red Man Jones feels a shiver along his spine. He licks his lips, excited and afraid. He hears the Giant walk—the deep reverberations travel an incalculable space. He catches himself, sneers. "Christ," he mutters, "get a grip. Probably nothing but a minor quake. Or maybe a rock slide." After all, he assures himself, it's only primitive people who make up such giants. "I don't need some mythical old gi-ant to explain my world," he reassures himself. Red Man Jones gets up, leaves his room, and doesn't look back at East Rock, too anxious to get to his math class on time.

The school bus churns its way into the parking lot at Sleeping Giant State Park. Red Man Jones sits in the far rear, smug, unwilling to show much enthusiasm. Some of the kids are a little afraid; this mountain is bigger than the one that rises above the school. This one looks like a man. It's kind of creepy, they admit. "Just another rock," he tells his seat mates. "Piece of cake," he assures them. "Anyway," he adds, "all we're going to do is look at some rock formations. Not like we're going to go off on the deep trails or anything."

The teacher gathers them, warning them to stay together on the Tower Trail. Red Man looks over to the legend on the big signs that greet visitors, quickly realizing that the Tower Trail is the sissy trail. Clear path the whole way. No ledges. No steep climbs. With a righteous grudge, he hangs back, reluctantly following the trail. But he loves his Geology class. So despite himself, he forgets his pose, gets interested, starts to have fun. Mr. Wilder knows his stuff. He stops the group, points to a boulder, rattles off all kinds of scientific names, throws out dates like there's no tomorrow. Tells them that about 15,000 years ago, the great Wisconsin glacier created all of this. How the face of the earth was changed dramatically and forever. How everywhere—if you know where to look—the Giant wears this great history. "Giant's an open book," he marvels. "You just have to figure out where the pages are and how to turn them."

Even though they stop often, it takes less than two hours to reach the watchtower from the easy trail. The group is young. The trail is easy, well-marked, so often traveled that it is compact, easy to walk. Gathering at the watchtower, they look out over Long Island Sound. They can see East Rock, think they can make out the outline of their school. While they are gazing out into the sea, wondering what it might be like to fall from so great a height, asking Mr. Wilder whether the rocks of the ledges here are the same as the boulders below, Red Man Jones slips away, walking so quietly you'd swear he had moccasined feet. He leaves the trail quickly, heading for the blue sign he can see in the distance. Blue Trail. Quinnipiac Trail. The one that leads to the Giant's left hip.

It is not long before he enters deep woods. Thick hemlock, huge oaks, so dense that sunlight barely enters except in weak shafts. A deep carpet of needles underfoot, his feet spring forward. Suddenly the trail emerges from the forest, makes a turn, starts to scale a high, vertical ledge. Red Man's heart quickens; he plants his feet for a moment, pivoting his hips. Then nimble as a mountain goat, he starts to climb. It is in the back of his mind that he has brought no climbing gear, that he could bring no climbing gear. Red Man Jones is scaling steep, vertical trap rock with nothing but his hands and his feet.

Finding just the right toe-hold, with incredible strength he hoists his body to the next shelf. His hands are bloody; his fingers quickly become numb. He climbs on, occasionally rubbing his bloody palms across his butt. He looks up but can see no end to the sheer, vertical rock above him. He tries not to panic. Trying to find another toe hole, his foot slips. He plants it again; it slips again. "O.K., O.K.," he lectures himself. "You're a great climber, Just calm down. You know what to do." He tries his foot again, placing it a little further to the right. His toe catches. Just as he pushes off, the rock beneath his foot crumbles. Tiny rock fragments let loose, tumble through space. He hears them hit against the ledges on their way down, imagining them bursting into a thousand tiny bits. Sweating profusely, he tastes the salt in his mouth. Beads of sweat drip from his nose. As the drips from his eyelashes run into his eye, he pays no mind to the shouts in the distance. He concentrates only on finding a better toe hold, one that won't crumble beneath him. He tries again, this time trying a spot a little to the left. His toe holds; the rock does not shatter. He pushes off. His hands reach and grab a ledge above and he pulls himself up. His fingers begin to ache again. He tries not to look, knowing his palms must be bloody raw. Another toe hold, another push off, Red Man Jones continues to climb. He cannot see where it ends. He stops trying to find out. He simply faces the rock, using his hands and his feet the best that he can. He finds a toe hold, pushes off again, pulls himself up. But this time the ledge his hands reach is flat, long. He pulls himself over it. Exhausted, he lays on his belly.

Two hikers come by, asking if he is alright. Ask what the hell he's doing up there without gear. That he should get down right away.

Red Man Jones stands. Tries to make a fist but his palms are so raw the pain stops him. "It's an experiment," he informs them. "A science project. To see how much stress the body can take."

"Well kid," they bark. "I'd call off the experiment if I were you. Look at you. You barely made it up that little ledge. What the hell are you going to do with the big ones?"

Red Man Jones looks up, to the left. The ledge above them is twenty times steeper and longer than the puny, little one he has just fought so hard to conquer.

"Look, face it buddy," the hikers warn, "you have no business being on this part of the Giant. Get off the blue trail. You have no right to be here." The point him to an easy trail that will lead him back to the Tower Trail, where he belongs.

Red Man Jones stands firm. Wants to scream, to cry. He does neither.

"Look," they say sternly, "either you get your ass back over where it belongs or we'll get the Park Ranger on your case. He'll throw you out of here."

Humiliated, raging, Red Man Jones walks sullenly back to the sissy path. Assured that he is leaving, the well-equipped hikers start up the steep, sheer rock of Giant's chin.

The easy path takes Red Man Jones through a smaller stand of hemlocks. Daylight enters here in wide shafts, the wind wending its way more easily. He breathes the deep hemlock air, forgetting for a moment his humiliation, his pain. The knees of his pants are torn away. His knees are gashed, bleeding. His hiking boots are scraped. The front of his shirt tattered. Suddenly it occurs to him that he's got to make up some story, some way to get out of all the trouble he's going to be in. He hears voices yelling for him. He sits at the base of a large hemlock tree, trying to figure out what to do. Red Man Jones hears a tiny voice, a strange tiny voice. He hears it above all the other voices shouting for him. Impossibly, he hears its tiny, insistent voice, drowning out dozens of frenzied search hollers. He cannot find its source. He looks up, down, but cannot see anything that could make such a noise. He hears water rushing deep beneath him, a pleasant, strong, rushing, muffled roar. His bloody hand touches a strange rock. Pieces of quartz gleam from it; so, too, veins of granite. He can identify these and two or three other kinds of common rocks. But there is a deep green diamond across its top; in the middle of the diamond, a deep yellow square. The rock is not large. He picks it up in his two hands, turning it over, analyzing it with his scientific eye. He blinks. Suddenly the yellow square moves, pulsates. The green diamond starts to move too, both now pulsating, growing, changing, growing out of the rock, catching the wide shafts of light that enter the hemlock grove. Red Man Jones puts the rock down, backs away. The rock opens for the briefest second. Red Man Jones catches the barest glimpse of a tiny frog, with a yellow crown and red eyes, singing a strange, haunting song. A tiny frog, with glaring red eyes, opening its mouth, singing an unheard of song that drives deep into his open ears. Overhead, the flapping of wings.

Red Man Jones races back to the Tower. When his party sees him coming, they think he has gone mad. Tattered, torn, wide-eyed, babbling about a frog in a rock that exploded in his hands.

He says not a word the entire trip back home. Although angry and disappointed, Mr. Wilder does not press him; he fears for Red Man Jones' mind. Mr. Wilder calls Doll Red Feather Bird Smith Jones, tells her that her son has had some sort of accident. She comes to the school to bring him home. Shocked by his appearance, by his vacant gaze, she almost brings him to the hospital. She decides instead to bring him home. One the way home he chants: "Inside rock, a world, exploding. Inside rock, exploding, a world."

Red Man Jones seems to have forgotten that strange day on the mountain. His wounds have healed, he has stopped saying impossible things, returned to his everyday high school life. He seems to have forgotten to remember what he saw that day.

The frogs wanted to take him that day. "He's ours," they insist. Grace Yellowbird Faith nods. She knows this is true. The frogs are insistent; they try to have their way. Grace Yellowbird Faith shakes her head. "No, it is not time," she warns. The frogs persist. They make their claim. They threaten—an ancient frog chant, with high lilting chorus, deep, reverberating notes.

Grace Yellowbird Faith holds up her hand. "No," she repeats. "It is not time."

Grace Yellowbird Faith holds firm with her iron will.

Two yellow birds appear, standing behind her. They snap their wings; the frogs fall silent. They know the yellow birds' iron will.

Red Man Jones seems to have forgotten that strange day on the Giant. His wounds have healed, he has stopped saying impossible things, returned to his everyday school life. He seems to have forgotten to remember what he saw that day. But if you could look over his shoulder you would see that on every sheet of paper he draws a tiny frog in the lower right hand corner, a frog so tiny you almost need a microscope to see its tiny red eyes. You'd need a microphone to hear its tiny screech.

If you could look into his mind, you would know that a blue diamond and a red square rotate there.

If you could look into his heart, you would know that he imagines himself dancing, chanting, in full, many-colored feathered dress.

For his eighteenth birthday, Doll Red Feather Bird Smith Jones gives her son a copy of his birth certificate and the beaded vest he wore as an infant. There is also a fresh-from-the-bank crisp, clean, uncreased one hundred dollar bill, a down payment on his name change. They are in the painted box that was Sanford Hitchcock's, the one that holds the family Bible. Inside the painted box also is the plain box that holds Elizabeth's family Bible. When Doll Red Feather Bird Smith Jones gives him these things she says "Whether you want them or not, these things are yours. Just like your name."

The key to the plain Bible-holding box has been lost. His mother is deeply sorry. The last thing Montowese Frog Jones did before he was escorted back to base was to write his son's name in the Bible. He told his wife where he hid the key. But she, alas, cannot remember.

That night Red Man Jones breaks the lock. Looks at his name written in a fine, straight, strong hand. Though it is not legal, he draws a line through Red Man, writing above it Robert M.F. He repeats this in the other Bible. Later that night, as he closes his eyes to sleep, he sees a green face. He gets up. He lifts open the painted chest, opens the plain box. He reopens the Bible, crossing out the Robert M.F. Writes above that Red Man. He repeats this in the other Bible. Starts back to bed, retraces his steps. Opens the painted box, opens the plain box, reopens the lockless Bible. To the right of Red Man, O.K. He places his crisp, clean, uncreased one hundred dollar bill in this lockless Bible, placing Ben Franklin face up. He opens the other Bible. To the left of his name, he writes O.K.

Red Man O. K.
O.K. Red Man

Red Man O.K. Jones falls into a deep and peaceful sleep. Double O. K., a twin red man falls into the sound, serene sleep of the newly born.

1968

Red Man Jones' SAT scores are disgraceful. The guidance counselor said it was proof that he was not college material. She urged him not to waste his money, not to bother to apply. He didn't. Instead he went to work on the night shift at the Winchester factory helping crank out the "Rifle that Won the West." He's been living at home, saving his money. A few years ago a new College opened. It sits right across the street from Sleeping Giant State Park, around the curving hillside road that hugs the ponds now owned by the Water Company. The road has been constructed over the ponds, effectively cutting them in two. A small bridge runs underneath, allowing the pond's water to flow into one another. He thinks about applying; it takes him almost four years finally to do it. He sent in his application, along with a fee. He thought about retaking the SAT but decided it wouldn't do any good—he'd probably do even worse since it's been so long since he studied anything. Probably all a waste of money, he worries, but fills out the application anyway. The essay stumped him completely the first year he tried to apply. He just gave up. He had nothing to say. After two more unsuccessful tries, Red Man Jones finally gets inspired. He decides just to tell them the truth. How his father jumped out a toilet window to see him after he was born and how that turned out to be a great thing since his father was dead soon after and couldn't have jumped out of a toilet window to see him if his father had waited. How his grandparents begged his parents to name him Red Man. How good a rock climber he is. How he wants to live across the street from the Sleeping Giant so he can climb the rocky edges of his face.

Red Man Jones reads over what he has written. Dictionary at his side, he makes sure every word is spelled correctly. Satisfied, he starts to put his application in the envelope. Hesitating, he takes it back out. Adds to the essay: "And I want to be near the Sleeping Giant. He has something to say to me." Red Man Jones almost erases that last line. Instead he puts the application in the envelope, licks its gummed top, closes, presses it tightly and chooses his stamp. He has four from which to choose, all part of this year's commemorative series. He sits quite a while, choosing among Leif Erickson, Walt Disney, Henry Ford and Chief Joseph. Finally he chooses Leif Erickson. He licks his back, places him head up in the corner of the envelope, ready to let him and the application he heads go forth on their doubtful journey. But suddenly Red Man Jones wants to take it back, to erase that last line. But, alas, it is too late. He won't waste a stamp. Especially not a Leif Erickson.

He has to wait for three months. When the letter comes, it is very thin. He knows before opening it that they have not accepted him. The skinny envelope does not contain forms for rooms, announcements of financial aid. He almost tosses it away unopened but figures what the hell? He's kind of interested in just how they tell you they don't want you. He is right: they will not be admitting him as a regular student. Therefore, he is not eligible for financial aid. Therefore, he is not eligible for a room on campus. But they will admit him as a "Special Student" for one semester, allowing him two classes. They mention that a short distance from campus there are rooms to rent, in case he is interested.

Red Man Jones has enough money to pay his tuition. He has one month to decide; it takes him two days. He sends in his deposit, both furious and curious to be a "Special Student." He makes a copy of his sort-of-acceptance letter and sends it to his old guidance counselor. At the top, he writes "I am so college material." He gets a small, but real, sense of satisfaction. He smiles at his own bravery, at his own wit.

Quinnipiac College mails him a copy of the course catalogue. Red Man Jones spends hours reading every description of every course, even though most have pre-requisites that he does not have. It's an agonizing choice. Red Man Jones has not told anyone how much he misses school, how much he really wanted to go to college. He is mindful that he must make the right choice, the perfect choice. These two courses are his first and they may be his last. Of course, he chooses Geology 101, An Introduction to The Science of Geology. In the description for this course: "Frequent field trips to Sleeping Giant State Park are required in addition to class and laboratory time." Almost as a supreme challenge, to prove to himself that he will be that special of all special things, the well-rounded college material student, he enrolls in English 103, section 3, Contemporary American Fiction. In the course description for this course: "We will study cutting edge, newly-published American fiction."

The last weeks at the Winchester Factory are painfully slow. Hot, boring, day after day on the same assembly line, Red Man Jones dreams of September, of the beginning of his college life. He works at the factory until the day before school starts; he is not stupid enough to believe he doesn't need every dollar he can scrape together. He has rented a room within easy walking distance of campus. He won't even need to buy a bike. About a week before school begins, his mother tells him that they must go to the Red Men's Lodge that evening. Before he can open his mouth, his mother's pointing finger shuts it. "You're going. That's all there is to it, young man. Period." The period does it. Red Man Jones knows she means it. After he gets there he is ashamed for having wanted so badly not to go. He is the first from the neighborhood to go to any college. They present him with a certificate naming him "An Honorary Red Man." It is rolled, tied with a red ribbon. When he opens it he can still smell the fresh ink—someone has written the document in beautiful calligraphic script. On the outside of an envelope: *Mr. Red Man Jones, College Student*. He hesitates; they urge him to open it. Inside, a fresh-from-the-bank, crisp, clean, uncreased one hundred dollar bill. Ben Franklin stares Red Man Jones in the face. They shake his hand, slap his back, urge him to do them all proud. A pot luck supper follows. Red Man Jones can't believe how delicious the food is. When the dancing starts, Red Man Jones is one of the first on the floor; when the singing starts, his voice joins the others. When the chanting begins, Red Man Jones feels something in his heart. He does not know what it is, but he hears it pound there, insistent, regular. Make us proud, Red Man Jones. Make us proud. Let your feet dance to the hum of the earth; let your heart beat to the sacred drum. Make us proud, Red Man Jones. Feather your head, bead your chest. Make us real proud, Red Man Jones. Listen to the waters rushing beneath you; listen to the voices of the rock. Make us real, real proud, Red Man Jones; listen to the tiny voice screeching in your red and white head.

Red Man Jones swaggers a bit as he walks to his first College class. His hair is cut in a duck's ass across the back, the front is swept up into a pompadour. He wears penny loafers, a clean copper Lincoln looking out from the slit in the top of the shoe. When he walks and the sun is just right, he makes flashes of gleaming light. He has on a blue oxford shirt, a narrow black tie. The legs of his black pants are pegged tight. Red Man Jones notices, though, that more than a few of the blonde-haired men have long hair, wear jeans. Crap, he thinks to himself, already out of date. But he still swaggers a bit, confident in his killer smile. His first class is Geology. The professor, Dr. Eaton, received his Ph. D. from the University of Connecticut, is nationally famous, has published many monographs. His specialty is basaltic rock formations; his current research is being conducted at the Sleeping Giant State Park. He is a Visiting Professor at Quinnipiac College. Red Man is lucky to find himself in such a class. He's studied Geology before; he knows his rocks. When he walks out of class his swagger is gone. Dr. Eaton's first lecture goes right over Red Man's head. He walks out, terrified of failure, terrified that the school guidance counselor was right. He finds himself in the middle of a group of students leaving the class. He is so relieved when one of them speaks up first, saying what they all feel. "Christ," the student says, "I couldn't understand a goddamned thing he said." The comradery is immediate. Red Man Jones still has his place.

The next day he has his English class. Mr. Bourne, a Ph.D. candidate at the University of Connecticut, is a one-year Visiting Instructor at Quinnipiac College. He has already published one article on modern fiction and presented two papers at major conferences. He is a shy man, slightly balding, older than Red Man Jones expected. Mr. Bourne speaks very softly; the class has to strain to hear. He tells them they will enter a world in this class like no other. A journey into the very best recesses of the human imagination. Meet wordsmiths so skilled they will marvel, feel awe. That they will be part of a great discovery. They will be uncovering the greatest new voices of their generation. It all sounds good, Red Man thinks, but a little too easy. Thinking he may have wasted his money on this one, he places his bet on Geology. After class, he finds himself part of no group. The students leave, each going a separate way.

The first couple of weeks whiz by. Red Man becomes more comfortable with Geology, gets the hang of Dr. Eaton's lecture style. Gets a B on the first exam. Is pretty pleased, especially since of the thrity students in the class, only two got an A and fifteen got D's. "Hard old bastard," Red Man mutters, "but knows a hell of a lot." English isn't going so well, however. Red Man Jones is increasingly lost. A collection of short stories by John Barth, *Lost in the Funhouse*, about did him in; even after two weeks of class discussion, Red Man Jones has no idea what is going on. They move on to Thomas Pynchon's *The Crying of Lot 49*. Red Man is lost in a house that isn't much fun. He's failing English, feeling his hard-earned money go down the drain. His face reddens when he remembers the money, the certificate, their make us proud refrain. He almost doesn't return to class, thinking that might save him a little face. But he does return. Something Mr. Bourne has written on his paper gives him a little hope. "You are very smart. And you write rather well. But it seems you have nothing to say about these works—nothing, that is, to say that you want to be saying, need to be saying. I hope you find the book that will give you something to say. That will make you want to have something to say." He added a p.s. "If you do find that book and have something you want to say, I will be willing to read it."

The F on his paper doesn't sting so much. Yes, he failed to understand that the title of Pynchon's novel referred to an auction of rare stamps. Yes, he failed to understand that, but at least he doesn't feel like a piece of worthless shit.

The next week they start Barth's *The Sot-Weed Factor*. It's very long: small print on over eight hundred pages. The first few pages are rough going, but Red Man Jones keeps going because of a phrase in the first sentence of the novel. The main character, Ebeneezer Cooke, is introduced as a "rangy, gangling flitch." Red Man Jones has to look up flitch; he's never heard it before. He finds three meanings:

1. A side of pork cured and smoked.
2. A longitudinal section of a log.
3. A bundle of sheets of veneer laid together in sequence.

He still doesn't know why Ebeneezer is called "a rangy, gangling flitch," but Red Man Jones is fascinated that he is called this. Fascinated that the words stay in his brain, almost like a chant. "Rangy, gangling flitch," over and over again, playing in his head. Soon Red Man Jones finds he cannot put the novel down, reading well into the early morning, starting again before dawn. The novel is fantastic, unbelievable, funny as hell, scary too. But what draws Red Man Jones the most is that Ebeneezer Cooke uncovers a history behind history. Another history, there all the time, waiting to be discovered, uncovered. Red Man Jones talks for the first time in class, then writes his essay with ease. He gets a B. In his comment the instructor notes that he thinks Red Man Jones is getting close to discovering his own voice.

Before they start their next novel, the instructor tells them that their next book has just been published. It is so strong, he is sure it will win major prizes. *House Made of Dawn* is an extraordinary book. Big print, just a little over two hundred pages. The first word throws Red Man Jones. "Dypaloh." He's never heard it before; he cannot find it in any dictionary. He goes to the library and asks but no one there can tell him what it means. So he returns, starts reading again. "There was a house made of dawn." He cannot make any literal sense out of this. But something deep inside him understands exactly what Momaday means. "For a time the sun was whole beneath the cloud; then it rose into eclipse, and a dark and certain shadow came upon the land." Red Man Jones thinks about the Giant, about how the light disappears as you hike into the deep woods. When he gets to the scenes at the Holiness Pan-Indian Rescue Mission, he thinks of the Red Men's Lodge. Starts to revise this way of thinking about it, his way of feeling about it.

"My grandmother was a storyteller; she knew her way around words. 'Storytelling; to utter and to hear.'" All the times Red Man Jones' grandmother tried to tell him stories, all the times he did not listen. Red Man Jones shivers: before him the beheaded Indian profile, staring straight ahead into space. Once again, in his mind, he walks past it, not wanting to look back. "The walls have closed in upon my grandmother's house. When I returned to it in mourning, I saw for the first time in my life how small it was." Red Man Jones winces. "There, where it ought to be, at the end of a long and legendary way, was my grandmother's grave." Here, where it ought to be, at what is still the beginning of another long and legendary way, Red Man Jones sets out to find his family's graves—or, at the very least, sets out to find his family's lives. An historical house is across from the corner of campus, a house painted red, salt-box style. A plaque on the door says it's the Dickerson house. Red Man Jones has a gut feeling that somehow it relates to him. He runs, crosses the street, and starts up the side of the Giant, leaping in long strides nimbly over the path. After he crosses the street he passes by the ponds. He knows he will return to them, before dawn—something timeless to see. In less than an hour he makes the summit, reaches the watchtower, and briefly looks out through the spider web window. Holds out his open arms, gazes out to sea. Scans the harbor, feeling the wind blowing through his pants, his sleeves. He has been letting his hair grow; he runs his fingers through it, letting it fan out in the stiff breeze. He leaps into the air, clenches his fists, plants his feet firmly on the rocky earth beneath. He has something to say, by God. He really has something to say.

Racing back to his room, he seizes paper and pen, writes furiously, forgetting to eat, refusing to listen to the gnawing inside his belly. He writes through the night. When he hands in his essay, his hands shake. The next week, he gets it back. A huge *A+* written on the cover. In the back, this note: "You have found your voice. Never give it back."

He's been on four field trips so far. Each time they have been enjoyable, he has learned something new and interesting, but he feels little excitement. This surprises him. He always used to be very excited to discover the scientific properties of the earth, to learn to read the layers of rock data deposited year after year. On the field trip today, something strange happens when they are looking at the rock that Dr. Eaton has cracked open. Instead of seeing distinct little lines, each showing the effect of heat or cold or water, Red Man Jones starts to hear tiny little voices, one building on top of the other. Startled, he realizes that there are histories behind history, just waiting to be uncovered. Startled, he realizes that without the bottom layer, the next layer could not be deposited. Without it, the next layer could not find its grip. And the layer that is now top, will it form the base from which a new layer grows? Are all layers fated to become a bottom layer? Are all people doomed to move from being a top to being a bottom? It strikes him: he can read the cracked rock face another way. Each layer has its own place, its own tiny voice. New layers come into place, but they do not crush the one below. All the layers, working together, finding strength both above and below, giving voice to everything that has ever been, voice to everything that ever will be. Red Man Jones listens little to the rest of the lecture. As soon as they return to the base and Dr. Eaton dismisses the class, Red Man Jones heads up the Tower Trail, crosses over to the Quinnipiac Trail where he has made a deposit. He has his climbing gear this time—this time he is ready to meet the Giant's face.

He quickly scales the small ridge on which he labored so hard on what seems so long ago. He can still feel the hurt in his hands, his fear as the rock crumbled below. He does not think of the strange rock; for now, it is safely beyond his mind's reach. Focused, intent, strong, with his ears open, his heart not shut, Red Man Jones casts his hook and rope high into the sheer rock cliff that is the Giant's neck. It is mid-morning; Dr. Eaton's field trips always begin before dawn. Red Man Jones is grateful; he has plenty of time to climb. No class until tomorrow. Having read ahead, he has no homework tonight. He is cautious, unafraid. Finding toe holds easily, his arms and legs very strong, he hoists himself higher and higher. He is careful to secure his safety ropes, remembering the girl plunging down East Rock. He does not look down. Great streaks of black rock veins are at his fingertips, shale deposits gleam in the sun. Mica, quartz bring colorful shine. Hard trap rock over his head, at his feet. He tightens his leather harness, ready for the steepest part of the climb. For a moment he hangs suspended in the air. He quickly catches his hook into a sturdy rock fissure above, pulls himself up. In that fissure, a tiny pool of water. Red Man Jones marvels, wondering if it supports any life.

He reaches the top of Giant's shoulder, decides not to climb higher today, and heads south, toward deep woods on a ridge. Inside, the sun appears in narrow shafts. He finds himself in a circle of hemlocks. Encircling the hemlocks, a circle of oaks. He sits at the base of the largest hemlock. Removes his backpack, letting his shoulders feel weightless. Glad he stuck food in his pockets, he eagerly eats. He notices the sun shafts slanting near the ground, guesses it's time to head home. Starts to gather his gear, start the pleasant, easy walk down the tower trail. After the great climbing he has done today, he thinks he deserves the sissy trail. He hasn't finished his apple. He could just pitch it over the cliff but he places it carefully by a large rock. For some strange reason, he pats the rock, as if it were a person's head. For some strange reason, he pats it again, letting his fingertips rest in its green moss, then straightens up, turns to leave. As he does, a tiny voice shrieks. Red Man Jones turns abruptly, just in time to see a tiny green foot dash behind the rock. He slips off his backpack, gets on his knees, tries not to breathe. He peers around the rock, just in time to see a tiny green foot dash to the front of the rock. Red Man Jones laughs, likes this little game. From the center of the mossy-topped rock, water rushes, deep beneath. He turns his body to face the front of the rock, sure he'll see a tiny green foot dash the other way. No green foot dashes. Disappointed, he gets up, puts his backpack on, heads home. About halfway down, he wanders from the path a few hundred feet. A little stream. So much mica on the stones here, the lowering sun makes hundreds of tiny rainbows dancing along the water's edge. He knows he's been by here a dozen times. Maybe the angle of the sun wasn't just right. He lies on his belly, drinks. The bottom edge of the sun is just touching the earth. As he stands up, he hears a shrill little shriek. Seeing nothing, he instinctively places his hands on a mica-covered round rock that sits partially in the water. From beneath it leaps a tiny green frog, with deep red eyes. On its back, a deeper green diamond. In its center, a bright yellow square. Red Man Jones tries to catch it. As he lunges for it, he falls flat on his face. As he pulls himself from the water, shaking off as much as he can, he sees the frog, sitting on another rock. The frog opens its tiny little mouth very wide. Red Man Jones doesn't know the language with which it sings.

Red Man Jones crosses by the ponds just as the top of the sun begins to touch the sky. Great white wings flap above; a snowy egret passes over his head on its descent to its pond nest. He isn't sure which he prefers—the snowy egret descending at dusk or ascending at dawn. Red Man Jones feels good, feels strong. Thinks of that slippery little strange frog, wishing it had not gotten away. Suddenly, the roar of enormous flapping wings. Across the last remnants of lighted sky flies a black bird. A huge black bird, with the face of a frog and bright yellow wings.

A prize assembly is held near the end of December, just before semester break. Red Man Jones receives an invitation to attend. Awarded the Quinnipiac Essay Prize, for the best essay written in an English class that term, he is given a copy of the complete poems of e.e. cummings and a check for $25.00. Curiously, he is not elated. Instead, he is afraid. If he stays at this school, he fears, he will keep hearing the frogs; if he listens long enough he'll have to start telling their story. After final exams, Red Man Jones gives up his room. He moves back to his mother's house, working for a few weeks at the Winchester factory. Doll Red Feather Bird Smith Jones goes to the Red Men's Lodge almost every night. She's been dating a really nice guy she met there. Calls himself Hawk Tail. Swift, mean, and clean, he laughs. Red Man Jones likes him. He works at Winchester's too, but in a different division. Red Man Jones just works on the assembly line. Hawk Tail is master finisher of the carved wooden shafts of their best models. Says he learned it from his grandfather, an English Presbyterian who knew his wood.

Red Man Jones listens to the radio, reads the papers everyday. The war is getting nastier, protests against it mounting. He doesn't take sides. He just knows that his draft number is about to come up so he gets the agony over with and enlists. As he pulls away from his mother's embrace, he sees the fear in her eyes. He also knows that his grandmother is very ill, will probably die before he comes back. Red Man Jones leaves the house on Montowese Avenue not knowing if he will ever see it again. The evening before, he went over to Mount Carmel, looked up at the Sleeping Giant, hoping that he was sound asleep. He did not enter the park; he just watched from across the road under the light of the first moon. Across the face of the moon, an owl flew. In front of the owl, the shape of a hawk, with a frog's face. Red Man Jones is not afraid. But he tries hard to close his heart to what the Giant is trying to say.

As he boards the bus that will take him to basic training, he sees East Rock in the distance. It makes him think of the Giant. "Just dead rock," he mutters. "Just a huge old Indian, long since dead, laying on his back, turned to stone," he stupidly insists. As the bus leaves the parking lot and turns onto the Parkway, Red Man Jones imagines the frogs are waving good-bye. If they had little fingernails, he's sure they'd be painted bright red.

He is a mediocre soldier. His bed is never made to the standard, the corner of his blanket always off. He messes up drill, his hair is too long, his belt buckle not shined well enough. He becomes a clown, doing anything to get a laugh. The other guys sort of like him but he's getting on their nerves, acting crazy. Wakes up sweating and screaming one night, muttering something about frogs crossing the moon. Crazy bastard, they think, as long as he leaves us alone. Wakes up another night, starts chanting in some strange voice, then yelling something about red eyes and yellow rocks. They tell him if he can't smoke weed without keeping them up all night, then he'd better quit.

Red Man Jones finds himself in the jungle. His scouting unit is one of the first to land. Army intelligence fears that North Vietnamese are nearby. He's good at tracking. He learned on the Giant how to look for the remains of old paths. Knew one animal track from another, could even tell one bird track from another. This jungle is way thicker than any part of the Sleeping Giant's deep woods. He feels like he's suffocating, the air is so dense, damp, heavy. Nothing but walls of green everywhere. The huge tropical leaves keep hitting him in the face. Strange insects hop onto his arms, his neck, his face. He swats them, smashing them, leaving their slimy green on his cheek. He hears birds in the distance, their song different than any song he has ever heard. Enemy footsteps behind him, he turns, rifle cocked. It is his platoon buddy. He forces himself onward, a thousand eyes upon him, watching, waiting.

The platoon slowly advances, careful to inspect every bush, every tree. They feel the earth inch by inch, their toes looking for hidden holes. Red Man Jones has strong toes. He trusts them to find even the tiniest slit in the earth where the enemy might hide. He forgets to keep his mouth closed; he almost swallows a huge spider web hanging from a large green frond. As the spider vaults, its green and red back displays its diamond pattern. He keeps low to the ground, pushing his way among the undergrowth, hearing the footsteps of his comrades at his back. The smell of fire, the flash of light, the shaking ground. From above, they are being fired on. From above, shafts of bullets, pinning them in the undergrowth. The rushing, pounding steps of the enemy advance. Their fingers grab him, thousands of them, claw-fingers, grabbing him. Deep red eyes staring at him, green legs jabbing at him. A thousand of them, crawling over his body. Tens of thousands of them, with deep red eyes, sprouting black wings from their little green arms. Tens of thousands of them, crawling over his body, croaking to the yellow sky.

Red Man Jones lays very low, a little red man, waiting for death. A very frightened little red man, waiting for the white flash of death.

After he is discharged from the hospital in Saigon, he returns to base for only a day or two. They put him on the first flight. Discharged from the army, no longer fit for duty. They assure him there is an excellent VA hospital in West Haven, at the base of West Rock where maybe he can receive some help.

Red Man Jones is back at the assembly line at the Winchester factory, once again helping to crank out "the Gun that Won the West." His grandparents are dead; his mother and her new friend have moved to Chicago. Red Man Jones rents a room just a few blocks from the factory, walks or rides a bike to work. He does not drive—automobiles scare him. His room is furnished with a bed and a dresser. He has added a hot plate so he can heat soup, water for coffee. The only real furniture that is his is at the end of his bed. There the plain Bible box lies within the painted box with its own Bible in it. Under these the beaded vest. Red Man Jones leads a quiet life. He reads a lot, everything from detective novels to the New York Times. He spends a lot of time at the main New Haven library on the city green. Two greens, in fact, mark the center of town. Once lined with great elm trees, they are almost all dead now. A terrible blight. Arborists from all over the world unable to defeat it. Only a few of the elms survive. Scientists study them, hoping to unlock their key to survival. He visits often the Peabody Museum of Natural History, especially interested in the skeletons of prehistoric birds. One has huge, strong wings, a great pointed beak, sharp teeth. Wondering what were the color of it eyes, he muses on the terrible irony of prehistoric. He does a little climbing on East Rock. Sometimes he takes the bus over to West Haven, climbs on West Rock. Hears climbers saying that some local historian now says that the Judges Cave was never on West Rock, that it was on Sleeping Giant. The judges had ordered the death of King Charles I when his son took the throne; two of the judges, William Goffe and Edward Whalley fled to America. Legend has it that these regicide judges hid out in these caves. Red Man really would like to know what the evidence is and how history could be so wrong. It's not like West Rock and Sleeping Giant are exactly close to one another. He almost tries to enter the conversation but decides not to. Red Man has become a very shy man. He dates little, probably will never marry. His is a quiet life. A decent, quiet life.

He has made friends with a man who attends his Wednesday evening group therapy at the Veteran's Hospital. He also was in Viet Nam. He has nightmares about his missing hand. His buddy fell next to him, shot through the head. Ace grabbed hold of his buddy's hand, tried to hoist him upward, to get him out of there. It might have been a grenade, maybe a machete. He stood there, looking down at his friend's body on the jungle floor. A foot or so in front of them lay their hands, clasped tightly, severed at the wrists, pooled with blood. Jagged edges, not a clean cut. He looked at his stump, appalled at the fleshy bits of tendon hanging down, of the gristle of jagged bone marrow protruding. Flesh on fire, hazy smoke. His nostrils still burn with the sting of dead flesh. Some days it's not too bad. Other days Ace is terrified to look at his arm. Red Man Jones and Ace Pierson go over to Jimmy's this Wednesday evening, a great restaurant out on Savin Rock, by the ocean, famous for its seafood. Red Man Jones always gets the fried oysters, the fried whole-belly clams. Only place around that gives you the whole belly—most places only give you the strip. The dark, moist, meaty whole belly, its smooth and mealy texture, its fleshy smell—this is what Red Man Jones will remember for days afterward. The taste of the whole gut on his tongue, sliding down his throat. They take the bus, sitting in the back. It's a warm night. The smell of salt air permeates the dirty interior of the bus on its Savin Rock run.

Red Man Jones was pretty quiet during therapy. Lately he hasn't had a lot to say. He sits looking out the window, watching the dark reflected light from the ocean's surface. The road runs right beside the water here—highway reflection and ocean water seem to blend. The seagulls are thick, noisy, the sound of their flapping wings almost deafening. Their white dung covers everything. They get off the bus, go get in line. They decide not to eat inside, taking their food out and sit on the shore. A three-quarter moon lights the beach, the sand is cool, the tide is high. They sit close enough to the water so that the waves lap at their shoes. Occasionally a piece of seaweed pushes onto their feet. Red Man Jones loves to pick it up and then pop the little bloated seaweed sections, enjoying the small explosion, the squishy jelly liquid running down his wrist. He wipes his hand on his jeans, takes another whole-bellied clam. Ace Pierson has been very talkative tonight. He's been telling Red Man Jones about going to a newly-formed meeting for Mohican Indians. That he's learned so much about his history. Met great people. Learned old dances, old songs. Says they are planning a powwow soon and invites him to come. Red Man really isn't interested. Ace Pierson leaves him alone.

They eat some more, listening to the water rushing at their feet. Red Man Jones takes a stick, plunges it vertically into the sand. When he pulls it out, the water rushes in, then the sand folds back over itself. All of a sudden Ace Pierson tells Red Man Jones that he has heard a story and it is driving him crazy trying to figure it out. It has come down from an old, old Mohican grandmother who says that it will be coming true. He pushes Red Man Jones' arm, asks if he wants to hear it. Red Man Jones shrugs O.K. He has nothing better to do anyway, although he'd probably rather just eat.

"Well, it's all about how the bull frog has to make his neck swell up so big in order to sing his courting love song. In the early days, long before we kept track of time with a clock, a great Thunderbird fell in love. He pined for this beautiful Thunderbird Woman, dreamed about her both day and night. He couldn't sleep. He couldn't eat. His massive strong wings became bony. Bull Frog asked him what the matter was. Thunderbird sighed, a sigh so deep and heavy that the earth shook beneath them, causing Bull Frog to fall over. Thunderbird helped pick Bull Frog up. Sighed again, more softly. Remained silent.

'Please, tell me why you are so sad,' said Bull Frog.

'I cannot, I am afraid,' cried Thunderbird .

'But why? I am your friend. I will help you,' Bull Frog assured.

Thunderbird thinks a long while. He puts his great wing around Bull Frog: 'Do you promise not to tell anyone?' he needs to know.

Bull Frog nods.

'There is a Thunderbird who lives across the bay. She has veins of yellow running through her lustrous black wings; glitters of red streak her deep, luminous eyes. I love her. But I cannot speak to her. Every time I think about asking her to come flying with me, my throat closes up, and the only sound I can make is a strange gurgling. I am sick at heart. I do not know what to do. I love her. I must tell her so if she is to know. But I cannot speak. It is as if something stops up my throat, killing my song before I even sing it.'

Bull Frog puts his green and slimy hand on Thunderbird's wing tip. 'Friend,' he says, in a deep, soothing tone, 'your song will yet be sung.'

Thunderbird does not understand. He looks at Bull Frog: 'But how?' he asks.

'If you will fly me across the bay, then I will speak to her. I will tell her what it is you want her to know. Then she will go flying with you. You can bring me home and then go off to fly around the great, vast, wonderful world with the one you love.'

Thunderbird roars with glee, whistles, sings. Wings outstretched, he twirls and he whirls till he becomes a black whirlwind. He turns so swiftly that he picks up the wind and whirls it into a circular cyclone. Before he knows it, he is spinning down into the earth, his whirling bird body driving a slit into the world. Bull Frog croaks a mighty croak. Thunderbird Man stops his whirl.

'You had better watch that,' Bull Frog warns. 'Such power. It might take you to the center of the earth. And what if you couldn't come back?'

Thunderbird agrees. He promises not to dance so fast.

Bull Frog jumps on Thunderbird's back. He lies low so the wind won't sweep him into the sky. They fly across the bay. Bull Frog cannot believe how beautiful this Thunderbird is. Lustrous black feathers with reflective glints and gleams of deep, soft, golden yellow. And her eyes. Never has red flashed so gently from such deep, dark eyes. No frog he has ever loved has ever had such colors. Bull Frog asks this beautiful Thunderbird to put her ear down to the ground so that he might whisper to her. Instead, she lays her wing on the ground, motions for Bull Frog to jump on. She lifts him gently in the air, level with her ear.

'Thunderbird has something to say to you but he is afraid,' Bull Frog begins.

She smiles, urging him to continue.

'He wants to tell you about the way you look.'

'Then please, Bull Frog, tell me what it is he wants me to know,' she trills gruffly, as only a thunderbird can.

Bull Frog does not intend to say what he says. He hears himself say 'He wants to know how you can call yourself a Thunderbird. No proper Thunderbird ever had yellow wings and red eyes. Silly yellow wings, crazy red eyes. Too many colors for a proper Thunderbird.'

She almost throws Bull Frog to the ground. Marching over to Thunderbird, she pulls back one of her mighty wings, crashes it across his unsuspecting beak. As she takes off into the sky, she spits over them both, raises her mighty wings, flapping dust into their eyes. Doesn't bother to look back.

At first dumbstruck, Thunderbird is soon angry, very angry. He calls on the Great Thunderbird Spirit for justice. The Great Thunderbird Spirit hears his son. From this day forth, Bullfrog will have trouble singing his own love song. He throat will swell, his skin stretching so far it will threaten to break open. He will look a silly, ugly thing. Big eyes, so big they pop out of his head. A belly of a neck, big, round, strange. Little blood veins will emerge on his big belly of a throat. His slimy skin will pulsate.

From that day forth the Bull Frog must sing his song of love through a swollen belly of a coarse throat.

Bull Frog is very sad. He misses his sleek throat, his clear, pure words. He fears his ugliness as he sings his love songs to those he loves.

'Will you ever forgive me?' Bull Frog asks of Thunderbird.

Thunderbird thinks a long time. He finally turns to Bull Frog: 'Maybe on the day we fly together in front of the moon.'

Mohican grandmother swears that someday the thunderbird and the frog will fly together in front of the moon. She swears that when this happens it will be a sign that some great change is coming to the world."

Red Man simply nods. Deep in his memory, he knows he had seen the frog bird fly in front of the moon. Deep in his memory, he knows great change is to come.

1992

There is blight on the side of the giant. Scientists confirm it is true. Red Man Jones hears it first on the local radio station, then he reads part of a report in the local newspaper. Botanists have recently discovered a very troubling occurrence of woolly adelgid, a hemlock blight, at Sleeping Giant State Park. There is no known cure and the blight has already spread so rapidly that part of Giant's left hip is brown. They note that it "secretes a white cottony coat around itself" and, under that coat of white protection, sucks the hemlock dry. It devours its sap juice, effectively desiccating the poor hemlock tree, leaving it a dry, brown shell of a thing.

Red Man Jones has a strange vision of a white man wearing a great coat. This strange great coat has feet around its wrists, a long tail down its front. He has to get up, go outside, he is suffocating. His head clears; he forgets the coat. But he is bothered by the report, knowing he has to return before the Giant's body becomes too disfigured. Wants to finish his climb up the Giant's face, see if he can catch that strange frog running around the rock. But most of all he needs to smell the hemlock groves before they die. He needs to sit in the narrow shafts of sunlight, hearing the water rush beneath him, imagining frogs dancing in the dark hemlock limbs.

Wanting to be in good shape, he starts training at the gym. He's too fat. His muscles are soft. He thinks it might take a few months. He is fat. His muscles are soft. After nine months he is strong enough to climb the Giant's face. On weekends he used to climb either East or West Rock, practicing for his return to the Giant. But now he sticks with East Rock. It's closer to home, he reasons. But whenever he climbs above the huge stone steps on East Rock the Giant's feet carved into the stone, Red Man Jones starts feeling a huge white coat being spun around him. A thick, cottony, furry yet slimy coat whose fibers prickle his skin. A coat that has teeth in its cuffs that gnaw away at Red Man Jones' bones.

It firms his resolve to return to Giant's sleeping mountain where he won't be gnawed away.

Red Man Jones is ready. He packs carefully. Fully equipped, he returns to the Giant. Plenty of food in his pocket. Just as he is about to lock the door behind him, he re-enters his room. Opens the painted chest at the foot of his bed. Takes off his back pack, opens it. Takes the beaded vest from the bottom of the box. Rolling it tightly, he pokes it down snugly into the side of the backpack. He opens the lockless Bible, takes out Benjamin Franklin, slips him into his back pocket. He closes the lockless Bible, puts it in its plain wood box. He places it back in the painted wood box, closes the painted cover. He runs his hand along the paint, feeling its faded strength. English strength, good strength. He opens his door, closes it behinds him, turns and locks it. He has no idea that he has locked his door for the last time, no idea that a week later his beloved painted chest and all it contains will be sold for a song.

He takes a cab to Mount Carmel just before dawn. Only a thin ribbon of reddish brown at the horizon. He walks by the ponds. Just as he approaches their western tip, he hears the flap of wings, the rush of wind: a great egret lifts itself vertically into the air. Red Man Jones watches from underneath, staring as its strong wings carry it aloft. It turns its head sideways. Red Man Jones swears for a moment that he sees a tiny green frog in its beak. A tiny green frog with big, deep red eyes. He laughs, sure it's just some weird reflection from the pond or the sky. He almost starts right on his climb but he takes off his backpack, gets down on his belly at the edge of the pond. Cars whiz by just feet away. He doesn't see it at first but on a pond lily pad a couple of feet from shore is a large frog, croaking. Red Man Jones lunges toward it. Quick as a flash, it dashes into its underwater cover. Red Man Jones laughs, almost thankful he didn't catch it. He stands up, puts back on his backpack, starts toward Tower Path. He follows it briefly, then crosses over to the blue Quinnipiac Trail. Just as he turns to go, the big frog reappears, croaks very loudly. Red Man Jones turns just in time to see the frog's back as it leaps into the suddenly-appearing water. On its back, red squares. In the middle of the red squares, yellow diamonds. He remembers Ebeneezer Cooke.

In record time he starts again to ascend the Giant's chin, finding himself at the very same spot when years ago he decided to stop his climb for the day. Almost noon, he eats quickly, making sure he has enough time to complete his climb to the top. He is amazed at how easily he can climb. Toe hold after toe hold, hoist after hoist, he gains the top of the giant face. When he feels his foot catch on firm rock at the very top, he pulls himself over the edge of the last trap rock ridge. With a convulsive shudder, he hauls his body completely onto the rock shelf. He lies there a few minutes, on his belly, hands spread out over the black trap rock ledge. He gets to his knees, then stands. With arms outspread he surveys the earth beneath. He does not linger, planning to traverse the top of the ridge, make his way to the center of the Giant's belly before dusk. There are the thickest hemlock woods; there Red Man Jones will spend this night.

In record time, he nears the center of the Giant's belly. His heart sinks. Many hemlock needles are covered in a whitish coat. "Woolly adelgid," he mutters out loud. A flash; it contains gelid. Gelid white coat. An image of a baby and a woman appear, bound together by the tail of a great coat. He shakes his head violently, clearing his brain. Making his way into the grove, he sits at the base of the largest hemlock he can find, leaning his back against the hemlock bark. Without knowing why, he opens his backpack, takes out the rolled little beaded vest, lays it at his side. He rests, breathing the spicy hemlock air, feeling its carpet of needles under his cheeks. He closes his eyes, almost sleeps. Suddenly tiny little voices. Red Man Jones cannot hear what they say. He cannot hear "We want him now. We want him now." He cannot see Grace Yellowbird Faith. He cannot see two yellow birds nod their solemn yellow heads O.K.

He gets up, tries to trace the tiny voices, his rolled little beaded vest in his hand. He takes his toes, pushes them into the earth in a dozen places. He moves out in an ever-expanding circle, shoving aside small rocks, digging little holes with his strong toes. A red-tailed hawk screams overhead, while yellow birds flock high in the hemlock boughs. Large, black, flapping wings in the distance. A tiny frog sits on his shoulder, lapping its tongue on his cheek. Red Man Jones pays too much attention to the frog at his cheek. His strong toes stumble into a vertical slit as it opens deep within the Giant. Red Man Jones disappears, waving the rolled-tight little beaded vest high in the air.

Red Man Jones lands wide awake inside the mountain, hearing the gentle rushing of clear, fresh water. Yellow birds circle above, chirping strongly, sweetly. Many creatures live here, among them two men and three women. Everyone and everything seems young, beautiful. There is an abundance of berries and roots and seeds. Grace Trap-Ridge Hitchcock approaches, holding the hand of Chief Montowese. He welcomes Red Man Jones, introduces him to their daughter, Grace Yellowbird Faith, who sits weaving her great blanket. Frog Bird and her son Yellow Tail Frog Bird Charles Sanford Hightower welcome him too. In the far right corner of Grace Yellowbird Faith's enormous blanket sits a large frog with great red eyes. On its back, a darker green circle; in the circle, a yellow diamond. The frog is sitting on a woven frog. On its woven bright green back, a yellow square; in that square, a red diamond. Grace Yellowbird Faith has been weaving this blanket for many years. She will be weaving this blanket for many years to come. The old people say that when she is finished weaving this blanket, the earth will be restored to itself.

Suddenly a vertical shaft of light opens high above. From it descends Thunderbird Man. He has the head of a great frog. His great black wings are tipped with the brightest, most golden yellow, and his eyes are deep, blazing red. In his beak, a fine, full red feather. He walks toward Red Man Jones, offering him the feather, then enfolds him with his great yellow-tipped black wings. Red Man Jones lays his head on the great breast of this wondrous bird beast. A feathery darkness enfolds him. He hears its heart beat strong, steady. Like a drum, he thinks. Like a sacred water drum.

Thunderbird Man calls Grace Yellowbird Faith to stand next to Red Man Jones. She is a large and powerful woman—striking in aspect, graceful in her speed. Her thick hair is parted in the middle, gathered into two great braids that fall to the middle of her back. The left side of her hair is the deepest golden yellow, brighter and deeper than the corn. The right half of her hair is the most lustrous jet black. If you look closely you can see each shaft of black hair has a tiny yellow gleam at its tip. Special eyes she has. Her left eye is the most brilliant blue— bluer than the sky, bluer than the sea. Her right eye is a deep hazel blue, flecked with brown, green, tiny streaks of black. Her fingernails are deep, dark, bright red. In the middle of each finger a yellow circle; in the middle of each circle, a green diamond; in the middle of each diamond, a red square.

Thunderbird Man admonishes Red Man Jones: "You have been reluctant, my son. Why?"

Red Man Jones hangs his head, does not answer for some time. Finally he says, reluctantly, "Because I have been afraid of what I have seen in the sky."

Thunderbird Man admires his honesty. "Are you afraid now?"

"I don't know," Red Man Jones honestly replies.

"Will you take her hand and let the Great Spirits' magic show itself?

"I think so," is his honest, if disappointing, reply.

Thunderbird Man shakes his head. The birds and the frog sigh. Thunderbird Man puts his wing on Red Man Jones' shoulder. "We will meet again when the next first moon lights Giant's sleeping belly. If you are ready, you will stay with us. If you are not, then you are free to leave."

"Free to leave?" Red Man Jones questions.

Thunderbird Man nods.

Red Man Jones nods back, already knowing that he has no desire to go free.

At the next first moon, Thunderbird Man reappears, descending swiftly, powerfully, gracefully through the vertical slit that opens in the rocky ridge above. Grace Yellowbird Faith has just finished weaving another section of her blanket. A great Thunderbird, a red-tipped arrow in its claws, a large stick in its beak. On top of that section sits a large green frog, with a yellow crown, and jewel red eyes. Thunderbird Man calls Grace Yellowbird Faith to his right side. Red Man Jones is at his left. Chief Montowese and Grace Trap-Ridge Hitchcock stand nearby. Frog Bird and Yellow Tail Frog Bird Charles Sanford Hightower join in. Two yellow birds hover overhead. Thousands of tiny frogs are in the wings; so, too, legions of little yellow birds.

"Are you still afraid?" Thunderbird Man asks Red Man Jones.

"No," is his simple and honest reply.

"Will you take her hand and let the magic of the Great Spirits show itself?

"Yes." He has in his pocket his little beaded vest, rolled tightly.

They join hands. Thunderbird Man calls the two yellow birds who come, each carrying two seeds in their beak. The male yellow bird drops two seeds into Red Man Jones' hand; the female yellow bird drops two seeds into Grace Yellowbird Faith's hand. Yellow birds give the signal. Grace Yellowbird Faith and Red Man Jones join hands. The frogs gather, thousands of them singing a croaking love tune. Thousands of yellow birds converge. From a far corner of the world, Mother and Father Thunderbird nod their heads, give their assent. Thunderbird Man takes the hands of Grace Yellowbird Faith and Red Man Jones. When he steps back, a frog sitting high upon a trap rock ledge speaks:

"What is given to you is a great thing." Folding his wings closely about his chest, Thunderbird Man twirls. As he whirls the tips of his wings turn pure yellow, forming a halo of light around them all.

Stopping, he takes from Red Man Jones the tiny little vest, unrolls it, and holds it up so the frog high on the ledge can see. The frog nods, solemnly. "It is good to have the vest in our hands. It is good that we will see the frogs dance front and back." The frog calls on Great Frog Spirit for strength and power. Great Frog Spirit hears his son. The vest in Thunderbird Man's hand begins to spin, to swirl and to twirl, doubling itself. There are two vests now, one in each hand, tiny little frogs running, front and back. Thunderbird Man asks Grace Yellowbird Faith and Red Man Jones to open their hands. In her right palm, his left, tiny creatures. Each creature grows rapidly to six feet. One has the head of a woman, the other the head of a man. Each has the body of a frog; from their sides sprout great black wings. Bright red feet, deep green eyes. On each, a tiny little beaded vest with frogs running front and back. Grace Yellowbird Faith and Red Man Jones love what issues from their seeded hands.

Thunderbird Man nods approval. "This is good. You have done well. It is now time to name these children. In their names will be the sign of what may be to come."

Grace Yellowbird Faith and Red Man Jones have no names. "We leave it to the Great Spirits to name these beautiful children," they agree.

Thunderbird Man nods. "It is well that you have done this."

They pray for guidance in the choosing of names. It is granted. The frog high on the ledge sings the names for all to hear.

So it is Red Faith and Frog Lily, twin child-beasts, who will henceforth be living and waiting in the belly of the Giant. The next section of the blanket their mother is weaving will be theirs.

Grace Yellowbird Faith and Red Man Jones give thanks again for such beautiful children. Everyone dances. A motley crew, they dance, hearing sacred water drums deep within the mountainy earth. A strange and alien nation, waiting. A special nation, in the making. A nation of impossible difference living as one.

1880

All of Mount Carmel talks about him. High up on the giant, mining the earth, David Tall Man believes the old legend. Before Kietan put Hobbomock to sleep, he took from the giant many treasures. Kietan's pockets could only hold a small part of them. David Tall Man is sure that there is a great store of treasure, just waiting to be found. He lives in a small abandoned cottage at the base of the mountain. He hikes to his mining spot on Ridge Hill before dawn everyday; he does not descend until a little after dusk. He seems to have no family, no friends. The town wonders about him, about where he gets the money to buy his food. They do not know that David Tall Man left his wife and son, that he came from Bridgeport with two-hundred dollars and a pick-axe. They do not know that if he does not find treasure before his two hundred dollars is spent that he will have to pick up his pick axe and slink back to Bridgeport. She warned him when he left that it was sheer foolishness. That it would serve him right if she and their son, David Pine Tall Man, left town.

David Tall Man lives carefully, spending as little money as he can. He eats berries and roots, has made traps for small game. He thinks he will be able to last until he finds the treasure vein. He's come close already: a thin vein of copper. But it ran out right away. A false start.

His back is broad, his shoulders massive. He excavates the rock with rhythmic precision. The sound of the metal against the trap rock echoes for miles. When he hits heavier, dense rock, it sounds like a drum. More than one person hearing it has joked that the Indians are at it again. The winter is icy. There have been many days that David Tall Man cannot make it up the mountain. These rocks can be slippery when dry. When wet they are difficult. When icy they are impossible. He doesn't want to break a leg so he sits in his cottage fuming, fretting, shivering. When the ice breaks, David Tall Man rushes up the giant, hardly able to wait till he can resume picking through more of the giant's body. An old, crazy woman sometimes makes her way up to David Tall Man's little mine. Mostly she just stares at him. But once, when he was picking away, she snarled: "Christ, you fool, stop it. Don't you think the giant feels that?" David Tall Man laughed, told her to get down to the road where she belonged. The old woman wagged her finger in his face. "That's a problem too. Road's where giant's warm blanket used to be. Someday he's going to get cold. He'll want it all back." She turns her back to David Tall Man, making her careful way down the path. Looking up, he drops his axe. He swears there are frogs dancing on her back.

He decides to quit for the day, rattled by that foolish old woman. On his way down he almost steps on a copperhead, moving out of the way just in time. Luckily he caught the diamond flash on the back of its head. That night he does not sleep well. He dreams of green birds with black and yellow wings. They appear in profile, flying across the face of a full moon. He hears voices, tiny, insistent. Quiet at first, then growing louder. "He's ours, you know," he hears them say. He wakes, drenched. It's just before dawn. He goes to the pond, plunges in the freezing water. Just as he plunges downward, the feet of a great egret swirl the water so that he cannot see. Waves made from their powerful ascent pound his face. He turns over, floating toward the surface. As his body breaks the surface of the water, his eyes open, watching the receding feathery underside of the great egret flying skyward. Its wing bones are stretched outward, the bony veins forming an intricate pattern on its wings. As he stands and hops onto the little shore, a tiny frog appears underfoot. His feet are huge, often clumsy. Snapping his foot back into the air, he sighs great relief as he sees a frog hop hurriedly away. The little creature turns its glinty red eyes and stares briefly at what seems to it a giant man.

Rushing home, he changes into dry clothes. Energized by his encounter with the egret, David Tall Man uses his strong legs to propel him up the giant. He abandons his mine, picks up his tools and moves them a few hundred feet down the giant's side. In the middle of a group of hemlocks stands the opening to a very shallow cave. David Tall Man had noticed it many times but now wastes no time, beginning to tunnel from the back of the shallow cave. It takes weeks. The trap rock here is solid, dense. He makes not more than a foot a day of progress.

Months roll by—still nothing. David Tall Man has taken to praying. Chanting out loud. Often during the day, sometimes at night. In a strange voice. Over and over again:

> "Little frog with red eyes
> Tell me where it is.
> White bird in the air
> Where do your wings go?
> Tell me

Tell me
Where to dig my treasure.
Little Red-eyed frog
You know where it is hid
White-winged bird
Soar overhead
Dip your wing
Show the hiding place
Of my treasure."

All who hear snicker. All who hear have no fear of the ramblings of a harmless crazy man who can't tell a poem or a prayer.

David Tall Man perseveres. He hears the water rushing quickly beneath. He worries that he may break through to water, drowning the treasure underneath. A great white wing hovers high above, pointing downward. Feverish, he struggles to control himself. He works very carefully. As he makes another inch, he sends his long fingers in to explore the narrow passageway. He has sensitive fingers that can tell copper from rock. His fingers hit something with smooth ridges all over it. He pulls it out. It is a beaded pouch with leather drawstrings closing the opening. David Tall Man's heart races as he tries to catch his breath. With a thousand thanks to green frog and white bird, he pauses, marveling at the intricate pattern. The bag is beaded with four panels. In the center of each, a thunderbird. Closing his eyes, he hears the sounds of their wings. With fingers trembling even more, David Tall Man carefully opens the beaded thunderbird bag. In it a single yellow feather.

He bursts into tears. He throws the bag back into its cave, races down the Giant's side. Abandoning the already-abandoned cottage, he disappears, feeling betrayed by the creatures to whom he prayed.

David Tall Man dies a bitter, lonely man. His wife and son are missing when he reaches Bridgeport. David Tall Man dies, a disappointed, lonely man.

Poor David Tall Man. In his hands, a miraculous yellow-feathered world. And all he knows to do is throw it back.

1895

David Tall Man's wife and son make a new life for themselves. They move to New Haven, rent a small flat on State Street. She takes in sewing, cleans houses. As soon as he is big enough, David Pine Tall Man works after school doing whatever he can. Sometimes he works in the fields, helping pick crops. Sometimes he runs errands for the shop owners. Jessica Hotchkiss Tall Man wants her son to finish the eighth grade; she works and drives herself so that her son can have what she never had. He finishes the eighth grade, goes to work at the New Haven Clock Company. At first he simply works on the assembly line, putting the cut-out steel arrows that point to the hour on the face of the clock. As the pendulum swings, a tiny spring moves the steel arrow-hands around the face of the clock. But after five years, he has become the floor manager, in charge of thirteen men.

Yet David Pine Tall Man has been thinking about other things. His mother told him that his father deserted them. He has never seen his father's parents. He knows nothing about them. He has never seen his mother's parents. They live in England. He knows little about them. His mother does not talk about them much at all. Few letters ever come. When he has asked why, his mother simply shakes her head no. So David Pine Tall Man is amazed when his mother tells him that his grandparents are coming for a visit. Linda and Earl Hotchkiss arrive the day after tomorrow. David Pine Tall Man can hardly concentrate on making clocks when the time to this visit ticks closer.

They are much older and more frail than he had imagined. They are exhausted from their trip. Their boat arrived in New York three days ago. They rested, then took the train to New Haven. Jessica Hotchkiss Tall Man is strangely stiff as she bends to hug her mother and father. A foot taller than either of them, they comment that her married name is a fitting one. David Pine Tall Man finds his grandfather's hand uncomfortably cold and bony. He falls in love with his grandmother's pale blue eyes and still-black eyelashes. Looming a good two feet above her, her head barely comes up to his mid-chest. She tells him he is more handsome than she ever imagined, joking that he must have gotten it from his father's side. The carriage ride home is exciting. His grandparents marvel at how large the town is, asking David Pine Tall Man a hundred questions about shops, restaurants, the theaters, the marvelous twin New Haven greens, lined with magnificent, mature elm trees. New Haven, he informs her, is the Elm City.

"Is that so?" asks Linda Hotchkiss.

"It sure is," beams David Pine Tall Man, feeling like a tour guide with wise and deep knowledge of his city.

"Did you know it used to have a different name?" she wants to know.

"Really?" he asks, unsure if this can be right.

"Long ago, before it ever was New Haven, it had a different name."

He thinks she'll tell what it is but she doesn't. She just stops.

"So, what was the name?" he prods.

"Dragon Town," she replies, simply.

His mother scoffs. "Oh, David, that's nonsense. Mother always likes to make jokes. Don't take it seriously."

David Pine Tall Man starts to laugh, then stops. His grandmother's placid smile tells him she is telling the truth.

"Are you sure it was called Dragon Town?" he hopes.

She nods. "Yes, David. I am sure."

Again he thinks she will say something else but she does not. His grandfather seems to be paying no attention to the conversation. His mother is looking the other way.

"How do you know it was called Dragon Town? And why Dragon Town? There are no dragons here," he fires off.

"How I know is one thing. Why it was is something else all together," she quips.

He senses he has to pick one at a time. "Well, why was it called Dragon Town?" he asks.

"Because when the English first arrived here, the harbor was covered with seals. They called the seals sea dragons. So since the seals guarded the entrance to this place, the place got to be named after the seals. The seals that themselves were named after the sea dragons."

He loves the way his grandmother talks— he could listen to her tell things all day. He's never heard anything like it before. It's not so much what she says. It's the way she has with words. The way she makes things sound. The way she makes him listen to every word, trying to catch what seems like another voice under hers.

He thinks about asking why they were called sea dragons but thinks better of it. "How do you know this?" he asks instead.

"Because one of those early settlers many, many years ago wrote a letter to someone back in England saying it was so. Told about coming to a place called Dragon Town. Told about meeting a race of people they called Quinnipiac. Told of hearing about a legend of two giants fighting. The loser was put to sleep on his back, turned to rock. He lies on his back, a sleeping giant. He said that when the giant woke up—and he was sure someday the giant would—that if he sneezed, the whole harbor shoreline would be changed. The force of his sneeze would force the water from the bay, leaving Dragon Town without a place of entrance." As she finishes, Linda Hotchkiss nods, purses her lips, then cracks a smile. She slaps David Pine Tall Man on the knee.

His mother frowns, avoiding eye contact. His grandfather has not said a word until now. "Now, mother, don't talk the boy's head off. Not with those silly old stories of yours." He winks at his grandson; in that wink a world of misunderstanding. David shifts uncomfortably, smiles feebly. All are silent the thankfully-short rest of the way home.

They have but a small house. His grandparents will share David Pine Tall Man's little room. It is summer; he will sleep on the enclosed back porch.

They have a modest but special supper: boiled corn, potatoes, fresh blue-fish. Coconut cake and coffee afterward. They turn in early. David is lying atop a Pendleton wool blanket. When he turns on his side, he can see through the porch windows, to the bottom part of the sky, a few of its many stars. Tomorrow, he plans to start cutting a hole in the ceiling. He will frame the perimeter of the opening, fitting window glass into it. For the rest of the summer he will lie under his created skylight, gazing at the stars.

Just as he is planning this, his grandmother knocks, opening the door that leads from the kitchen to the porch.

"By the way, David, in that letter was something else."

David quickly props himself on his elbow. "Really?" he asks.

She nods her head, smiling widely. She whistles through the gap in her mouth; she is missing four front teeth. "Yes, really" she returns.

He's already used to the game. "So, grandma, what was it?"

"A big, bright red feather, that's what."

He laughs so hard his stomach hurts. When he stops laughing, his grandmother has long since disappeared to what is now her room. He turns over, looks out the porch window. He hears a noise— a scraping, hopping sort of noise. A little groan, almost a croak. By the back door, trying to fit itself into a little gap between the door and the sill, a tiny green frog with shining red eyes. David Pine Tall Man hops out of bed, gently opens the door, setting the frog safely free.

He returns to his sleeping bag bed, lies on his back, closes his eyes. Drifts off, starts to snore. Has dreams about waterways changing course, of towns he can't find the entrance to. He wakes frequently, tossing, turning, dreaming. In the early morning hours, he hears the fog horns. A huge frog appears, with a gold medal around his neck, holding up its claws. They are painted a bright red. David Pine Tall Man reaches out his hand to this frog; the frog takes its bright red claw-nail and writes on the back of David Pine Tall Man's hand. He looks, trying to make out the letters. He cannot read them. They begin to fade. He squints, tries to read the fading red ink. But he cannot make them out to see. When he awakens he does not remember this dream.

At breakfast he is tired but eager. His grandfather wants to rest. As he puts it, "A body's not made to be on the road more than a day at a time. Gotta rest it in between. Otherwise, it's likely to run out on you." His grandmother, however, says, "Hmmmph. Blamed nonsense. God didn't give us legs if He didn't want us to be moving." She gets up from the table, freshens up, ties on her best straw hat, the one with a deep red lily on the side, and waits for her grandson to take her arm. They strut outside, promenading downtown. She wants to swish her way over the twin downtown greens under the leafy canopy of elms. She has on a great skirt of black taffeta. When she walks, it crinkles. There is a black-on-black pattern of diamonds set on edge, quivering, pulsating as she moves. On her feet, smart boots with mother-of-pearl buttons running up the outside of her ankle. Holding her grandson's arm, she feels as she might have felt fifty years ago. But it is not fifty years ago. She is old; her strutting days are almost done. She is all but exhausted by the time they make the twin greens. They sit for hours on one of the benches, thick with pigeon shit underneath. Too tired to get up, she is too tired to care that dozens of pigeons gather at her feet, impatient for her to share her meager lunch. They peck at her toes; she shoos them away. They return, peck her some more. When she throws them some bread, they converge, fighting over the crust. They finally leave. She holds her legs out, looking at her boot. They have pecked a tiny hole. A tiny hole, with ragged edges, atop her fine leather boot. With pigeon shit clinging to her heels, Linda Hotchkiss begins a long, loud laugh.

Finally she has rested enough. Taking her grandson's arm, they rise and begin the rough, long journey home. David Pine Tall Man wants to hire a carriage, assuring her he has enough money. She will have none of it. "If God didn't want me to walk," she says, "he wouldn't have given me two good legs." He laughs, hugs her. He has promised her that they will do this tomorrow and the day after tomorrow. He does not have the heart to have it otherwise. David Pine Tall Man does not have the time off from work he told his mother he had. But there are stories he just must make time to hear.

"Your father wrote me one time. Addressed just to me. Your grandfather was not pleased. He wanted to see. But I closed the letter, put it between my dress and my breast."

David Pine Tall Man has been waiting for days to hear her say something about his father. They sit on the twin greens, as they do everyday. She brings the pigeons scraps, gives them something right away. They have made a bargain, it seems. She feeds them when she arrives; they leave her feet alone for the rest of the day.

"You know your mother was very brave, to leave for America with your Aunt Faith who was dying. The doctors thought a change of scene might restore her. She always wanted to see New York. It was her dream. We all put together what money we had. She sold her house and her furniture. They sailed in August. She lived till November, saw the New England fall. But that left your mother, a girl of eighteen, alone in a new land. She heard about good jobs at factories in Bridgeport, Connecticut. She took the train there, was hired at a clothing factory. She sewed buttons on collars fourteen hours a day. Almost ruined her eyes. I know she was often sick. I could tell it from her letters. Well, letters at first, that is. Then just a note. Then hardly a line. Then we got the announcement. That she had married your father, bore a son. We didn't know what to think, what to do. We had given all of our savings to your mother and aunt. We had no more. We could not come."

She paused abruptly, shook her head, laughing ironically. "Now, David, now that we have sold our house and all our furniture, now we have the money to come."

David's eyes widen. Not a temporary visit flashes in his brain. He wonders if his mother knows. He'll have to fortify his porch before winter.

"Your grandfather was suspicious, I admit. Said right from the start that something must be wrong. Otherwise we would have had an announcement about the wedding first. I tried to think he was wrong, but I guess I knew he was right. But as I said to him, if that be the case, then we ought to be mighty thankful they got wed. Not that we're righteous, mind you, because that we are not." She breaks into a belly laugh, showing well the large gap in her front teeth. She hugs her grandson, confesses, "'Cause, well, I was in the same way, so to speak."

He's proud she talks to him about such adult things.

"Your father was a proud man, David. A very proud man. He wanted me to know something, so he put it in a letter. He did not write very well. But he wrote just well enough that I got his point. I never met him, but I've got a feeling I would have liked him. An honest man. A direct man. When he had something to say, he said it."

David Pine Tall Man barely remembers his father. In fact, he does not think he does remember him. The only memory he has of him is an image he has probably created from his mother talking about him. David Pine Tall Man wishes desperately that he could have known his father. Swears that if he has a son, he will never desert him.

David can stand it no longer. "What did he write?" he urgently questions.

Linda Hotchkiss straightens her bodice, fluffs the back of her hair. It is as if she is preparing finally to play a part she has dreamed about for years and wants to make sure every prop is in place. "Well, David, your father wanted us to know that he had Indian blood in him. His mother was half Quinnipiac. His father was part Mohican."

David Pine Tall Man is speechless. Mouth open, he tries to speak. Just hollow spaces where the words should be.

"He also told me that his mother's father, Franklin Long Water, told him that that name came from the English. They called the place where the Quinnipiac lived long water. His father-in-law said that he kept the name given to him by the English because it fit. Sounded nice. Sounded right. That he wanted to name you David Pine Long Water Tall Man but your mother said it was too silly, too long. That Tall Man was bad enough."

They sit, silent, for a long, long time. Dusk is beginning when they leave the bench, make their way home. As they turn the corner onto State Street, they pass by little shops that have just opened. They sell old furniture, old dishes. Linda Hotchkiss takes her grandson's hand. "David, I told you that we sold the house and our furniture to pay our way here. There is nothing for you to inherit. The only thing I have to leave is my Bible, my family Bible. When it is time, it will be yours."

Don't blame a boy of seventeen for not realizing that he is being handed down a little treasure. How could he know the thrill he will feel when he opens its covers and reads:

October 22, 1878. Born: David Pine Tall Man. My grandson.
November, 1879. Correction: David Pine Long Water Tall Man. That is who my grandson is.

He asks his mother. Jessica Hotchkiss Tall Man waves her hand, says "Why, no. Not likely." Her husband never told her any such thing. As far as she knows he was part English, part French Canadian, maybe some Irish or Scottish. His parents died very young. She never met them. But she is sure she would have known what their backgrounds were. Says her mother's always telling outlandish tales. "If she doesn't stop, I'll have to confront her," she warns. David Pine Tall Man backs off; he wants no confrontation. He knows now, too, that he will have to keep his grandmother's stories to himself.

He is very worried. And perplexed. Two very different versions of his father's history. Which is true? Both can't be true, he reasons. But which is the true one? And how do I find out? he asks himself.

David Pine Tall Man starts going to the library. Starts reading history books. He thinks that maybe if he studies history, he'll somehow discover how to tell if history is right. He has long since been fired from his job, has long since stopped feeling humiliated by his mother's disappointment. "Like father, like son," she muttered, just loud enough for him to hear. Mornings he walks to the green with his grandmother. Afternoons, he leaves her on the bench while he goes to the library. Evenings, he lies on his now-fortified enclosed back porch and looks up at the sky through his personally-designed ceiling sky eye. His grandfather dies suddenly of what probably was a heart attack. They hardly seemed to notice, except that for a while they set an extra plate at the table. He spoke little, said even less. Hardly moved, except when he absolutely had to. "But a good man," his wife often protested against imagined attacks. "A decent good man. No nonsense. Worked hard. Dull, maybe, but he always did the right thing. That's why I married him. Had a good head on my shoulders." David Pine Tall Man probably should be ashamed. But he hardly knew his grandfather and he can still feel his cold and bony hand. At the funeral, he thinks of other things.

At the library David feels lost. There is a huge, cavernous reference room, filled with hundreds of volumes of history. That was the snappy answer the librarian gave when he asked where the history section was—the reference room, rs rolling. Stung, he backed away, tip-toed over to one of the large wood tables that line the center of the room, slunk in, stayed quiet. After a while, he gets brave. Straightens up, gets up. Walks over to a shelf, picks out a book. Volume One of *The History of America*. After an introduction that gives a brief glimpse of Columbus, this historian argues that Captain John Smith should be credited with laying the foundations of what would later become the United States. Captain Smith reached New England in April of 1614. His party intended to take many whales but he records: "*We found this Whale-fishing a costly conclusion: we saw many, and spent much time in chasing them; but could not kill any.*" A few lines later he records: "*Now because I have beene so oft asked such strange questions, of the goodnesse and greatnesse of those spatious Tracts of land, how they can bee thus long unknown, or not possessed by the Spaniard, and many such like demands; I intreat your pardons, if I chance to be too plaine, or tedius in relating my knowledge for plaine mens satisfacton.*" David Pine Tall Man admires Smith's honesty about the whales, unashamed of his failure. But David Pine Tall Man is deeply troubled by the second passage. These shores are unknown only to those who can write that they are unknown. But does that make them, then, known? He pushes beyond the obvious, that there are at least two histories of America. Of course, there is the one that the English wrote. And even if the Indians didn't write one, David Pine Tall Man believes it is there. In stories handed down instead of in a page in a book. But what nags at his brain is this: his growing faith that there is a third history, behind or below these two. A little voice, an insistent little voice, always now sitting on his ear.

Randomly turning pages, he happens upon a long and strange poem by Ebeneezer Cooke titled "The Sot-Weed Factor." In it he mentions "*Scotch-cloth Blue.*" David Pine Tall Man almost jumps from his chair with excitement. He starts thinking how many blues there can be in the world. So a Scot knows blue because a certain dye has been used to make cloth for his shirt. Is that the same blue as an Irishman's blue? Or a Londoner's? Is a Massachusetts blue the same as a Connecticut blue? How do you know blue is blue? When is blue not blue? His mind spinning, David Tall Man thinks he is thinking deep and heavy thoughts. They are new to him— we will give him that. But his grandmother, Linda Marie Longfellow Hotchkiss, sits on her bench on the twin greens, the pigeons at her feet. Her hand is empty; they have eaten all the crumbs. They do not leave her alone. They want more, their insistent coos growing louder. They peck at the toes of her shoes; she does not kick them away. Her head is slumped on her chest. She does not snore. Her hands grow cold, her fingers stiffen. She has had such thoughts for years. She has had glimpses of the third history behind the other two. She does not scoff that the giant who sleeps will sneeze once more. But now Linda Marie Longfellow Hotchkiss is herself a giant of a little woman, sitting, sleeping the stony sleep of death, in the middle of Dragon Town.

Her funeral is at the Center Church on the New Haven Green. She visited there shortly after she came to New Haven. For her, religion was not a difficult thing. She did not belong to any church. Instead, she liked to visit many. Theophilus Eaton founded the Center Church in 1683. Theophilus: loved by God. A fine name for the founder of a fine church, she thinks. A crypt lies underneath. Buried there is Mrs. Sarah Whiting, *"the painfull mother of eight Children."* Linda Marie Longfellow Hotchkiss likes honesty in a woman, feels comfortable in the Church that buried her. It is a very simple service, much like the one held for her Earl. She will be buried next to him in the Grove Street Cemetery. Jessica Hotchkiss Tall Man thinks about buying a plot for herself but decides it is not the time. The funeral starts at ten o'clock; they are home before noon. A very few close friends come to the house afterward. The vice president of the New Haven Clock Company comes to the funeral, telling David he is so sorry. Now he understands that David needed time with his dying grandmother. Considers a minute and then says that he may come back to work if he wishes. David Pine Tall Man shakes his hand, says he will think about it. Thanks him, really means it.

The few friends who have come by are gone by one o'clock. David goes to what used to be his room. Taking the Bible from its place in the bottom drawer of the chest, he carries it to the back porch. He has decided to keep the porch as his room; he is comfortable there. If it gets bitter cold, he can always spend a night or two inside. He opens the Bible, thrilled that at least some of his family history is here. He sees many names he does not recognize. His family is traced back at least four generations. Written with a calligraphic flourish is his mother's birth date:

April 2, 1860. Born: Jessica Longfellow Hotchkiss. My daughter.

There are two final entries on the page:

October 22, 1878. Born: David Pine Tall Man. My grandson.

November, 1879. Correction: David Pine Long Water Tall Man. That is who my grandson is.

He notices a tiny red arrow at the far right of the page. Above it is written Isaiah 45:8. He turns to that verse, reads: "Let the earth open, that salvation may spring forth." At the end of that verse, another arrow. Above it, Revelation 19:17. As he opens to that verse he finds, neatly pressed between the pages, two feathers—one deep red, the other, golden yellow. His heart races as his mind tries to connect all these strange things. Long Water, he keeps repeating to himself. Long Water. His grandfather's name. The one his father wanted him to have. Suddenly Tall Man isn't good enough. From now on he's going to be David Pine Long Water Longfellow Tall Man.

He muses the rest of the afternoon and evening. He doesn't talk much with his mother. She stays in her room. He hears her crying. He reads until very late, then lays on his back looking at the stars. Mind buzzing, he is afraid, anxious, excited. And very sad. Deep inside, an empty grandmother space. He cries softly at first. Then he cries long and hard, so long and hard he almost chokes. Gets up, blows his nose. Lays back down, his throat dry, tense. He closes his eyes, hoping for a little sleep. Sensing a sudden darkness, he opens his eyes. The skylight is just a blank black space. Frightened, he hoists himself rapidly to a sitting position. As he does so, he looks up and sees taloned feet resting on the glass. With wings outspread Thunderbird Man lands on the skylight, closing off the stars from David Pine Long Water Longfellow Tall Man's little view. He closes his eyes, opens them again, just in time to see a frog face pressed to the glass. David Pine Long Water Longfellow Tall Man sees himself reflected in Thunderbird Man's deep red eyes.

Thunderbird Man lifts his wings, continues his journey through the night sky, leaving a perfectly clear view of the bear chase that never ends in the center of the skylight. Thunderbird Man wings his thunderous way over the New England night sky, musing on the young man with so many, many names.

After his magnificent vision, David Pine Long Water Longfellow Tall Man becomes small and afraid. Finding himself tongue-tied with so many names, he begins to call himself simply David Man. A timid man, he marries a timid woman, Penelope Winter, after his mother is dead. He returns to work at the New Haven Clock Factory. He works his way up again to the rank of manager, staying at that rank for the rest of his career, managing men with ordered precision. He spends most of his spare time reading the classical works of English literature, especially the Renaissance. His favorite author is Sir Philip Sydney; his favorite work *Astrophil and Stella*. Late in life, in the fall of 1928, he and Penelope have a child. He is bitterly disappointed it is not a girl child; he wanted to name her Stella. The best David Man can think to do is to name his son David Sidney. David Man takes from its place in the bottom drawer his family Bible. Into he adds this entry:

November 3, 1928: A son, David Sidney Winter Tall Man. He underlines the i in Sidney just to make sure everyone knows it's Sidney with an i not a y.

Penelope is a diligent and thrifty soul. She wastes nothing, always buys goods on sale, has become legendary for her ability to trade to her advantage. Their son is smart, does well in school. They have enough money to send him to high school. He will win a partial scholarship to one of the local colleges. They will be able to supply the rest of the funds so that he may live in one of the dormitories on campus.

David Man lives a quiet, timid life. He has forced from his memory whatever memorable visions he might have had. His temperament has become regular, even, like the ticking of a pendulum on a clock. Dull, predictable—his grandmother would have been crushed to see what he has become. When David's and Penelope's son is in the eighth grade, they chaperone his class to an outing at Sleeping Giant Park. David Man leaves his wife with the other wives, follows the men who are following the boys up the Trail. The climb is difficult. But he puffs his way up foot by foot, finally reaching a large hemlock grove in which he decides to rest. He waves the others on, sits with his back against a tree, his knees bent, wiping his sweaty brow. Water rushes below, an exciting and soothing sensation. The water's force vibrates the ground beneath him. David Man allows himself to do something he has not done in years. He luxuriates in the spicy hemlock air. He closes his eyes, starts to doze. Awakened by an annoying pawing on his leg, he glimpses a tiny frog hunting a tiny fly that has landed on his trouser. The frog's tongue darts out, catching the fly. Just as it does, David Man's unthinking hand smashes it, leaving a sticky green residue in his palm. David Man's day is ruined. He washes his hand in the stream below. He cannot rid his ears of the ungodly little shriek the small frog made as David Man's giant hand was about to erase its tiny little life.

David Man is a haunted man from that afternoon until his death. He has dreams that will not let him return to sleep. Yellow feathers on red wings, red feathers on yellow wings. Frogs with wings, crossing the sky in front of the stars. A fly crawls into his inner ear, buzzing there incessantly. Penelope finds her husband a burden, wondering what evil luck God has sent to her and why. She shakes her head, yet perseveres.

David Man grows worse. He lives only two weeks after he retires from the New Haven Clock Company. He lingers on the verge of death, lying with the gold pocket watch the Company presented to him open in his hand. He does not die easily, at peace. Penelope stays by his side. Heaving himself from his bed, he shakes the house with his tremors. Just before he dies he holds out his hand, letting the open pocket watch fall to the bed. He turns his hand, looking at the back of it and utters a sound. At first it is a whisper, then a scream. In red ink, the words bleed. He screams. It is during one of these screams that the veins in his head burst. With blood gushing from his eyes and his nose, David Man leaves this earth a terrified, haunted and timid man.

On the back of his hand this:

Eaton
1638-Coat
1683-Church

It is, of course, invisible to Penelope who is as terrified and timid as her now-dead husband. David Sidney-with-an-i Tall Man is at school when his father dies. When he comes home, his mother tells him that his father is at rest, that he died peacefully while taking a nap. David Sidney-with-an-i Tall Man doesn't care. He just wants to know if he gets to stay home from school tomorrow.

1960

David Sidney-with-an-i Tall Man is an accomplished scholar. The years since his father's death have flown by. He has graduated from college, gone on for an even more advanced degree, and is now living in New Haven again, teaching ancient history at the college from which he graduated. He is proud to be named after the man who wrote *Astrophil and Stella*; after all, he imagines himself a worthy Renaissance Man. In truth, he is somewhat of a prig; indeed, at times a bore. At times a superfluous idiot, Davis Sidney-with-an-i Tall Man is often an insufferable thing.

He has had one date in his life. His mother paid her friend's daughter to accompany him to his senior prom. At the stroke of midnight the young woman disappeared, keeping her contract literally to the minute. He didn't seem to care, sitting all evening anyway, never once asking her to dance. The only thing that excites him is genealogy. He loves to trace family trees of people he does not know. When he was a teenager he began to trace his own but gave up when it became clear that there was no written trace of one side of his family. Incompleteness is what he hates above all, so he just pretends that his own genealogy doesn't exist. He visits local graveyards, taking trace etchings of epitaphs. He has done all the ones in New Haven, most of East Haven and West Haven, and is working his way through Hamden to Mount Carmel. He's most interested in the Dickerson family line. They have the best epitaphs.

Jane Eliza Dickerson	1789-1822	Born too late, died too soon.
Elijah Dickerson	1735-?	Never found his body. Is he dead?
Robert Dickerson	?-1852	Birth too easy; can't remember it.
Jane Ann Dickerson	1854-1858	Saved from Life.

He's thinking about a scholarly monograph on early New England epitaphs. He's sure there will be a market for it; after all, if he enjoys them, there will a lot of others who will too. Might be a little hard finding a publisher, but he assures himself that he can do it.

He also collects old family Bibles when he can buy them very cheaply. He used to be able to get all he wanted for less than a dollar at the local thrift store. But lately they've been appearing in the antique shops along State Street, often selling for over ten dollars. If a volume looks very, very special, he'll pay that much. After all, he already has hundreds; they take up most of the bookshelf space in his office. The rest are in his small two-bedroom home on Orange Street, where he has turned one bedroom into an office. There, too, the shelves are filled with Bibles. The walls are covered with tombstone etchings that he has framed. He finds great comfort sitting among these family tomes. Some have gilded covers, bound in leather, others are placed in decorative outer boxes, and still others have torn covers, missing leaves. Some have colorful illustrations, some have none. A few have black and white engravings. In all, however, one thing in common. Carefully entered records of births, weddings, deaths. He has three or four that cover at least eight generations. When he holds these, even David Sidney-with-an-i Tall Man gets excited, tries to find imaginative faces to match the names. Even he feels his heart beat faster, trying to make up the stories of the lives of the people whose names his finger rests upon. Once he started trying to write down the story as he imagined it, but it frightened him. He feels safer if it's just up in his head. That way, he figures, it's just his and nobody can change it on him. Nobody can steal it from him. He had that happen once. After a conference where he had given a paper. Three months later it appeared in *Annals of Ancient History*. He almost pressed charges but did not think he could prove malicious intent. The guy was smart enough to give him a footnote.

Being a footnote stung deeply. So he got smart. Let things just stay up in his head till he was ready to write the complete paper and then send it immediately to the editor. After all, he cautions himself, have to be able to compete. And he has: he has earned early tenure and looks forward to a long and satisfying career. Especially since he has such an exciting project so close to home, he never has to worry about what to do on weekends or evenings. He's on his way back from the Grove Street Cemetery where he wanted to recheck the spelling of a name when he decides to go over to State Street where he'll stop for a pizza. On his way back, he stops in the antiques shops that line lower State Street, treasures often spilling out onto the sidewalk. He loves looking through them. Sometimes he lands a little treasure. Not long ago he found a liberty eagle dollar; not long before that a first edition of Samuel Butler's *The Way of All Flesh*. And these weren't in the high-priced upstairs. Lately, David Sidney-with-an-i Tall Man only buys from the basements where the dealers put the stuff they don't care about. He spends hours sifting through piles of trash, emerging dusty, tired, and sometimes victorious. Today he finds nothing until the basement of the last shop he visits. It is an album filled with postcards and letters and newspaper articles. There's one about an old cemetery not far from Sleeping Giant State Park. There's a photograph of an old tombstone in the newspaper article: he can see clearly the name John Dickerson. He closes the cover of his treasure, hugging it to his heart. Races upstairs, pays his dollar. Still clutching it to his rapidly-beating heart, he runs home, panting with excitement as he sits down at the old oak roll-top desk in his study. With trembling fingers he opens the album, lays it across the wood's grain. Page by page, turning them slowly, he immerses himself in yet another part of a family history that is not his.

Whoever made this album meant it to be an emerging history of Sleeping Giant Park. There are lists of dates when land was acquired, there is an article about the Observation Tower being built by the WPA, there are legends about how the Giant went to sleep. There are articles about which Indian tribes used to live at the mountain. In 1638 it was sold by Chief Montowese to Theophilus Eaton. Eaton founded New Haven, founded Center Church in 1683. David Sidney-with-an-i Tall Man wonders if those dates are correct, whether there might be a simple transposition. Just too neat and too uncanny. Postcards showing photographs of the Sleeping Giant. An old article about the Mount Carmel Trap Rock Company. A society page article about a wedding held at the base of the Giant's feet. This catches his eye:

Tragedy at Sleeping Giant

The Sleeping Giant Park Association regrets to announce the tragic disappearance of a woman and her son. Both elderly, they had been helped to the unfinished watchtower by the members of the Association who had gathered there for a picnic and a meeting. They made it to the top of the ridge without incident. The elderly woman and her son were just walking around, looking at the tower, taking in the sights. The Association members sat in a circle, discussing business matters. They heard a strange sound;* when they looked to see what it was, they realized that the elderly woman and her son were nowhere in sight. They immediately formed a search party. One of the Association members is a detective, well-trained in search techniques. The search was conducted according to scientific principle. No trace of either the elderly woman or her son have yet been found. The detective is not hopeful; he says that the brush on the Giant's side is so thick, they could search for a thousand years and still not find them. "Ironically, they could be right under our noses," he said, "and we wouldn't be able to see them." The Association expresses deep regret and deepest sympathies for the victims' families. The Association also reminds people to be very careful when hiking on the Giant; the hills are steep, the rock ledges slippery and most dangerous of all, the plant thickets are dense and impenetrable. Since it can be dangerous, they advise extreme caution.

*Correction. In our earlier report we failed to include the eyewitness testimony of one of the Association members. He swears a huge black bird flew overhead, larger than any living bird he has ever seen. He swears its wings were tipped with yellow and that its head was green, like a frog. It had red eyes. He swears he was not imagining it.

David Sidney-with-an-i Tall Man is so excited he cannot breathe well. He starts packing his bag right away. He will take the bus over to Sleeping Giant. There's a motel a few blocks away where he can stay. He still has some research funds. He'll need to visit all the graveyards, talk to anyone in Mount Carmel who knows anything about this mystery. An ancient history might be lurking here and he wants to be the first to get it published. He's heard before of strange disappearances in conjunction with old sites held to be sacred to primitive peoples. He might uncover an ancient religious site, or even a forgotten religion. Of course he knows that there is no mystery about these people vanishing; he is sure there is a rational explanation. He is also sure there's a book waiting to be written about the history of the place they disappeared.

He spends three days and then every weekend and vacation researching the Giant and the history of the mountain and the surrounding towns. But he comes to many dead ends. Frustrated, and sensing that his work might well remain incomplete, he abandons the project.

2002

Ivan L. Hollar, a savvy antiques dealer, knows he's got a treasure. An early New England painted chest, paint all original, finish unrestored, no repairs. An early one, probably 1720, maybe earlier. Almost a miracle to find one in such pristine condition. Of all places, at a yard sale. In the corner under a pile of junk labeled "make me an offer." He doesn't betray his interest, throwing the seller off-guard.

"Hey, I've got a kid setting up a house. How about ten dollars for the whole pile?"

The seller shrugs his shoulders. "Suits me just fine."

Ivan is beside himself. Like a lunatic, he clears his chest, throwing all the other stuff—a carpet, a vacuum cleaner, a cracked crock—into the air. He picks up the chest, tottering at first beneath its weight, and brings it to his car. He always carries moving blankets, rope. He wraps it carefully, secures it in the back of his Ford Bronco. As he is driving away he cannot hear the man holler "Hey, what about your other stuff?" as the seller shakes his head, making circles with his finger about an inch from his temple.

Inside is a very plain box. Early, too, but not interesting. Two old Bibles. Neither is worth much. No colored illustrations, no impressive calligraphy. He puts the chest in his back room. He needs to think a while before offering it for sale. May just sent it to Sotheby's— it's that good, he thinks. Before he leaves his own shop, he takes the box and two Bibles downstairs, puts them on the bargain table.

David Sidney-with-an-i Tall Man is sixty-four, depressed, at a loss for how to account for his only mediocre success. He is a Professor now and will retire at the end of this academic year but has not produced the great book that would change his field. He's taken a leave this semester. In the back of his mind, still the hope that something will come. Many years ago he thought he was on the right track toward success with genealogy or with the rocky giant but it came to a dead end. He shrugs now to think of it, how foolish it all was. Just a random stone formation, the chance deposits left by the great Wisconsin glacier. That's all there is to its history. Everything else just a myth. But in his better moments, he knows better. He has studied myth all his life; he ought to know better.

He has taken to wandering up and down Chapel Street in the heart of New Haven. For a couple of years he stayed on upper Chapel Street, across from the big university campus. But lately he goes down to lower Chapel Street, where the Dollar Store and the Liberty Pawn Shop are. He sits outside on the benches where people wait for buses. Buses come and go, passengers get on and get off, but he sits there, all day, day after day. Sometimes, especially when it's cold, he'll go inside, pretend to shop. He walks over to Wooster Square most days for lunch. Almost always pizza pie, sometimes a calzone. He's become friendly with an older woman who also sits on the bench, watching the buses and people come and go. When he invites her to eat with him today, she readily accepts. An old scarf is tied tightly around her head. She is missing many teeth. Her eyeglasses are vintage cat's eyes, from the sixties, black with rhinestones in the corners, forming fake diamonds. Her coat is long, brown tweed, missing a button. Her bunions are big. She has cut out portions of her shoes, letting her red wool socks show through. Fingers long, remarkably strong, nails painted red with tiny bits of glitter scattered throughout. In the center of each nail, a yellow square; in the center of each yellow square, a green circle. It's her indulgence, she notes proudly. An artist does them. She has lived here all her life and has many stories to tell. They order a medium pie, with green peppers, mushrooms, and black olives. She gets cherry soda, he gets root beer.

"I'm the family historian," she confides.

"Really?" he marvels.

She nods. "I have stacks and stacks of letters and diaries and Bibles and all sorts of things. Whenever anybody dies, they give all this stuff to me."

"Have you tried to organize it?" he wonders.

She shakes her head, laughs. "Good Lord, no. That's the last thing I'd want to do with it. Try to organize things too much you lose their sense. I read them better when they're in bits and heaps, scattered about. More fun that way too."

He agrees, even though he has no idea what she means. It makes no sense to him at all.

"Plus," she continues, "there's a lot of it that isn't written down, at least not yet, at least as far as I know. All the old stories from the old people. The ones that have come down through many generations of time. Those are the one that matter most."

Their pie arrives, crust bubbled and browned from the wood-fired brick oven. They wait for it to cool.

"Are you going to write them down? If you don't, they'll be lost. I mean, what about after you're dead?"

"That's the hell of it," she replies. "Because if I do write them down they get lost too. Not meant to be read. Meant to be heard. Story will change from the way it was supposed to be."

"But isn't it better changed than dead?" he tries to persuade her.

"I don't know but I don't think so," she offers.

They eat, ask for a bag to take the ends of the crusts with them. They return to Chapel Street, walking up to the twin greens. Finding an empty bench on one, they sit. She throws out the crusts in small bits to the flocks of birds that descend. The great elm trees have almost all died; maples still young are struggling to provide shade. The day will come when hybrid elms will shade the twin greens. Elms free from Dutch elm disease. But today Sidney-with-an-i-Tall man is a little annoyed that she feeds flocks of starlings, crows, pigeons, a few sparrows. Undesirable birds.

"Why do you feed such ugly, nasty birds?" he snipes.

Ignoring him, she throws out more crusts.

"All that's left here in town are dirty, undesirable birds," he complains.

She looks him square in the eye. "Well if that's what's left, you feed what you've got."

He realizes that's why he has befriended her. She makes him see things in a brand new way. He's also been collecting local lore as a pastime and she is full of it. Almost every day she tells him another great story about the area. How the Dickerson house across the street from the Sleeping Giant came to be abandoned. Starting long ago, whenever a Dickerson descendent tried to move in and live there, they couldn't stay because the house was haunted. There were voices yelling "Goddamned Grace." And worse yet, the head of a big buck deer, huge antlers, would hang in the air, sometimes inside, sometimes outside, even knocking itself into the front door. Pieces of underclothing hung from its antlers. Stuffed in its mouth, strange papers. One grabbed the paper from its mouth but when she did it burst into flames and burned her hand. Another tried to grab some underpants but they wound around his neck so tightly he almost choked. So the Dickersons rented the house to outsiders, figuring the ghosts would settle down. They just got worse. They couldn't sell the house so they gave it to the historical society. Guess the ghosts liked that; they've been quiet ever since.

How Hezekiah's Knob, one of the ledges on the Giant, got its name. Seems like an old woman lived on the Giant. Knees so bony and crippled, they looked like knobs. She was sitting on one of the numerous trap rock ledges and she died. They found her sitting upright, her legs dangling over the side. On her knobby knees, the outline of a little frog. In each hand, a feather. One red, one yellow. So they buried her nearby and called the area Hezekiah's knob.

David-Sidney-with-an-i Tall Man scoffs at this one. "The outline of a frog?

No, that's too ridiculous," he insists.

Yellow Marie shrugs her shoulders, screws up her nose, whistles through the gaps in her teeth. "Too ridiculous? Really?"

He shakes his head yes, laughs.

"Small minds have small borders they can't get past," she snarls. "That's what's too ridiculous."

Shocked, he stands up, wounded worse than when he was a footnote. But he sits back down. They sit silently for a while. Someone has left a copy of the local paper on the bench. Each takes a section, reads. Nudging her, he reads aloud:

Biologists discover colonies of deformed frogs at Sleeping Giant State Park. They have no idea how to account for this phenomenon. They will be studying the water, the plants, even the rocks around the ponds and streams. Some have no back legs, some have fused back legs. Some have many toes, some have no toes. Some have misshapen heads, some have shortened tongues. So far, no polliwogs have been sighted. Only adult, deformed frogs. The biologists are deeply concerned. Frogs are the best indicators on the planet of a polluted environment. They are especially sensitive to environmental imbalance.

"Isn't that strange, Yellow Marie?" he asks, his voice trembling.

"Strange happenings on the Giant these days," she agrees.

"Is something else going on?" he wonders.

"The hemlock's dying of blight," she responds.

"Do you think the two are connected?" he hopes.

"Blight's just the beginning. Frogs are just the start. Giant's waking up," she nods seriously. In that nod a universe of understanding.

On his way home he stops in Ivan L. Hollar's antique store. Heads straight for the basement. Sees the Bibles, leafs through one of them. When his eye spots Dickerson, he scoops it up, holds it tightly to his chest. With his free hand he fans the pages of the second Bible; when he sees feathers red and yellow, he slams it closed, picks it up, hugs it tightly to his breast. He gladly pays his twenty dollars, goes rushing from the store. Panting when he gets home, he can hardly breathe he is so excited. Something's going on with the mountain Giant. He'll head there tomorrow, after he's had a chance to read and think. He casts out of his brain the voice that says he's crazy; he invites in the tiny, insistent voice that lets him believe that frogs can live in knotty knees.

Ivan L. Hollar hollers after him. "Hey, Mister, they're only a dollar." David Sidney-with-an-i Tall Man doesn't hear him and wouldn't have cared if he did. He is finally ready to cross a border. Mind small no more, he will run out of his everyday world. No timid man, when he sleeps tonight he will dream great things.

As he rushes across the green to the library, he stops to see a starling take off into flight. It has strong, beautiful wings. There's a shimmering, almost sparkling, jewel-like iridescence to its black feathers. It is beautiful, but he knows it is out of place. It was brought here, let loose upon this nation. Many native species have been driven out, or worse. He runs up the steep library steps, springs into the reference room. He looks up Dickerson, finds names similar to the ones in his recently-purchased Bible. Opening volumes of encyclopedias, he sees the catacombs of Rome. The caves under St. Louis. Building the subways under New York City. Reading from a history of New Haven, he is surprised to discover that the greens cover the graves of twenty or thirty thousand people. Gravestones that were found were moved to the Grove Street Cemetery but not so many as all the bodies that were left. This shocks him. So many dead buried beneath the green. Who were they? Why has he not heard about them? Why are there no legends about them? He reads on, coming to the building of the Center Church on the green. Theophilus Eaton, 1683. The entry confirms that many bodies were dug up when it was built and bodies moved to Grove Street Cemetery. A church. A starling. Both displacing something so it could make its own space. A starling. A church. Both imports to America. Both forcing others to leave to make room.

Mind racing, he instinctively looks through older volumes of American Indian History, then newer volumes of Native American History. He looks up Quinnipiac, then Mattabeseck. These entries are very short. Of the Quinnipiac only that they were so dispersed by 1880 that they ceased to function as a tribe. O.K., he thinks to himself, dispersed. But can't they still be a tribe? A culture? he wonders. He moves on to a book on New England legends. Tries to find Hobbomock—he is not there. Tries to find Kietan—he is not there. Volume after volume, David Sidney-with-an-i Tall Man searches hopelessly.

He leaves the library, spends some time on the greens. Thinks about the starlings. The birds they dispersed—surely they are not all extinct. Some moved elsewhere, lived on the margins, adapted. He remembers the coelacanth, thought extinct for thousands of years. Then one turns up. Then a whole colony. Then many more colonies, in different oceans. They were there the whole time, invisible, unrecorded. And then by chance, history is rewritten. The impossible become possible. All the bodies under the green. Covered up. Invisible. An alien world deep beneath the surface of the street. Under the manhole covers, under the watery tunnels that run beneath. Another layer, underneath the underneath, living, watching, waiting. Humans and birds and reptiles and beings that are all three. With the eyes of a hawk, the amphibian lungs of a frog, and the power of a hybrid brain. Crossing all known borders, a new race of being. Holds out his hand, then the thrill of slimy green fingers in his own. His hand grows accustomed to the strange feel, begins to think it is his own. No longer slimy, he begins to like his cool, green hide. In his brain he watches a rock explode. From its pieces flow a black river. From this black rock river flows the body of a giant. First the head, then the belly, finally the feet. Over it flies a large white bird, flapping its powerful wings. Drums from beneath Chapel Street, voices, singing, emerge from the manholes. He hums, at first softly, then more loudly. Letting his chest expand, he breathes deeper than he dreamed possible. A drum's vibration under his feet, David Sidney-with-an-i Tall Man looks down, catches sight of a tiny frog leaping into the sewer drain at the corner of Chapel and Temple Streets. Not for a moment does he believe it is impossible. "Chapel, Temple," he murmurs aloud. "A sacred song, a sacred water drum song has led that frog to me," he says in a voice that seems from the deepest part of him and yet seems not of him at all. "Down a sewer drain. Alive. By choice?" he needs to know. If there's one frog, there have to be more. He doesn't just reason it; he just knows it. You feed the ones you've got, he remembers. Deep underneath, frogs feeding with what they've got. His mind is racing so fast he doesn't realize his feet are running, have been running for blocks.

As he turns to go up the steps to his house, it is already well after dark. Hesitating, he turns and faces the rising first moon. He looks up, sees a large bird fly in front of the moon. A large black bird. On its back, a frog. A deep green, large frog. In its hand, a yellow arrow from which trail a thousand stars.

David Sidney-with-an-i Tall Man opens his hands wide, arches his arms over his head, hoping that even one tiny star rains upon him. Even the tiniest fragment of the tiniest star is all he needs.

With constellations revolving in his brain, he dreams many dreams this night. His fingernails are painted with yellows, reds, and greens. Yellow birds fly the perimeter of his room. The soft buzz of their wings tickles his ears. Tiny frogs dance across his bed, their red eyes flashing. He is in a coat with feet around its wrists, a long tail on its front. Eaton is written in red across its back. A drum beats. His heart regulates itself to the beat of the drum. He sees himself dancing. In full headdress, he is dancing. Beaded moccasins on his feet. On each toe, a tiny frog that leaps every time he lifts his feet. At the watchtower on top of the Giant, he looks through its spider web window. A copperhead snake stares back. A strange- looking woman is weaving a blanket. Frogs sit on her shoulders, yellow birds light at her feet. The drum beats and strange, beautiful, compelling songs are sung. Voices more than human. More than human voices. Hundreds of frogs gather. In unison, they say "We want him. We want him. He is ours." He wakes up, very disappointed to discover it is but a dream.

He dashes from bed, throws on his old, comfortable clothes, the ones he likes to wear when he visits bargain basements. Puts on boots. He's been saving a hundred dollar bill. He folds it so Ben Franklin's cut-in-half face stares at him. David Sidney-with-an-i -Tall Man stuffs Franklin's half face in his back pocket. Opening one of his Bibles, he removes the feathers yellow and red. He places them carefully in his breast pocket. Calls a taxi. Doesn't bother locking the door.

He starts at the Giant's feet. As he crosses in front of the ponds, he hears the rush of wings. As the egret rises, he swears he sees a red feather in its beak. Then he gasps more loudly—there is also a yellow feather in its beak. As it soars higher, David Sidney-with-an-i Tall Man watches its powerful feet. In them, a drum, maybe a water drum. On its sides, four red circles. In the center of each circle, a green diamond. In the center of three of the diamonds, a yellow star. In the fourth, a yellow bird, flying, a frog on its back. Turning, he crosses the entrance to the park, greeting the frogs sitting on the tops of all the signs. A fly lands on his shoulder. Grasping it, he holds it between his fingers, offers it to the frogs. They nod, croak, let the fly escape. David Sidney-with-an-i Tall Man, a Ph.D in ancient history, croaks back. Bounds on the Tower Trail. Two hours later, he reaches the watchtower. Yellow Marie is there, waiting, with her red socks showing through her holed shoes, holding out her arms. He leans his head against her breast, relaxing to the steady beat of her heart. Yellow Marie holds up the backs of her hands. They look through the spider web window overlaid with greens and reds and yellow. A many-colored world before them, with earth and sky netted into one intricate and beautiful webbed whole. At this moment, as the sun rises higher in the sky, he sees a rainbow of colors dancing on its rim. At this very moment, he sees a slit open in the top of the sun. From it emerges a black-winged bird with a frog's face. On its back dances tiny yellow birds. He nods, and in that nod a world of belief. The rock formation on which he stands sends a signal through his feet to his brain. Not dead, he knows, just sleeping. Just sleeping, on the margins.

They walk toward the Giant's hip, moving closer to his belly. Suddenly, a grinding sound, like trap rock grating against trap rock. Overhead, two great black birds: massive wings outstretched, enormous beaks, powerful, watchful eyes. He takes from his breast pocket the two feathers. Putting the red one into her hand, he grasps the yellow one in his. They hold their feathers aloft, letting them move to the breeze. They seem to fly. The human hands that hold them become mighty flying wings. The earth opens. Yellow Marie and David Sidney-with-an-i Tall Man go under, holding hands, feathers held aloft. Hand-in-hand, they parachute into the magical marginal, entering a world even beyond what Sydney dared to dream.

Thunderbird Man is waiting. He hugs Yellow Marie, thanks her for a job well done. He turns to speak to David Sidney-with-an-i Tall Man:

"You have been difficult. Very reluctant. Just a rock formation, you said," Thunderbird Man sneers.

"I know," he replies, hanging his head.

"We have had to work hard to make you hear."

He nods.

"The great book that you have wanted to write. It has been here all the time. You didn't even know where to look."

He nods, again. There is really nothing he can say.

Thunderbird Man calls the yellowbirds. Each sits on one of David Sidney-with-an-i Tall Man's shoulders. Thunderbird Man snaps his fingers. All of sudden David Sidney-with-an-i Tall Man finds that he is standing, laughing, in a thick carpet of bird shit.

Thunderbird Man gives the call. Chief Montowese appears, holding hands with Grace Trap-Ridge Hitchcock. Frog Bird and Yellow Tail Frog Bird Charles Sanford Hightower appear, smiling welcome. Grace Yellowbird Faith comes forward hand-in-hand with Red Man O.K. Jones. With them, Frog Lily and Red Faith. Thousands of frogs convene. The underground sky is yellow with wings.

Thunderbird Man points to the blanket that Grace Yellowbird Faith is weaving, has been weaving for many years. "There is one more section of the blanket left to be woven. The time draws closer. Blight has appeared on the Giant's side. Earth frogs are deformed. The time is close at hand to stop the destruction."

Grace Yellowbird Faith returns to her weaving. Sitting where her weaving will continue is a strange and beautiful creature. It has a woman's body, the feet of a frog, and the wings of a bird. Its wings are tipped with yellow, the tips of its feet are red. Around its neck, a large medallion of mother-of-pearl. In its center, a green square. In the square, a yellow diamond. In the diamond, the red outline of a human hand.

In the distance the faint, insistent song of a sacred water drum.

In the distance, the sound of water, rushing.

A strange new nation, waiting, in the magical margins.

The well-concealed vertical rock split above opens. Descending in the shaft of light is Yellowbird Woman. She is small but strong. Her feathers are almost a translucent yellow. If you look closely, you can see that each feather is tipped at its very end with red. She has a human face, with skin a smooth, deep ebony, and human feet of the purest white. Around her neck, a deep green necklace made from pond lily pads; interwoven through them, a chain of red beads. Her eyes are a deep and gentle blue, containing oceans. She alights, holds out her shimmering wings, gives Thunderbird Man the signal to begin.

Thunderbird Man calls Red Faith and Frog Lily to his side. Giant needs a healing ceremony, a hybrid healing ceremony. Conditions above deteriorate rapidly. The blight has spread over most of the Giant's chest; the deformities among frogs are frightening in their frequency and severity. Worse yet, vandals frequent the Giant. They have scrawled obscene things on his back, his face, his feet. Trash sometimes litters the ponds. Volunteers organize, clean up, but the trash persists. Even worse, botanists and biologists have found nothing to explain the blight, the monstrous frog births. They simply shake their heads, stand by, watching things get worse. Thunderbird Man may be the one to find the strength to have the creatures of the earth unite to save the Giant, to recover his warm green coat, to restore the frogs that sing upon his back and swim in his watery veins. If the ceremony does not take place, then Grace Yellowbird Faith will have no choice but to rush to finish her blanket. But Thunderbird Man is worried. Daniel Dickerson Harrington IV is going to need a lot of training, a lot of persuasion.

Red Faith and Frog Lily hurry to Thunderbird Man's side.

"We will need twin strength for this difficult mission," he warns.

They nod, unafraid. "Tell us what we must do," they say in unison, "and it will be done."

"It will not be that easy," he cautions. "Even if you do your best, you may not succeed."

They say nothing, waiting for clarity.

"You cannot make the heart of a man feel what it won't. No matter how hard you try, he may resist you. His father did, and his father before him. And his father for many generations before that."

They nod, starting to understand the risk of failure.

"The above ground world is not an easy place. It will be difficult for you. Even dangerous," Thunderbird Man sternly warns.

Red Faith and Frog Lily raise their joined hands in the air. "We have been told many stories of the world above. We know that it will not be easy. But we have our languages to help us. We speak more than one human tongue, frog and pond lily tongues too."

"Yes, that will help" he agrees. "But that will not be enough. You must also be able to hear many languages," he corrects them.

They nod. "Of course. That is most important," they acknowledge.

Thunderbird Man holds his hand under his frog's chin. "But speaking and hearing what is said is not enough, either, you know."

"It isn't?" they ask, surprised, confused.

"You must be able to hear invisible words. You must be able to learn the languages you do not speak, do not hear."

"But how will we do that?" they wonder.

"Grace," he replies. "Have Grace."

They nod, wondering still.

He continues: "And you must be very patient. It may take a long time. Each of you must undergo a physical change before you journey upward. Red Faith, you will become the shape of a pigeon. You will flock with the other birds on the twin New Haven greens. He eats his lunch there every day, no matter how cold or hot, no matter how rainy or snowy. He is a man of habit. You can count on that. You will have to stand your ground. Many pigeons will push and crowd around his feet. Few, though, will have the sense to sit at his ear. On the back of a park bench, new voices can be heard."

"But how will I know which one he is the first day? And does he have a name?" Red Faith wonders.

"You will hear the silent words he does not speak. His name is Daniel Dickerson Harrington IV. Know this, too: he will respond to another name if the time is right."

"What is that?" they ask, curiously.

"When the time is right," Thunderbird Man confides, "he will be Red Hand Man."

Thunderbird Man turns to Frog Lily. "You will become the shape of a white frog. You will have spots of red on your back. You will be waiting deep within a now-hidden cave on the belly of the Giant. If this cave is discovered, then you will be there to begin the ceremony."

"But what if the cave is not discovered?"

"Then it will be time for the blanket to have its final hand," Thunderbird Man sighs.

Thunderbird Man calls all the underground citizens who quickly gather. Chief Montowese and Grace-Trap-Ridge Hitchcock kiss Frog Lily and Red Faith goodbye. Thousands of yellow birds tip their wings to the strength of the twin pair. Frog Bird and Yellow Tail Frog Bird Charles Sanford Hightower hug the twins close to their breasts. The frogs converge, croaking farewell. Red Man O.K. Jones and Grace Yellowbird Faith, hand-in-hand, walk slowly toward their children. Embracing each in turn, they cry together. Thunderbird Man softly reminds them it is time. Thunderbird Man spreads his mighty wings, bends them toward the rocky floor. Red Faith and Frog Lily climb on, holding tightly to the deep, lustrous black feathers with tips of gold. Everyone waves, everyone fears, everyone hopes. As Thunderbird Man begins to ascend, a hazy halo encircles them. As he ascends higher, the haze clears. A white frog with red spots and a pigeon huddle together in the middle of his strong and bony back, encircled in rainbow light. Cooing and croaking, Thunderbird Man takes flight. The tips of his wings glow. High above, a slit of light emerges. As it opens, the great bird with his strange and wondrous cargo flies into the light. Behind them, Yellow Bird Woman lifts herself into the lighted slit of sky.

As the shaft of light high above closes, Strange Creature still sitting on the blanket has something to say. It taps its frog feet three times, flaps its wings four times, turning first east, then south, then west, then, finally, north. It taps its frog feet three times again. Crafted from mother-of-pearl, a medallion circles its neck. In its center, a green square. In the square, a yellow diamond. In the diamond, the red outline of a human hand. The human hand moves, waving its fingers. Strange Creature, an odd poet indeed, opens its mighty mouth and sings:

> "Pigeon and Frog
> On mighty wings
> Have soared to the world above.
>
> A pigeon and a frog
> Cooing and croaking
> Their way above.
>
> A pigeon and a frog
> And a red hand.
> A red hand the pigeon of frog
> A hand red the frog of pigeon

Pigeon Frog's red hand
May save the day
May Frog Pigeon's red hand
Save the day."

All join her in tapping their feet, their wings, singing, praying "Pigeon Frog's red hand may save the day. May Frog Pigeon's red hand save the day." When Strange Creature raises her wings, all cease their singing. She pleads: "Keep Frog and Pigeon in your hearts. Have faith that a red hand finds its proper heart." They all vow to keep heart and faith, then disband. Grace Yellowbird Faith returns to the blanket, slowly weaving its final section, next to Frog Lily's and Red Faith's section. She begins what will become the outline of a red hand.

Daniel Dickerson Harrington IV is a man of great outward faith. Every Sunday he sits in the back left pew in the Center Church on the New Haven green. He never needs to open his hymnal; he knows every word of every song. He almost never needs to open his Bible; he knows almost every word on every page. He spends hours each week contemplating the wonders of words. At least three times a year, he re-reads Jonathon Edwards' *Personal Narrative*. Like Edwards, Daniel Dickerson Harrington IV wants to lie low before God, to empty himself to become a proper vessel to be filled with the wonder of divine light. Unlike Edwards, he has yet to be able to prostrate himself before his God. Every time he tries, his mind gets in the way. "But I am me," it always says. "I am I. I cannot be empty of me," it complains. Disgusted, Daniel Dickerson Harrrington IV castigates himself. He prays more fervently, studies holy words more intensely, trying to feel what it is he thinks Moses must have felt when he saw the bush aflame. Daniel wants to be struck by the power of a miracle, to feel the white heat of a divine fire, to know the thunderous touch of a divine hand. But, alas, these things have eluded him. He has words, and more words; he has hymns, and more hymns; he has stories and more stories. What he doesn't have is the heart of faith.

He is not an unhappy man. His life is quite full. Never married, he has devoted himself to his career as a Professor of Archeology. He is well-known in his field. His textbook is used at most colleges and universities. It has made him rather rich. He lives in a large house on Hillhouse Avenue, owned by Yale University. They have given it to him, rent-free, in honor of his achievement. His nest egg is almost ponderously large. Daniel Dickerson Harrington IV has his eyes set on the prize of early and comfortable retirement.

Lately he has begun to do two things. He frequently visits the rare book library. He knows the research librarians there who allow him use of any and all manuscripts. He is not looking for any particular volume. He is just looking. Yet he has begun a systemized search. Beginning with Z, he will methodically work his way back to A, confident that there will still be truly rare books to read well into his retirement. And he has begun to compile a family history. Not the usual genealogical tree, really. It's important that he knows who descends from whom but it is not crucial. As long as he has some of it right, he's satisfied. He knows that he descends from the John Dickerson who helped found Mt. Carmel. Knowing that is enough. What is crucial to him is that he tries to record as many of the stories that have been passed down as he possibly can. He means to compile them and pass them down to his nephew, Walter Reed Redcar. Daniel Dickerson Harrington IV's only sister, Grace, who married Andrew Redcar, died in an automobile accident ten years ago. The irony of it all strikes him. Driving a red Thunderbird, she was struck head-on by a red Eagle. Despite wearing a seat belt, she was killed. The Eagle scalped the Thunderbird—sliced its top clean off, taking with it the head of Grace. Her body still in the topless car, her head was a few feet away, gazing out over the highway. Andrew still grieves. Walter Reed cannot bring himself to speak about his mother's death. Daniel Dickerson Harrington IV doesn't think about her death; he thinks about the family history that gave her life. So he is collecting things these days. He is helped in his task by his great grandfather, Buster Dickerson Harrington, who began to preserve family legends over a hundred years ago. He deposited them into a camel back trunk that has been passed down through the generations. Each generation has made its own deposits, though he is the first of these generations intending to make sense of all these things. He looks at the now-impressively large collection of clippings, photos, cards, stories, books. Even a beaded purse into which had been placed a slip of paper. The purse is beaded with the black outline of a thunderbird, its body filled with beads of jet. In its beak, a red cross. In its talons, a white frog. On the frog's back, red diamonds. In one of the diamonds, a yellow star. Long ago, Daniel Dickinson Harrington IV opened the purse, took out the slip of paper, read this: *"Have Grace."* Long ago, he put it back in the bag and closed the lid of the camel back trunk. Today he knows that he is going to open it again. First the trunk, then the bag, and then the Have Grace slip of paper. He will be looking for Grace; he is positive she is in there, waiting to be found. If he finds her, maybe she can help him live with the memory of his dead sister, his beloved beheaded Grace.

He heads toward the green, thankful his favorite bench is unoccupied. He piles his books on one end so no one will sit there. He becomes unreasonably angry when someone insists on sharing the bench; it spoils the rest of his day. That's why he's especially fond of inclement weather—then he can be sure he has it to himself. He brings his lunch every day except Saturday and Sunday. Then he gets takeout from the Golden Wok, or a small pizza from Pepe's, or soup from Grandma's Kitchen. Sometimes Center Church offers a lunch after services. Daniel Dickinson Harrington IV wraps his in a napkin and proceeds to the park, where he sits alone with pigeons and starlings at his feet. Contemplating mighty thoughts, he sits there, eating slowly, daring anyone to share the bench, amassing dozens of begging birds at his feet. They coo and caw. He shifts his feet, sometimes kicks the air to make them scatter. They persist, flocking back, pecking at the ground under the bench, strutting back and forth waiting for their tossed crumbs. His fingers pry off a bit of bread. Opening them, he casts his bread bit to the ground, delighting in the rush of feathers and wings and beaks. Guessing which birds will win, he slaps his thigh when he guesses correctly. But there is a soft spot in Daniel Dickinson Harrington IV's heart. He always watches to see which bird hangs back the farthest. Which seems the shyest, the weakest, the oldest or the youngest. As he leaves, he always gently tosses a bit of bread or cake at the marginal bird's feet, standing guard until it eats. Today the marginal bird is a small pigeon with a streak of yellow on its wings. Very unusual, he thinks. As he turns toward home, he gives the pigeon a wink. He blinks as pigeon winks back.

He goes back to his office, returning to his painstaking work on paintings found inside caves at East Rock and Sleeping Giant. Although these mountains have been searched many times, and hikers by the thousands have climbed all the trails, the caves had lain undiscovered until a few years ago. Their opening hidden by deep underbrush, it was by accident that off-trail, illegal hikers literally stumbled upon them. These caves are not very deep, but they are wide. Water trickles down their sides. Bats hang at their backs. On their walls, cryptic pictures. Strange beings. A beast with a bird's body and a frog's head. Another creature with a woman's head and the feet of a frog. Yet another with a human body and bird's feet. Birds fly across the wall in abundance. One wears some sort of necklace. On one wall, the figure of a frog with spots drawn on its back. The figures in each cave are similar to those in the other caves. But in the cave at Sleeping Giant there is a figure that does not appear at East Rock. Someone has drawn the outline of the Giant. Out of his belly emerges a strange, shadowy yet blank shape. What is even stranger is that a disembodied hand reaches out from somewhere, stretching its open fingers to touch it.

Daniel Dickerson Harrington IV studies this shape, has been studying this shape, will be studying this shape for some time to come. If he stares at it long enough, he hopes that he can see what sort of beast lies under the beckoning blankness. Fascinated by a floating hand, a hand floating free, trying to touch a shapeless shape rising out of a mountain belly, he sits, muses, stares, and ponders. What sort of history is emerging here, he does not know. But he senses that he will have to revise his textbook when he finally unravels the mystery. Tired, he daydreams a bit, gets up, stretches. Is about to put the photographs of the paintings back in their folder, leave for the day. As he turns his eyes back to the one from the Sleeping Giant cave, he stops dead in his tracks. There, in the middle of the emerging blank space that rises from the Giant's belly, a hemlock twig. Swaying from its tip, a tiny green frog, with bright red eyes. He closes his eyes, rubbing them hard. When he reopens them, he does not find a swaying little green frog. He sees a thunderbird flapping yellow-tipped wings. He closes his eyes yet again, rubbing them even harder. He opens them once more. There is no thunderbird there. Instead, there is a red hand. Sitting in its palm, a pigeon. On the pigeon's back, a tiny white frog with red spots on its back.

Daniel Dickerson Harrington IV is a man of great outward faith. But he quickly closes the cover on this hymnal. He cannot hear the songs it contains, cannot read the language of the cave book. He must believe—he must believe, he thinks—that what emerges from the belly of the mountain giant man is nothing more than the shadow of a shape. No, he thinks, my textbook will need no revision. Just fanciful paintings. Some old Indian just having fun, making strange beasts where there were none. And me too, he laughs to himself. Starting to see strange things. So when the tiny white frog with red spots on its back winks, Daniel Dickerson Harrington IV has already deposited it, along with the rest of its fanciful tribe, into a folder, placed the folder in a filing cabinet, and locked his office door.

When he gets home, he opens the camel back trunk as he had promised himself that he would. When he takes out the beaded purse, sweat beads on his face. Heart racing, he feels faint. As he holds it, his hands shake so that the beads become a blur. In the corner, dancing, a tiny white frog with red spots on its back. He runs his fingers over the beaded beast, its heart beating. Daniel Dickerson Harrington IV throws the bag from him, sinks to his knees. He cries out: "He reveals deep and mysterious things." And this: "I was appalled by the vision and did not understand it." And finally this, in a voice deep and seemingly from another body: "Go your way, Daniel, for the words are shut up and sealed until the end of time."

Hoping that the winking frogs are safely shut away, he closes the trunk, vowing to abandon his project. But it is no use, Daniel Dickerson Harrington IV. The outline of a red hand has been winked into your heart. The shut-up words are here, near Dragon Town. Go your way, Daniel. Open your mind and your heart to the shape of your fate. Have Grace, Daniel. Open your ears to the language of the hymnal under your feet.

Daniel notices her, has been noticing her for the last few weeks. She sits on the bench opposite his on the south side of the first New Haven green with her back to the myriad groups gathered waiting for the Chapel Street bus inside the little sidewalk enclosure. At her feet, many pigeons, starlings, sparrows. She is reading—she is always reading, except, that is, when she is staring at him. David was eating one day and felt that strange sense that someone was looking at him. At first he turned his neck and looked backward, not realizing at first that she who stared was right in his face. Right in his face she was, but from the very safe distance of the other side of the green. He stared back. His rule of law says that rudeness begets rudeness. Or, as he likes to put it, "If you're rude enough to stare at me, I'm rude enough to stare back, damned it." But he tires of his own rule of law rather quickly. He prefers now to set his eyes on his book, on the ground, or crane his neck to the side, pretending to see something to the east or to the west. And he finds himself sneaking looks at her, just to see if she is still staring at him. When she is, he gets angry, or blushes. When she isn't, he gets angry, or blushes.

He doesn't have much time today. He needs to be back at the office early for an appointment with an art historian he has asked to look at the cave paintings. Daniel is afraid he is tired of them, has lost interest in them. How else can he explain his unprecedented reluctance to study his subject? At first he had been tremendously excited. Now he does not even want to open the drawer where they are filed. And he just cannot, for the life of him, tell why. He's surprised that the northern breeze at the back of his neck is so warm, suddenly realizing a small pigeon is sitting on the back of the bench, next to his left ear. So close that its feathers touch Daniel's cheek, soft as silk. He shifts enough to look the bird in the eye, noticing for the first time how multi-colored its irises are, how multi-colored is the iridescence of its wings. He notices a streak of yellow on its wings.

"Well, little pigeon bird," he coos. "How is it that you have yellow wings when all your fellows have none?"

The little pigeon bird scratches the back of the bench, ruts its head into Daniel's shoulder.

"Here you go," he says as he gives the pigeon a bit of bread.

As he does, dozens of birds from the ground fly up, landing on Daniel, landing on the back of the bench, pecking at the yellow-winged little pigeon bird, driving it away. Daniel is angry, very angry, but checks that anger. After all, he says to himself, it is just pigeon's way. And then he chides himself, saying he should have given the other birds something first. And he probably shouldn't have fed one on the bench—he broke his own rule. His leg feels wet, strange. When he looks down he sees himself besmeared with pigeon shit. He takes the paper wrapper from his grinder, quickly wipes off as much as he can. He throws the rest of his lunch on the ground, scoops up his books, runs home, hoping that the shit hasn't seeped clear through to his skin. He keeps making the wrong turn, having to backtrack countless times. Having quickly changed, throwing his soiled pants on the back porch, he runs as fast as he can. Daniel is an unhappy man when he reaches his office. For the first time in his life he is late for an appointment. Very hastily, he begs the art historian to assume the project. Daniel watches with relief as the woman leaves his office with the photographic reproductions in a folder held firmly in her hand. She seems familiar to him. He tries to place her face but cannot. He is struck by her ring. It is a very large green stone. In the center of the stone, a red triangle. In the center of the triangle, a yellow bird.

A few days later, he is once again sitting on his bench, with his back to the north, against the front steps leading to the public library. Once again, he sneaks a peek and knows that the woman is staring at him from the south side of the green. Quickly concentrating on his open book, he hears feet shuffle, his books scrape along the bench. His heart is in his mouth; he cannot swallow his food. Like a chipmunk, he pushes it aside, into his cheek pouch. She has slid his books down the bench. They touch his thigh. She has sat down. He does not raise his eyes. Sandals on her feet. Each nail is painted red. In the center of each, a green triangle. In the center of each triangle, a yellow star. Gulping, his stomach growls, on the verge of a belch.

"I was positive it was you, so I thought I'd say hello."

"I didn't recognize you," he stammers, almost choking.

"I've been looking over the photographs and am making a trip to the cave at East Rock next week and to the one at Sleeping Giant the week after that. You'd be welcome to come, if you'd like. I don't know why you gave up the project. It's fascinating. I'm intrigued. I think there's a real story here, waiting to be told."

Daniel nods. But he really isn't listening to her. His eyes stare at the pin on her left chest. It is a bird, set all over with deep yellow stones. The tip of its wing is outlined in green jewels. It has a red stone eye. Its back wing is hidden.

Its front wing is on a little spring. It flaps when she breathes. Every time Mercy Pond takes a breath, the bejeweled yellow bird on her chest flies.

"You know there's a lot of trouble on the Sleeping Giant."

He nods. "I've read about the blight. A terrible thing. Like the elm blight that destroyed almost every elm tree in the city." He glances quickly at the newly-planted hybrid elms. Sighs.

"More than that," she answers.

"More than that?" he repeats.

"Acid rain," she continues. "It's hurting the mountain laurel. Burning weird designs into its leaves. Its flowers are brown and its growth is stunted. New bushes are only growing four or five feet high. A terrible thing."

He shakes his head. "And frogs are deformed there—and everywhere around," he adds. "The Connecticut Extension Agency said that they have found deformed frogs for at least 100 miles around Sleeping Giant."

"Why didn't you want that project?" she needs to know.

Startled by her abrupt shift of topic, it takes him a moment to recover. "I really don't know," he says, never having intended to be so honest.

"Why don't you know?" she persists.

Having the briefest glimpse of something waving, he knots his brow, trying to focus. But it remains a shadowy shape. "I just really don't know."

They sit without speaking. A small pigeon alights on the back of the bench between them.

"Well, hello, little fellow," Mercy Pond laughs. Her laugh is soft, easy, familiar.

Daniel sees the distinctive yellow wing streak. He is afraid to speak.

She takes a bit of crust from Daniel's sandwich. But before she can offer it to the pigeon on the back of the bench Daniel stays her hand. "No, don't," he urges. "At least not until we feed the others." He has grasped hard her hand. When he releases it, he sees the red print of his fingers on her skin. He apologizes profusely, explaining what had happened a few days before. Rubbing her hand, she scoots a little farther away from him. He hands her some crusts so she can help feed the birds at their feet. He gives her a choice bit of bread. She offers it to the pigeon between their heads.

"Will you go to the caves with me?"

"I don't think I can," is his lame reply.

She dismisses the lameness. "You can do better than that. Just yes or no" she demands.

He is about to say no. The pigeon nudges his right ear, pecking his earlobe, gently, insistently. Its beak descends into his ear canal. "Go, for the love of Grace. For the love of Grace, go."

As soon as he hears himself say yes— loudly and firmly— a dragonfly appears with blue translucent wings. On its back, in the design down its needle-shaped torso, is a mirror into another world. All Daniel can think is that it will be sewing his lips shut, sealing them until the end of time. The pain in his lips is terrific as the flying beast sews shut his bleeding lips. In and out, over and over, driving its needled body through his skin, pulling tight a silken cord it seems to have spun out of itself. In and out, over and over, prick upon prick. With each stitch, he finds it harder to breathe. With each stitch, he finds it harder to speak. Waving his hands wildly about him, he flaps them up and down. She is laughing so hard she is crying. A grown man, flapping his wings on the New Haven green in the middle of the day, mumbling something about being sealed up until the end of time. "End of time, end of time" he chants as he races around in a circle, flapping invisible wings.

Mercy Pond catches his arm, stops his bird dance. They fall to the bench, she still laughing, he gasping for air. They sit for quite a while. She finally gets up, says she'll meet him here tomorrow. Her arm is still imprinted with Daniel's red hand.

As Daniel runs back to his office he cannot get these words out of his head: "And as he finished speaking all these words, the ground under them split asunder; and the earth opened its mouth and swallowed them up." He runs faster, trying to stay ahead of the words. The words have open mouths and sharp teeth; they are at his heels, nipping and pulling his ankle flesh. Daniel runs for his life, jumping up the staircase, and slamming the door on the words made beasts beating at his back.

Panting, he runs to the bathroom, vomits. On his knees, he prays: "Our Father. Forgive us our trespasses as we forgive those who have trespassed against us." He can remember no other lines. Shutting his eyes, he tries to see. It is no use; his words are incomplete. Leaving his office, he runs home to his camel-back chest, takes the beaded bag from the bottom where he had buried it. Opens it, takes out the paper, holds it to his chest. Do not laugh: he swears he can detect the beating of a heart in the waving lines of ink. The ink seems red with blood, searing and scorching his chest as he holds it against his own beating heart, heart beating live with terror, fear, and the beginnings of ecstasy. He begs the frog to dance. It does not move. He begs it to wink. It does not wink. Daniel Dickerson Harrington IV is a more than desperate man. He falls to his knees, clutching the little beaded bag to his chest, over the slip of paper already at his breast. Just at this moment—just when he falls to his knees—the top of the bag opens and emerging from its belly a deep, loud, vibrating croak. He fears it is not the grumbling of his stomach. He swoons, hearing a giant's footsteps approach, thundering toward him from the east. Louder and louder, they crash their inexorable way. Frozen in place, he covers his head, looks up to see a gigantic sole hovering above. He waits for it to descend. But the giant turns, brings down his foot a safe distance away, a yellow bird riding on the top of the giant's foot. It dips its green-tipped wing to him. Daniel is a dazzled man, a man opening his heart to a strange and alien nation, a man capable of praying to wondrous fathers in many shapes.

When Daniel rises, he realizes his vision: the shape emerging from the Giant's belly has the body of a thunderbird, the head of a frog, and the feet of a man. What he doesn't realize yet is that in a dim corner of the cave, painted on the wall, in red, is a human hand, pointing east.

Daniel sleeps fitfully, is awake before dawn, fully dressed, standing on his porch, gazing at the stars, wondering what they might have felt when looking at the North Star. If they had doubts about their journey, if their faith ever wavered. Now a man of inward faith, there is an excited calmness in his heart that he has never known. He thinks of his beloved beheaded Grace, looking out over a highway of destruction. Red cars killing a Redcar—he wonders if the irony occurred to her. She must have had consciousness for a few seconds after her head was severed from her body. What was it like, he tries to imagine, to be on the brink of entering some other existence? He doesn't think of heaven; he doesn't think of hell. Hearing waters rushing deep within the earth, he sees winged creatures emerge from fissures in cave walls. A great coat, with a long tail down its front, and feet curling around its cuffs, squeezes his wrists, a tail roping around his neck. A picture in the trunk. A woman. Black hair in braids. Headband beaded with birds, frogs, strange shapes. Strange shapes of things, strange things. His great-great grandmother, carrying one of her woven baskets on her back, peddling. Finding the Big Dipper, he quickly locates the little one. Suddenly it hits him: trespasser. The Center Church on the green: trespassing. The twin greens: trespassing. The library: trespassing. His God cannot help him now. His God, he fears, is trespassing.

But Daniel does not fall to his knees. Instead he opens his heart, his ears. From a far distance he hears the beat of a drum. A tiny drum voice at the beginning, it grows steadily louder. He raises his feet. His mind reminds him that he has no idea how to dance to this water drum; his spirit tells his mind to shut up. He raises one foot, and then the other. At first stumbling, he suddenly begins to twirl and to swirl and to whirl around the yard, swirling and whirling and twirling under the stars. Tears course down his cheeks, falling upon his chest, his hands, finally his feet. He does not wipe them away. As he sees the first pinkish-brown glimmer of the sun coming over the horizon, he opens wide his hand. He places it before his face and looks at the segmented, webbed sun ascending to its daytime place.

Packing quickly, he calls her office, leaves this message: "Mercy Pond. Sleeping Giant is calling me. I am going to its cave. Please come if you can." Though he seldom uses it, he has bought a new car. He slides into his Toyota hybrid, turns over its purring engine, and glides his hybrid creature onto the highway. He exits at Route 10, makes his way up Whitney Avenue, crosses over to Mount Carmel Avenue, passing the Giant from head to foot. He abandons his hybrid car near Quinnipiac University. Dawn is coming on full when he crosses the road, passes by the ponds. When the great white egret ascends straight up from its pond home, he witnesses the strong, bony wings rising. Dazzled, delighted, Daniel believes what he thinks he sees—a tiny frog on the egret's back, waving. Daniel waves back. Passing a stand of mountain laurel, he reaches out to touch one of its flower petals. Soft, like velvet. Thick, smooth, white tinged with red. He looks more closely—on its back, a black smudge. He looks at a leaf. Cut into its surface, veins that seem to bleed. The mountain laurel whimpers. Daniel kisses softly the bleeding branch. He runs to the park entrance, waves to the frogs and birds sitting atop the signs, then leaps onto the Tower Trail, surprising himself with his strength. About halfway up he realizes that he has no idea where the cave is located. As far as he knows, only a few researchers know and he hadn't thought to look at the sealed envelope containing directions. He simply left it in the folder with the photographs. He remembers hearing that the hikers who found it tried time and again to trace their steps but could not find their illegal find again. About halfway up he realizes he need not panic. Even without written directions, he has faith that his feet will lead him where he needs to be led.

As the watchtower comes into view he sees a shaft of multi-colored light cut into prisms through the spider web window. He turns, spots where the shaft of colored light disappears into the brush. On hands and knees, he descends. About twenty five feet down, he sees a ledge. Under that ledge, he realizes as he hops over it, is the entrance to the cave. Mercy Pond is already there, waiting for him. Deep inside, he is not surprised. Deep inside, he knows it is as it should be.

"So, you are already here," he remarks.

She nods. "I have always been here." The bird on her chest flutters.

He nods. "What is it I need to do?"

"You must be open to the signs. Much depends on you."

"But why me?" he needs to know.

Overhead, a great sweeping wind. As they look up, Yellowbird Woman begins to descend. Her translucent yellow feathers are tipped red. She has a deep ebony woman's face, bright white feet that land noiselessly on the rock ledge outside the cave. Eyes deep black, almost blue black. In their depths Mercy Pond and Daniel-Soon-To-Be-Red- Hand-Man are reflected beautifully.

Yellowbird Woman addresses Daniel: "You ask why you are given this great task. This is not what you should ask. You should not ask anything."

Ashamed, Daniel hangs his head. hoping the mountain will open wide its mouth, swallow him whole.

"I will do or die," he responds.

She shakes her head no. "If you do not change your I, the earth may die."

He nods— in that nod a faithful heart, a willing spirit. Mercy Pond takes his hand, squeezes it hard. As Yellowbird Woman touches their shoulders with her wings, they move forward toward her breast, letting her envelop them in her embrace. Daniel hears her steady heart beneath her feathered breast. She backs away, says goodbye, quickly ascends, disappearing into an opening in the sky.

They enter the cave, waiting for their eyes to adjust to the darkness. He has brought a flashlight. As they study the walls, water rushes beneath them. A red-tail hawk screeches overhead. He does not know how he knows it is a red-tail; he just knows that he knows. They study each painting in turn but he cannot see any more than he saw at his office. He becomes angry, frustrated, worried. Fearing failure, he knocks his fisted hand against his thigh. He sits, closes his eyes, hoping he can clear his vision. Daniel begins to drift, swaying back and forth, seeing twin feathers, red and yellow, fall at his feet. Scooping them up, he holds them to his chest. A searing pain rips through his back. He is about to fall from a horse. Clinging tight, he holds on. An explosion of light behind his eyes, a deep vibration from the center of the earth below. Atop a fast horse, with a beaded vest on his chest and back, he rides into the wind. At a window, looking in, he is reflected in a child's eyes. A scream. Falling, beaded blood runs down his back. Opening his eyes, he gets on his hands and his knees. Moving toward the back of the cave, he crawls on his belly. Nose to the ground, he crawls, inhaling layers of earth. Damp, moist, fecund earth. The back of his nation's cave.

There, a few inches from the cave floor, painted in red, the outline of a human hand, pointing east.

He scurries back to the center of the cave where Mercy Pond awaits.

"It's a red hand. Pointing east."

She nods. "So we move east?"

He nods. But before they start he has something he must say.

"I had an ancestor named Buster Harrington," he begins. "I'm not sure whether he was a great-great-grandfather or great-grand-uncle or what. But that doesn't matter. He always told stories. But one in particular he told over and over again and it got passed down all this time, even to me. My father used to tell it to me often; I begged him to tell it at least once a week. Seems Buster had just moved into a new house. I don't know where it was. Sometimes Father said it was where the Giant's right hand used to be. Sometimes it was in another State. But that doesn't matter. Buster said he had just lain down when his blanket—a great blanket made from the fur of a bear— was ripped off of him. There was nobody else in the room. Some invisible hand must have done it. So he reached down, grabbed the blanket, pulled it up around his ears. Closed his eyes. The blanket just ripped off of him again, winding itself around his feet. Said it was wound around so tightly that he couldn't have gotten up if he tried. So he unwound it, pulled it back up around his ears, and, from underneath, held on to it with his fists. And sure enough, it ripped off of him for a third time, and floated in the air at the end of his bed. Just as he was about to reach up and grab the blanket, something whizzed by his head. A tomahawk was driven in the headboard, not an inch from where his head had been."

Mercy Pond listens intently, says nothing, waiting for Daniel Red Hand Man to continue.

"For a long time I thought it was just a funny ghost story. Then for a long time I thought it was an allegory."

"And now?"

"I think there's another history behind the blanket exchange."

They leave the cave, head east, moving along the side of the Giant, facing Dragon Town.

They walk a few hundred yards. Suddenly a pigeon arrives, wings streaked with yellow. Pigeon alights, walks behind Daniel Red Hand Man, pecks his heels. Remembering his race against the words made beasts, he turns, asks Pigeon to speak.

Pigeon scratches the ground, preens its feathers, shakes itself. "Grace. Say Grace," it coos.

Instantly he remembers his father at Thanksgiving dinner, saying grace. Turning to the sky, he opens his arms, closes his eyes. The tiniest of tiny croaks comes from the dense underbrush at his left side. Diving down to earth, on his hands and knees, he crawls into the thick brush. Pushing the dense growth aside, he forms himself a tunnel through which he enters the mouth of a cave hidden so well that no one has found it yet. He forces his way further along the passage. A few feet into the cave, it becomes much wider and higher. Upright, his eyes adjusting to the darkness, he scans the walls, casts his eye over the cave floor, the cave ceiling, its unpainted walls. Dizzy with excitement, his footing is not sure. Out of the corner of his eye, he has a glimpse of a tiny white frog with red spots on its back. He intends to move quietly toward it. The tiny white frog looks up, sees what to it is a giant foot about to crash down upon its tiny head. Daniel Red Hand Man teeters on the edge but he loses his balance, falls, his foot landing a safe distance from the singing frog.

> "He has come, at last. At last he has come.
> The twin powers of Pigeon and Frog
> have brought his feet to us.
>
> Frog and Pigeon given
> Powerful arts to lead his way.
> At last comes he who may yet
> Save the day.

Great Thunderbird hear us now.
Do not abandon us.
The ceremony must begin.
Show us how."

The white frog with tiny red spots on its back hops to the front of the cave, making its way to the open side of the Giant where Mercy Pond and Pigeon await. Daniel Red Hand Man follows. When he reaches them, he turns his eyes to the sky, opens wide his arms, his hands, his fingers, stretching their webbed, connected selves as far as he can. Thunderbirds emerge, blackening the sky with their translucent light. A great rush of wind brings Yellowbird Woman and Thunderbird Man to his side. Pigeon's feathers become arms as his beak changes into lips. Soon Red Faith is shaking the red hand of Daniel Man. Tiny little white frog with red spots on her back hops excitedly. Frog soon changes too. Her webbed feet elongate; her back lengthens and straightens. Soon Frog Lily too shakes the hand of Daniel, part Red Man, who holds out his hand.

Thunderbird Man speaks first: "You are given nine years and nine months, time you need not know. You must leave the Giant and return to Dragon Town. You must warn the people. You must rewrite history even before it is written."

Daniel Red Hand Man needs no questions.

Yellowbird Woman speaks second. "You will leave the Giant. You will plant the seeds of what can grow into the grace of faith. In nine years and nine months we will know if your seed takes hold, whether it grows roots deep into the heart of earth from which can emerge the flowers of a graceful faith."

He asks no questions; he needs no answers.

Thunderbird Man and Yellowbird Woman speak in unison. "The twins will once again go with you. They will assume different shapes. Be watchful."

In a great rushing wind that sounds like the water rushing underneath, they ascend, disappearing into the darkening, translucent sky.

2012

Daniel Dickerson Harrington IV Red Hand Man finds himself on his park bench, on the north side of one of the twin New Haven greens, pigeons and starlings gathering at his feet. On his shoulder, a sparrow. On the back of his hand, a painted dragonfly. At first his mind is a little foggy, but in a few minutes everything is clear. He remembers all he must remember, forgets what he must forget. He looks across the park. Mercy Pond is there, waving.

He goes straight to his office, even though his clothes are disordered and he hasn't shaved. Slightly balding, he keeps his hair short, neatly parted, combed precisely to cover as much blank scalp as possible. Shirts and trousers well-pressed. Always a leather belt— he likes the clear dividing line at his waist. Practical, sturdy shoes. He dresses comfortably, sensibly, conservatively. He draws no attention to himself. He is safe this way. But today he does not care. The departmental assistant almost gasps when she sees him. David Red Hand Man is in more disarray than he realizes. His hair goes every which way, his shirt hangs out of his belt, and his eyes have become wild. He dismisses her concern, goes to his office, locks the door, writes. Barricaded for seven days, leaving only to use the bathroom or to get something to eat, he writes furiously. Coming from the writing man's mouth, strange chants, in a language no one who hears him understands. He misses classes, he does not sit on the park bench, and he does not attend church. The writing red-hand man empties himself upon the pages he creates. He disavows much of what he has previously proven about the history of Dragon Town and Sleeping Giant. He disavows many judgments he has made about the advance of culture. He rethinks what it is he thinks he has learned from the relics uncovered in the harbor. He begins to read an invisible history, not inscribed on material tablets delivered from a material sky. For seven days and seven nights, he travels into the spaces between words, into the impossible places beneath the spaces, hearing voices under the greens, insistent, multiple, multiplying. For seven days and seven nights, Daniel Red Hand Man's fingers tap out words and sounds on a mechanical keyboard, spewing forth words made beasts, wondrous human-beasts, who wear coats of many colors. Disheveled but not distraught, he brings his revised manuscript to its conclusion. He calls his editor, asks to have it included in the next printing of his textbook, due next month from the publisher. He calls his minister, asks that he be allowed to present what he has discovered at the Sunday meeting of the Church elders. He calls the office of Native American Studies at the University, asks to meet with the Department. He calls the Algonquin Tribes Council Headquarters, asks to meet with the tribal elders immediately. He has three meetings scheduled in the next three days. He faxes his revision to his editor who assures him he will get back to him in a day or two.

Daniel leaves his office and heads to the green. His favorite bench is full of what he is sure are high school kids. They come here after school, hoping to get one of the college students to notice them. "Silly asses," he mutters, shaking his head. He looks across the park. Mercy is at her usual bench. He walks over, sits. He is ill at ease, thrown off balance. From an entirely different direction, it is not the same green anymore. Center Church is to his left; it should be to his right. He likes his back to the library. He does not like his face to it. He is in a foul mood. "Damn those stupid ass kids," he sneers. Mercy Pond calms him, reminds him that they are not important. He laughs a little at his angry, displaced self. They go to Louie's for lunch and return to the bench.

"I'm afraid," he confides.

She does not dismiss his fear. "Why are you afraid?"

"Because I do not think I will be believed."

"Why?"

"Because I remember Jeremiah. He was not believed, either," he reveals.

"But you are not Jeremiah and this is not the Bible," she notes.

"I know," he nods, "but I am still afraid."

"Of the ridicule?" she taunts.

"A little," he admits. "But mostly because I have never believed. I know how they will be."

A thin little sparrow hops on his shoulder. He turns his ear to its beak, hoping it will speak. But, alas, it has nothing to say. He looks at the dragonfly on the back of his hand. It is still; it does not fly. He looks to his left, toward Temple Street. A fully restored, shiny black Thunderbird is coming down the street. On its hood, a silver thunderbird ornament. Painted flames race up its back, mimicking the painted flames racing up its trunk. As he passes their bench, the driver waves. Daniel Red Hand Man feels again his faith and his despair.

He meets first with the Native American Studies Department. He has sent ahead his revised chapter on early Algonquin history and the geography of the area, arguing that long ago great Thunderbirds saw in Hobbomock, the legendary but real Giant, the same self-destructive tendency that the trespassers would bring, that the Quinnipiac, and the Mattabeseck and other local tribes would also have. After all, they had seen him reach up, try to catch the yellow birds, intent on crushing them if he could. They put Hobbomock to sleep so that they could preserve him. That if the Indians who thought they could sell him and the English who thought they could buy him didn't come some day to realize that they have to preserve him, then they would awaken him. But in that awakening day, the Thunderbirds would not allow Hobbomock to walk the earth again. He would remain on his back. But from his belly would pour forth a whole new nation to replace the one that bought and sold him simply because they thought they could. But more than that: with the aid of a sacred water drum, this new nation would restore the Sleeping Giant and all his lands around him to the way it was the day before the trespassers set foot on his land. Daniel closes with a plea that they believe that this has been happening, is happening, and will be happening.

Listening politely, they seek his proof. His tribal affiliation. A list of Native Americans he has interviewed. He shows not proof enough. He is not believed. He is not trusted. After he leaves they say "Just nonsense. Not a scholarly chapter at all. Not well-documented. How can we credit this?"

He meets next with the elders from the Algonquin Tribes Council. Repeating his story, he gives again his warning. They, too, ask for his proof. They, too, wonder about his tribal affiliation. They want to know why it is that they have heard no such legend? Surely, they say, we would have heard about it. Thunderbird is sacred to us. After he leaves they say "He is too white. We cannot believe him. We do not trust him."

He gets a short email from his editor. "You prose is poor. Your argument unsound. We cannot accept this. But you may resubmit a thorough revision."

He meets with the elders of the Center Church. Once again he presents his pleas for belief, reminding them of the strange appearances and disappearances on the Giant, beginning in the seventeenth century. Once again, they want to know his proof. They want to know if he is an Indian. They want to know what material evidence he has. After he leaves they say: "He is too Indian. We cannot trust him. We do not believe him."

But the editor's assistant—well, that's a coat of a different color. Chief Joseph Eleven Many-Colored Coats, as he calls himself, has read the revised chapter. He has secretly copied it, distributed it among his fellow group of letter boxers. They hike the Giant every weekend, hiding boxes with paper inside them, writing elaborate and precise instructions, then try to find the boxes. They all have a special stamp. When they find a box, they stamp the paper inside with their singular stamp. They go off-trail legally; they have the Park Ranger's permission. They know parts of the Giant that few people know. Skilled rock climbers, skilled hikers, they are fit to journey the entire mountain. They can scale the sheer vertical rock of his chin. On hands and knees, they go into the deepest underbrush. They have heard things, seen things, felt things. They are willing to believe. Twelve believers find Daniel Dickerson Harrington IV Red Hand Man on his bench on the north side of the green, his back partially shaded by a strong-growing hybrid Liberty Elm Tree. It resists disease. Its leaf-veins are at peace. They do not bleed. Gathering at his feet, they form a half-circle. Forming a larger half-circle, pigeons and sparrows and starlings coo and chirp and strut. In the center of these two half-circles sits Daniel. Lips unsealed, he is heartened by the faith gathered at his feet.

Chief Joseph Eleven Coats of Many Colors assumed his name when he was adopted by the Quinnipiac Tribal Council, a group of Connecticut citizens, some Quinnipiac, some from other tribes, some European, some Asian, some Muslim, dedicated to preserving Quinnipiac culture and revivifying Quinnipiac history. Once a year the group held an adoption ceremony. Anyone who wished to could attend, persuade the council that he or she had studied Algonquin culture and had an honest and earnest desire to reclaim New England history. If persuaded, the Council would allow the adopted individual to participate in a public naming ceremony. John Mailer has many bloods— Quinnipiac, Mohican and Pequot, maybe Mattabeseck. Irish, English and Scottish, maybe French. So he thought long and hard before being publicly adopted into this group. He did not wish to erase any of himself by identifying with one group over another. But he felt a fierce desire in his heart to salvage a precious part of New England history that had been virtually erased. He had heard many times the legend of Chief Montowese, Theophilus Eaton, his coat and his eleven bolts of cloth. He had heard many times the legend of Joseph and his coat of many colors. So this name seemed to him the perfect way to blend his many parts.

He was very active in the group until it disbanded. It fell apart for all kinds of reasons. The usual political disagreements about what constitutes race. The usual problems with funding. The usual difficulty with getting volunteers actually to do what they volunteered to do. And for some not so typical ones. They were having a lot of success in the Fair Haven area of New Haven. Convinced the schools to add to their history curriculum, were given permission to put on a powwow at the middle school. Students were taught Native American mythology as they were Greek mythology. That is until the Board of Education stepped in. Stopped the group from coming to the school. Said that it was "unfair" to have some students "exposed" and not others. The group was small and didn't have the heart or the resources to fight back. So they just disbanded, as so many of their ancestors had done so long ago. To help him get over the bitter irony of it all, Chief Joseph Eleven Coats of Many Colors began hiking at Sleeping Giant. By chance, he saw a notice in the Mount Carmel newspaper that anyone interested in letterboxing should meet at the entrance to the park on Sunday afternoon. If there was enough interest, The Park Association was going to explain this popular British sport and would allow letterboxing on the Giant. Sunday afternoon, at two o'clock, twelve trusty and hearty souls began their letterboxing careers, unaware that they were setting out on a different sort of search.

Anna Webb is a cosmetologist. At twenty-three, she has finally gotten her life onto a productive track. Dropped out of high school, she did odd jobs, going nowhere. Her father, a Presbyterian minister, wouldn't admit it, even to himself, but he was ashamed of her. Everyone in his family, for as many generations as they could count, was responsible, hard-working. Each generation had done better than the last. Backsliding, he feared. Her mother, however, wasn't as worried. Most of her family took a few twists and turns before they settled down in a straight path. Just time, she insisted. At twenty, Anna took up rock climbing by chance. At the local mall, a sporting goods store was doing demonstrations on a fiberglass rock wall. She figured she had nothing to lose, so gave it a try. She couldn't explain why she thought it so thrilling to have her toe take hold in a little crevice and to push herself off, reaching for the next crevice with her hand. When she swung out away from the fake rock wall on her safety harness, Anna Webb tasted a gleeful joy she had never known before. Suspended in the air, she felt the power of her calves, of her fingers, of her toes. A convert before her fifteen minutes had expired, she started working full-time at the local discount store, studied for and passed on her first try her GED exam, and saved enough money for climbing gear and some professional lessons. By twenty-two she enrolled in cosmetology school and now has a job at one of the local salons. She's spent a lot of time on the Giant and is ready for a new challenge. She is small—only five feet and two inches—but she is strong. She lifts weights, can bench one hundred thirty pounds with ease. Anna laughs that she is one of the only pure-bloods around. As far as anybody knows, everybody in her family is English. Just English. Only English. All English. Her father has documented the family lineage on both sides back to the Mayflower, an historical fact about which Anna feels ambivalent. Proud she was baptized a Presbyterian but seldom attends Church. Even more seldom does she read the Bible. She wants a more interesting God than the one she finds in her father's sermons, than the one she finds on her Bible's pages.

At forty-two, Peter Bogdonoff is one of the older members of the group. The great-grandson of Russian Jews who immigrated to America, settling on Hester Street, he is a struggling artist. With a small studio on upper Chapel Street, he sells just enough to keep himself supplied with canvas and paint. Working part-time waiting tables at a restaurant, he also works now and then delivering papers and advertisements. Divorced, his wife and two sons live in

Manhattan. He sees the boys once a month. Peter is fair when he talks about his wife Sarah, admitting the troubles were more his fault than hers. He misses his sons, Owen and David, but he also admits that he likes being single again. Free to keep whatever schedule he sees fit. He sleeps little and has for years. Four hours a night is enough. He rises early—usually before four o'clock. He's already worked a couple of hours before dawn. He often climbs at East Rock or Sleeping Giant from early morning until early afternoon, paints until four, then works at the restaurant until late evening. Peter used to be religious, believing the Torah. But that faith has faded. He seldom goes to synagogue except for weddings, bar-mitzvahs, other rituals. Yet he quite often reads parts of the Old Testament. He still finds something in it that speaks to him. He reads aloud. The words are weighty, assuming significance on his tongue. Drawn to the sound of the language, often unsure of the meanings behind the words, Peter neither believes nor disbelieves. He is curious, open, wondering, a little reticent. He will be the first to wonder if he has just heard the flapping of enormous wings.

Marcus Smith is a devout man. He is a Buddhist, having converted ten years ago. Wanting to be filled with the calm fervor of total belief, he realized, finally, that Christianity could not claim him as he wished to be claimed. He took a class on World Religions as a senior in high school. Timidly approaching the Buddhist group on campus, he was welcomed. Finding peace there in his contemplations, Marcus began to study yoga. A serene, thoughtful, peaceful man, Marcus began climbing as a sort of pilgrimage. When he started climbing Sleeping Giant, he wondered why it is not widely recognized as a holy site. He still wonders. At twenty-seven, Marcus is a successful financial advisor. Part Lebanese on his mother's side, he is also descended from slaves on both sides. Much of his family history is lost. He collects bills of sale. Although he chides himself for buying such offensive relics of the hegemonic past, he argues that they may be better in his black hands than in the hands of anyone else. At least he feels their horror. The tallest of the group at over six foot three, he is wiry, strong. His hair is long, thick, gathered in tight braids with many-colored beads on their tips.

Frances Piccerillo chews gum. She swears. Has the proverbial heart of gold, the steel will of a tarantula. What she wants, she gets hold of, and doesn't let go. She's nineteen, just out of high school, ready to start college in the fall. She's Catholic. Her Italo-American family is Catholic. She's fourth generation. Like so many, she isn't as devout as her ancestors. Olive-skinned, she has deep brown eyes, thick black hair, slightly curly. Smart. Almost a perfect 1600 on the SAT. Already published two poems in literary journals. Fiercely passionate about poetry, Frances pays attention to the sound of language. Her ears are always open, sensitive to the slightest pitch, undulation, tone. She listens, always and intently, even when she is chewing her incessant gum. She listens to the world; it gives her poems. Her father and mother own an Italian Import Company on State Street in Hamden, near the Mt. Carmel line. They have done well. Have a large house and a larger nest egg. When Frances gets married, they tell her, nothing less than a nine-course meal at the reception. Wedding cake at least three feet high. Good people, her stock— hard-working, God-fearing, good folk. Having been rock climbing since she was twelve, hiking is second nature. She is rather tall at five foot ten. Her feet are huge—she's almost outgrown a size twelve. But they don't slow her down one bit. She fits them into toe holds no matter how small, then uses their size and strength to propel her up the mountain. Jokes are her salvation. She remembers hundreds, able to handle the punch line with the best of them. She's not especially sensitive about her ethnicity but she doesn't like mob jokes. She loves animals. She has four cats, a dog, and a canary. Her keen ears will be the first to hear the teeny croak of tiny frogs swaying in the trees.

Thirty-two -year old Red Cloud Morgan is the pessimist of the group. His father is Irish; his mother a mixture of English, Mohican, French. Red Cloud Morgan does not like how he looks. He has dark skin, dark eyes, thick, curly red hair. It's the red hair that bothers him. He read that in the nineteenth-century English imagination, anyone with red hair was a devil. He knows it's ridiculous but it bothers him nonetheless. The best climber of the group, he is very muscular and strong. His neck is thick, his thighs massive. He rappels with great speed and flexibility as well as strength. He volunteers for Meals-on-Wheels. He is a dentist specializing in endodontics. His patients dread him. Rock climbing helps him forget. Red Cloud Morgan claims no organized faith but he is a deeply spiritual man. He cannot understand his own pessimism. Quiet, he hangs back from most conversations. But with a glass of beer or two, he transforms. His pessimism disappearing, he tells stories all night long. His wife Edith says that it sometimes seems he is two different men. His daughter, Rachel, agrees. His mother has yet to tell him (and he has yet to ask) why she named him Red Cloud. Entering her ninth month of pregnancy, she dreamed that the clouds rained blood, the blood became fertile when it reached the earth, and from the loins of the land—her loins, her land— sprung an unwanted child. No wonder he is a pessimist; no wonder he does not know why. Red Cloud Morgan will be the first to hear the sound of water, rushing, deep beneath.

Eugene Dvorak is the oldest of the group. At fifty, he is fitter than most thirty-year olds. A fitness buff, he is at the gym seven days a week. At the Winchester factory for almost thirty years, he has just heard that it will be closing soon. "The Gun that Won the West" will be made in China beginning next year. He is sad, mad, but resigned. And worried. It won't be easy for him at his age to find another job. He has little education— he quit high school, was drafted. He lost part of his scalp to shrapnel—a million-dollar wound, they called it. Sent home, alive, still able to walk and talk. Been at the factory ever since. He's been hiking and climbing for decades. His wife and children loved it too. Lisa, his wife, died ten years ago of breast cancer. His daughter, Anna, is away at college. His son Roy is married, living in Oklahoma. Gene, as he likes to be called, has become more devout since his wife died. He seldom misses Mass. He attends Novenas. He reads the Bible every day. He believes in miracles. An unbeliever that the Bible is literally the word of God, he is a believer that the Bible is a divine hand, a divine mind. Gene also studies astronomy and astrology. His father is Czech, his mother Lithuanian. Gene's favorite holiday is Easter. He is a master at painting Easter eggs. Tiny, mosaic pictures, tiny multi-colored geometric shapes forming intricate, swirling patterns. Inside the empty egg space, an elaborate scene. When you open them, you gasp at the steadiness of the hand that creates such a miraculous, tiny, perfectly detailed world in such a tiny little space.

Amy Sun is an accountant for a large mortgage brokerage firm. She's twenty-five, very petite, with long, lustrous dark hair that she keeps in a bun. Very athletic, she is perhaps the one with the most endurance. Her cardiovascular health is astounding. A five-mile run seems but a warm-up. She has run a number of marathons and always has finished in the top ten. She has to remind herself to get off the elliptical. Optimistic, outgoing, she belongs to the racquetball club, a philology group, plays chess twice a week, and volunteers at the local children's hospital. Engaged to a real estate lawyer, her life is happy, productive, promising. Her father is Korean-American; he immigrated to the United States about twenty years after the war. He still can feel the barbed gazes that often met him on the street even after all that time. After he married Ethel, his Polish and Irish wife, the gazes softened. He was secretly relieved when Amy was born with round eyes. He thanked whatever god was responsible for giving her an American face. Amy thanks no god for anything. While she won't deny that there may be some spiritual force in the universe, she believes that we create the gods we need. Morality for her is a personal thing. Salvation too. She will be the first to see the shape of a large black bird cross the face of the moon.

Hating his name, and intending to get it legally changed some day, is seventeen-year-old Jesus Rodriquez. He's tired of people pronouncing it wrong. He's stopped bothering to correct them: " Hey, it's Hey-sus." He tries to make himself believe it doesn't matter but it does. He has so fallen away from his family's Catholicism that he resents having been baptized. His heart does not respond to liturgy. The closest he has come to belief is at the beach, at night, tasting the salt air on his tongue, watching the waves roll toward shore. Their wavy fingers caressing the shore, then taking part of the shore back to its watery death in its wavy embrace. Then Jesus believes that creation and destruction are one-and-the-same. Love and death are but different sounds for the same word. The rhythm of all life is a dragging toward the rhythm of all death. As the seaweed washes up around his ankles, he thinks that if there is a god, it is like a great umbilical cord. It nourishes you but always threatens to wrap its cords around your neck, your feet. Jesus is a very handsome young man. Just under six feet, with wavy, dark hair, large, round dark eyes, even white teeth, he has a very muscular body. Well proportioned, he is the picture of healthy youth. He has a mild laugh, smiling eyes, and can laugh at himself with ease. Despite his philosophy, he is a happy man, looking forward to becoming a partner in his parents' business. The owner of three convenience stores, his father is an ironic American success story. He and his wife illegally crossed the border from Mexico. Stayed underground, worked very hard, saved every penny. Made their way to Connecticut, bought their first store. A tiny carry-out, in Fair Haven, selling lottery tickets, soda, candy bars. Worked very hard, saved every penny. Now the owners of three large convenience stores, they have a large house in Cheshire, a son about to graduate from high school. Their son, born here, is safe. But Hector and Luisa Rodriquez look over their shoulders a lot. The epitome of the American Dream, they are illegitimate in the country that they love. Devout Catholics, they pray that Jesus will come home someday.

Sarah Simpson is blonde, blue-eyed, beautiful. She gathers her thick, golden hair at the nape of her neck, braids it, often winding a blue or yellow or red beaded band around the base of the braid. It falls below her waist. When she is climbing or hiking she winds the braid into a coil at the back of her head, securing it with her grandmother's hair comb trimmed with mother-of-pearl inset with tiny red diamond-shaped stones. Maybe rubies but probably just colored stones. Sarah is ambivalent about her mixed religion, mixed race. English and Irish, she feels a war within her. Her English mother is Protestant, her Irish father Catholic. Pulled between the two her entire childhood, Sarah finally refused to go to church at all. A close friend invited her to synagogue where Sarah immediately heard the language of grace. The cadenced, rhythmic Hebrew was ironically her tongue of flame. Understanding not one syllable, she knew instinctively what it said. After many years of hard study, she converted to Judaism. But lately her ears have closed themselves to the rich old Hebrew voices. She has lapsed from Judaism as well. Restless, searching, Sarah hopes to find a new spiritual home. She seldom sees her parents, lives in her own apartment, has been a teller at a bank for ten years. A single thirty-year-old woman, she's secretly grateful for her good looks. An avid solitaire player, she is her own best competition. She's only been climbing a couple of years, but she is already damned good.

Luke Christmas used to be sure he had found his spiritual home. An evangelical Baptist from his early youth, he was sure and comfortable in his deep and abiding faith in conservative Christianity. But Luke now finds himself in a terrible conflict. At sixteen, the youngest of the group, he is also the most unhappy. When he realized he was gay, he thought he could be comfortable with his sexuality. But the religion he so loves damns him for it, making him deeply uncomfortable. At war with himself, climbing and hiking, he has discovered, help him silence the grenades going off in his heart, in his head. Part Italian, part Spanish, part English, he has dark hair, hazel eyes, and is of medium build. His parents were both born in America, as were their parents. A life of material comfort is his. His father is a pediatrician, his mother a nurse. Luke has wanted for nothing, save for a soul that can accept the body in which it is housed. A little shy, very kind, and adventuresome, Luke volunteers at the local animal shelter and at a summer camp for underprivileged children. A winning smile, a strong handshake, makes Luke a pretty popular young man. But, at night, alone, Luke Christmas is haunted by terrible ghosts that threaten to eat him alive while he tries to sleep in his own bed. He will be the first to see the shape of a frog soar over the face of the moon.

At forty-two, White Dove McNamara is on her second career. Having taught elementary school for fifteen years, she realized that she hated it. She went to night school, learned woodworking, and has started her own business making reproduction furniture. To her surprise, she also found her religion. Taking her hand-held tools to the virgin wood, watching a shape emerge from a blank tree trunk, White Dove McNamara witnessed the hand of her faith take shape. Happening upon a book titled *Religion in Wood* has led her to an intensive study of Shaker culture. Her studio has become her chapel: there, in the smell of wood shavings, surrounded by saw dust at her feet, she feels a spiritual power and wholeness that leaves her feeling complete. Hidden in each piece is a small slip of paper. Written in red: *here is a soul that has made peace with its earthly face.* Hiking and climbing, she finds that the Sleeping Giant becomes another sort of studio. In the hemlock woods she smells grace; in the stands of dense oak, she hears divine murmurs. In the pond from which the egret rises, she sees the strength of an angel's wings. Divorced since she was twenty-five, the mother of a son in the army, she has few regrets in her life. She loves Christmas but she is not sure she believes in Christ. She might call herself a pantheist but she does not like labels. That's why she likes her name so; that's why she never changed it when she married. Part Naragansett, part Irish, part French Canadian, part Swedish, she refuses to identify with one over another. Solidly Irish, McNamara has a deep, loud, reverberating ring to it. White Dove: as soft as a rippling brook, the gentle breeze of wings going by. It is a perfect name for her, coming from the natural world she loves so well. White Dove McNamara will be the first to doubt that she has seen what she has seen. And she will be the first to come to believe that she has seen a thunderbird cross in front of the moon with a waving frog astride its back.

Daniel Red Hand Man motions for his gathered faithful to be quiet. A sparrow has alighted on his shoulder, putting its beak into his ear, whispering. He smiles, nods. A dragonfly appears, circling overhead. When it alights on the back of his outstretched hand, the group utters a unified gasp of awe. Its needle-like translucent body, its nearly invisible wing— a material representation of the fantastic, they think. Even the pigeons and the starlings observe a moment of silence; they, too, contemplate the hovering, winged thing.

"I cannot tell you how much I thank you for coming here," he begins. He stammers, then continues: "for believing what I have written."

They nod. Chief Joseph Eleven Coats of Many Colors adds: "And we thank you. It is finally written. People must hear."

Daniel laughs ironically. "Ah," he says, "it is not so easy. You are the only ones who have been willing to listen. All the others have shut their ears."

Mercy Pond slides on the bench. Daniel smiles, thankful she is here. "Why are you so willing to believe?" he needs to know.

White Dove McNamara speaks first. "We have heard and seen mysterious and strange things on the Giant. At first I did not believe that I had seen what I had seen. Now I am sure that I have seen."

"Same with me," Jesus Rodriquez affirms. "I thought I must be crazy. Now I know that I'm not."

"The first time I heard the water rushing underneath, I was O.K. Just natural springs. But then the voices. Tiny, insistent voices speaking a language I couldn't understand. Creeped me out," confesses Anna Webb.

"And the frogs, swaying on the tips of hemlock trees. I wondered what might have been in my tea," Amy Sun confides as she makes circular motions near her temple.

Gene Dvorak has a worried look on his face. "I thought that God was trying to speak to me. And I was afraid. I covered my ears."

"I thought maybe I had stumbled into some undiscovered species of frog. I thought about calling a biologist," Luke Christmas admits.

"I can still hear the flapping of those great wings. They covered the face of the sun. An eclipse when there shouldn't have been one. I huddled there in the momentary darkness. But a minute later, the world was bright again. But I kept seeing the head of a frog on a black body with wings tipped with gold. I couldn't get it out of my head, no matter how hard I tried. I kept telling myself this is no close encounter of any kind." Peter Bogdonoff trembles excitedly as he recounts this.

Smacking her gum, Frances adds, "Damned straight. Thought I was going to shit my drawers the first time I saw that egret take off. A damned little red-eyed frog sitting on its back, waving to me."

Sarah Simpson nods agreement. "Just how I felt when I saw frogs sitting on top of all the signs. Figured I was crazy as hell."

"I wondered if the earth was ready to redeem itself. An old Buddhist belief that the earth will stand only so much abuse. And then it will send signs. I wondered if I was seeing the signs," confides Marcus Smith.

Chief Joseph Eleven Coats of Many Colors notes one more thing. "Now I wish we had spoken of these things. But each of us saw things at different times, different days, different years. All the times we were together as a group, we saw nothing, heard nothing. So none of us really believed what we saw when we were alone. So we didn't speak about it. So we didn't make any connection."

Daniel Red Hand Man understands well all they say; he, too, has only recently made the connections. "The Giant is in trouble. The blight spreads, the deformed frogs grow in number. The mountain laurel is stunted, its leaves in pain. They bleed. And who knows how much more is going on that we have not yet seen."

"What can we do?" they ask, unified.

"We must have a healing ceremony."

"But how?" they ask. "We know nothing of such things."

Daniel Red Hand Man hesitates. "Somehow we will know what to do when the time comes. I know that we must bring together many different people. Of all faiths. Of all races. Otherwise, we do not have a chance."

Each takes a different part of the city, of the surrounding towns; each will try to persuade, one by one, group by group, as many people and agencies as they can that the Giant is in danger. Though numerous reports of his decline have been published over many years, there has been no widespread belief in the need for action. Daniel has already secured air time at the radio station at Quinnipiac University, across the street from the Giant sleeping.

The night of Daniel Red Hand Man's radio address there happens to be the night that two meetings are simultaneously held at Quinnipiac University: meetings of the Connecticut Historical Society and The Greater New Haven Conservationists. After his address, he requests that anyone interested in further information to please gather at the University's large auditorium. As the historians and conservationists are leaving their separate meetings, they see people gathering, are curious, investigate. They stay, curious, intrigued. Soon the room is full, with people gathering in the hallway, down the stairs, outside. University security forces arrive, demand explanation, assert control, and threaten arrest if their numbers grow, breaking fire codes. The media suddenly appears. Daniel Red Hand Man and his motley band of would-be-listeners are on the evening news. Word travels, spreads. He is called to the news station for an interview on the late night news. He is clean-shaven, well-dressed, persuasively articulate.

What he says is this: "There is no need to believe me. First thing tomorrow morning, send a photographer to the Giant's side. Stand in front of the radio station. Look up. That is all you need to do. You will see the blight. He is disfigured. You can photograph that blight. There is no need to believe me. First thing tomorrow morning, send a photographer to one of Giant's many springs and rivulets. You will see the plight of the frogs. They are deformed. You can photograph that deformity. There is no need to believe me. First thing tomorrow morning, send yet another photographer to the Giant's mountain laurel grove. The flowers are stained, the bushes are stunted, the leaves have swollen veins. You can photograph that stain, that stunt, those veins that seem to bleed. You do not need to believe me."

Shaking, he leaves the studio, refusing to say anything more. Mercy Pond walks him home, helping him to fend off the reporters still at his heels. After a few blocks they give up, let him go in peace. Exhausted, exhilarated, he climbs his front steps. On his door, a note is tacked: "Way to go, my man." It is signed C.J. Underneath the initials, a sparrow and a dragonfly on the back of a man in a many-colored coat. Daniel Red Hand Man laughs deeply, feeling the hand of Grace waving in his direction.

Response is swift, furious. The Quinnipiac Council quickly reassembles and the local Universities pledge research funds. Conservation groups flock to East Rock, to West Rock, to Sleeping Giant. Protestant and Catholic Churches pledge support. The local Synagogues add theirs; so too, the local Mosques. A trust fund is established in care of the Sleeping Giant Association. In less than one week, contributions total over two million dollars. The letter boxer group does not wait two weeks to reconvene; they meet again after only one. Not understanding the sacred importance of place, they initially had envisioned a small healing ceremony of maybe a few hundred participants. They could easily fit on the greens. Daniel Red Hand Man had already applied for the permit. But the greens cannot possibly hold the crowd that promises to gather. Gene Dvorak has the idea to ask Mount Carmel to close off all streets near the Giant, to ask Quinnipiac University to clear its parking lots, and to hold the healing ceremony at the base of and up the side of the sleeping mountain man. At first officials think it will end in a nightmare; they cannot understand how they will control such a crowd. But within days, compromises are reached, within days the arrangements are made. Within hours after the last contract is sealed, announcements are made. On June 21st, beginning precisely at dawn, they shall gather. No cameras, no laptops, no cell phones, no radios, no media.

The concerned, the faithful, and probably a few of the merely curious begin to gather the afternoon before. All traffic—save for essential services like port-a-potties, medical and police equipment set up at the far end of the University parking lot— has been forbidden for blocks around the mountain. People are urged to take buses to Mount Carmel. They are forced to leave their cars, their bikes in designated area well away from the Giant. People walk to the Giant. Those who cannot walk are pushed in wheelchairs, or small wagons. Police are massed at the far end of the University parking lot, dressed in unnecessary riot gear. The massive crowd that gathers here has neither violence nor disobedience in its heart. All evening, all night, pilgrims arrive. All night, they sway, arm-in-arm, singing, chanting. Filling the air, songs of many nations, many languages.

A small, high platform with an open front has been erected at the entrance to the park. On the platform, sitting, cross-legged, Daniel Red-Hand Man, Mercy Pond, Chief Joseph Eleven Coats of Many Colors and the eleven members of their faithful band. Daniel Red Hand Man rises, gestures for silence. A sparrow sits on his left shoulder. Hovering over his right, a mutli-colored dragonfly. A silence deep and profound envelops the sea of people gathered at the Giant's base. As dawn breaks, a great white egret rises from its pond home as a collective gasp vibrates through the crowded Giant. At Daniel Red Hand Man's signal, a shaman, in Mattabeseck headdress, appears. His headdress is short, barely reaching the top of his back. Suspended on catgut around his neck, a ruby-eyed frog carved from quartz rock dances on his chest. He faces north, then east, then south, then west, singing a sacred song. As he sings, he dances. On his intricately beaded moccasins, tiny green frogs leap and dance in the air every time he lifts his feet. In his hands, a leather drum. The massive crowd has closed its eyes, swaying to the beat of the drum, opening themselves to the sound of a human voice carrying itself in waves across the Giant and the congregation at his feet. From the distance comes the sound of another drum, a sacred water drum, beaten by an invisible hand. But its beat grows louder, and louder. Tone pure, lasting. As suddenly as it started, it stops, leaving only the receding echo of its beauty.

Throughout the day the shaman dances, drums. His audience sways silently, fervently to the sound of his words, to the beat of his feet. Crossing the sky overhead, sparrows and starlings. Crossing the sky overhead, red-tail hawks and golden yellow birds. On the platform, hopping, a hundred tiny frogs with red eyes. As soon as they appear, they disappear. The crowd, eyes wide, still swaying, praying.

As dusk begins to descend, Daniel Red Hand Man and Mercy Pond slip away, stealing up the Tower Path, quietly, quickly, with Sparrow and Dragonfly at their ears. Reaching the watchtower easily, before an hour has passed they look through the spider web window at the descending sun, the ascending moon. Water rushes deep underneath, strong wings flap above. In the hemlock trees, swaying on the branch tips, tiny frogs, green and yellow with jewel-red eyes, and tiny, sharp claws. Daniel Red Hand Man and Mercy Pond start down the side of the Giant's hip, toward the deep underbrush. Just as they are about to get on hands and knees, a narrow lip opens, swallowing them without leaving a trace.

They land upright, unharmed. Thunderbird Man and Yellowbird Woman embrace each in turn, wrapping first him, then her, against a warm, feathered breast. Gathering around them, in a circle, come Chief Montowese and Grace Trap-Ridge Hitchcock. Red Man O.K. Jones alongside Grace Yellow Bird Faith. Frog Bird and Yellow Tail Frog Bird Charles Sanford Hitchcock join the welcome. Red Faith and Frog Lily, restored to their original bodies, hug and greet Daniel Red Hand Man and Mercy Pond. Strange Creature leaves its place on the blanket, joins the greeting party. Yellow birds flock; frogs gather.

"You have done well," Thunderbird Man says.

"Better than we had dared to hope," confides Yellowbird Woman.

Daniel Red Hand Man draws a deep breath. "But have we done well enough?"

"We do not know," reply Thunderbird Man and Yellowbird Woman, in unison. "We do not know. It will take time to know. So we must wait. We can be patient a little while longer."

Grace Yellow Bird Faith returns to her blanket. Strange Creature follows, sits at her feet. Every day Grace weaves another part of the last section of the blanket. Every day she adds another inch to the shape of the hand. It is a massive hand; it will take many more feet to weave its giant thumb. But every day, she weaves another inch. Inch by inch, every day the outline of the red hand moves closer to its finished shape.

Deep underground, a nation new.

2051

Impossibly old, Daniel Red Hand man sits on his bench on the north side of the green, facing south. The twelve tribes as he fondly called them that used to gather at his feet have long since dispersed, reduced to despair as one agency after another withdrew support as soon as the blight appeared gone. Within months, the blight returned. Not yet visible to most eyes, it began spinning its wooly white coat of death. It's been years since anyone found any Dutchman's breeches. The swans have disappeared from the ponds at Giant's feet. Daniel Red Hand Man dreaded the day when the egrets could not lift themselves into the sky.

The first to lose faith in the world's desire to dedicate itself to the Giant was Gene Dvorak. Disturbed by what he saw as growing complacency even by the Sleeping Giant Park Association, he created a monument to the Giant in one of his Easter eggs, preserving him as he should be. Gene covered him with vibrant life, leaving no holes. Giant was warm when Gene went to bed. But in the morning, just before dawn, Gene found the egg cracked, throwing his created world into disarray, leaving Giant with gaping holes. At noon Gene found the egg miraculously whole. But before the next dawn, it had cracked again. Deep down, he knew the Giant was cracked and that surface resurrection only leads to more cracking.

Anna Webb was startled from faith while doing a client's hair. For the hundredth time she heated her curling iron, creating ridges and swirls where there were none. Added volume and curl to straight thin hair knowing that it would all disappear within hours—less if it rained. Like Giant's hair, she realized. From a distance it is nice and thick. From the thousands who attended the ceremony to less than twenty at the last SPGA meeting—so much has interest waned. The Giant was hot and then he was not. He'll be cold again, she fears. His chest will be covered with holes. His leg will be exposed. Chilled with the thought of deep cold shaking him awake, she retreats. The inevitability of it all shook her faith that she could do something, that she could matter. They're going to strip him anyway.

Skeptical from the start, Peter Bogdonoff was the least disheartened by growing disinterest in the Giant. When he last visited, he spent a long time in the mountain laurel groves. They had grown tall, towering above him, looking recovered. But Peter kept staring and the longer he stared the more he was sure that the veins started to pulsate, to throb. The more he stared, the more he felt them start to bleed. Realizing that he could do no more, he turned Giant over to the power behind giant wings.

Rummaging in the State Street antiques stores, Marcus Smith found photographs of a bill of sale for rights to parts of Sleeping Giant to the New Haven Trap Rock Company. He stopped dead in his tracks. The weight of repeated history almost crushed him. Over and over again, a surge of interest and outrage. But over and over again, outrage abates, interest wanes. And more rights will be sold. As he touched the many-colored beads on the tips of his braided hair, he knew deep in his scalp that Giant's hair was unkempt, thinning in spots still hidden from common view. He knew, too, that it will be restored by hands other than only human ones. Resigned, he believed he would not live long enough to see that day. Abandoning his group, abandoning his faith, he imagined Giant's resurrection.

Red Cloud Morgan knew the Devil still walks the earth, waiting to damage the Giant. Until the earth radically transforms, it cannot rid itself of its devils. He imagined Sleeping Giant exploding, millions of bits of exploding trap rock burying everything all the way to Dragon Town. He also saw new devils arising out of the rocky ashes.

Looking into the clear night sky, Anna Sun was jolted to realize that the moon's pocked face was unhidden even for a moment by a large bird shape. Its translucence allowed the diseased face no cover. She ran from New Haven to the Giant hoping to exhaust herself, to let herself faint, to fall into even temporary oblivion. Though gasping, she did not fall at Giant's feet. Gulping the air, her throat burned, her chest heaved. Clarity almost blinded her. The Giant's salvation has nothing to do with her.

At the watchtower, Jesus Rodriquez was suddenly choked. He felt a cord around his neck. He struggled against it, trying to get his hand under it, push it away. The cord cut deeply into his hands. They bled. "But blood leads to renewal," he screamed. "But only if the body that bleeds destroys everything in its path," another voice screamed back. In a flash, he saw the face of the god he loves and hates. In another flash, he glimpsed other gods emerging from his belly.

Playing solitaire in the hemlock woods, Sarah Simpson stopped often to fondle the yellow beaded band at the nape of her neck. She plays with a stacked deck. She slipped an extra card in the pack so she can never win. Like the joker who made her think she could win against the apathy and the greed, that she could really band together with others and stop the blight. Staring at the cards, she read the destiny of the Giant. She surrendered her need to stop the destruction as she placed the extra card, a seven of diamonds, on the ace of hearts. As she did so, she doubled over as an arrow pierced her back. As she started to scream she realized that it is but an illusion—both the deathly pain and the resurrection from it. Gathering her cards, shoving them in her pockets, she slowly descended from the Giant, profoundly sad, utterly alone. She didn't see the frogs wave.

Luke Christmas was holding Gracie Creature Girl, an old cat found nearly starved to death. Ears terribly disfigured—disfigured both outside and deep inside—and rotten teeth. Her breath was nauseating. He dreaded her kisses. He tried not to breathe. He feared the frogs. They looked normal but their croaks were cracked. Surrounded by hypocrisy, Luke's head was filled with grenades. He thought of setting them off, attacking the false voices that promised to help the Giant but have abandoned him again. When he was visibly sick and it was the popular thing to do, they paid attention. But now they have moved on to other things. The last time he was at the Giant, he saw the expedition party from Mount Carmel Oil and Gas. He felt their boots tear Giant's flesh. He wrote a letter to the editor. The newspaper sent a reporter, declared Luke mistaken. Just some employees enjoying a short hike at lunch time. So he walked away from what he couldn't stop, haunted by knowing what evil a body can house.

With many months of intense labor, White Dove McNamara constructed a miniature watchtower, complete with spider web window. She used pliable willow wood to make the ramp. When finished, she carved initials on the east and west sides on the window. Tired, she did not sand the edges smooth. The next evening, about dusk, she returned to the tower, sandpaper in hand. A spider was trapped by an unnoticed splinter. Trying to rescue it, she pulled off one of its legs. She cannot get its shriek out of her brain. She rushed to the Giant, seeking refuge in his hemlock woods. A deep murmur of evil assaulted her. Holding her hands over her ears provided no protection. The Giant was pulling his blanket up. After descending, as she passed the trail legends at the park entrance, she looked toward the ponds. Flying across the face of the moon was an egret, blindfolded.

Chief Joseph struggled long and hard before he lost his faith. First New Haven and then Mount Carmel secretly baited pigeons, so their downtowns could be free of pigeon shit. Sitting on a bench, facing the New Haven Public Library, he saw how easily a photograph taken today would record an unnatural history. A false face. Or a more natural face? It hit him hard. Pigeons aren't native. Do we have to erase history to get a true face? He starts crying, lowering his head. Stuck in the slats of the bench, a feather, translucent gray, tipped with golden yellow. He longed for Daniel, longed to be sitting at his feet. For a brief moment, the greens were alive with history underfoot, waiting to be released. He never dreamed that the history underfoot might be equally unnatural. Blinking hard, he was disappointed that the feather was still stuck there, buffeted by wind. As he stood, facing the library, he felt the weight of all those volumes on his chest. He gave up his faith, giving over to resignation.

The last to lose faith was Frances Piccerillo. Watching her struggle so broke Daniel's heart. At the healing ceremony, she had full faith in the power of language, the cadence and rhythm of tongue. That gone, she slouched toward whatever will be born after Giant recovers himself. She slouched toward whatever will die when he is resurrected. Lying on her belly looking into the ponds at Giant's feet, Frances greeted a small white frog, red spots on its back, singing atop a pond lily pad. Leaning closer and closer to hear what it was singing, Frances lost balance, plunged into the pond. Rose amid the pond lilies. On their underside, written in red, *died for me not*. In yellow, *here before you, here long after you*. In green, *forked tongue*. Crashing through the water's surface, pond lilies and algae wound around her neck, Frances feared the language she loved so well had betrayed her. She ran home, eager to try to find solace in her beloved Yeats, resigned to wonder what will be the face of Sleeping Giant's second coming. A vision struck: Dragonfly sewing Giant's lips shut.

Just before dawn, on Friday October 13th, Daniel Red Hand Man holds his hand in front of the left side of his face to shield his eye from the rising sun. The Liberty Elm at his back casts dense shade. But looking up he sees the tips of every leaf is curled, browning. A bread truck rumbles by. A tiny frog hops out of the sewer, poised on the narrow iron grate. It jumps into the street, running into the park, racing to Daniel's bench. Claws red, extended, it salutes. Daniel's forked tongue darts from his open mouth. As he laps the air, he catches a dragonfly. Frog leaps onto Daniel's tongue. Dragonfly dances its wings; Frog croaks a song. As Daniel closes his mouth, Dragonfly darts out, tickles his chin as Frog leaps down.

Removing his hand, Daniel lets his eye squint with the rising sun. Dragonfly hovers over the bench while Frog rests in the grass at Daniel's feet. Frog's legs grow large, its thighs widening. With a convulsive leap, it jumps over the moon, barely visible in the brightening sky. Daniel stares as Frog squats atop the moon, spreading thunderbird wings. Dragonfly whispers in his ear. When he looks again to the sky, Dragonfly is trailing words from its needled torso. Deep gold words, with long teeth, and sharp tiny beaks.

Throwing his head back, he opens wide his mouth, catching fragments of falling words. As their sharp tiny feet prick his tongue, he smiles, stands, faces the library. As he looks up Orange Street, he wonders how many bodies lie under the concrete. As he starts home, he tries not to step on any cracks.

On his way home he walks by the Peabody Museum of Natural History.

The original museum burned down over a decade ago. In its place is a small, glass-walled building. They gave up trying to reconstruct the remaining fragments of bones. Hung pictures instead, easily able to gather them. The original museum was a very popular tourist attraction. It provided a service—have your photo taken with a reconstructed mastodon or archaeopteryx for a small fee. Hundreds of photos were donated. All they had to do was erase the human beings. School children still take tours to the museum but they quickly pass by the exhibits, hardly gasping.

Suddenly he turns and heads away from home, hastening toward what used to be the Edward Malley Company, the finest Department Store in New Haven's history. He remembers buying a Max Factor solid perfume—a golden frog with green jewel eyes. Lied. Said it was for his sister. He still carries it everywhere. He reaches into his pocket, pulls it out, letting it sit in the middle of his palm. Opening its mouth opens its entire top half. He can still smell the perfume even though it is small, dried, cracked. Pungent, old and spicy. He closes its mouth, holds it tight before returning it to his pocket darkness. Turning toward home, he scurries, head down.

He falters on his steps but, resolute, ascends, unlocks his front door. Removing his shirt, he takes golden frog out of his pocket, sets it in the sun on the dining room table, mouth wide open. He stuffs his pockets with old newspaper clippings—articles, warnings, promises. Bare-chested, he leaves his house, the front door wide open.

When he opens the garage, he sees his well-protected, ancient hybrid. Slides in, turns over the engine. After a few short gasps, it beats regular, like a drum. Daniel smiles. Without thinking, he heads out to West Haven, to what once was Savin Rock. Just shore and water and hills left. No amusement park. No restaurant. A huge billboard overlooks the shore, advertising the investment potential in developing the area. It hits him: Developed. Destroyed. Redeveloped. Redestroyed.

Unsettled, he heads back toward New Haven, down Grand Avenue. Thinks briefly about going over the Ferry Street Bridge and make his way to Nathan Hale Park. Instead goes straight down Grand Avenue, past the site of the old Pequot Theater. Takes a left, drives another block to the Fair Haven Cemetery. He loves one of its stones—the one for Eunice Hotchkiss, aged 4 years and 3 mos. A stone lamb rests atop the stone, keeping her warm. He kisses the lamb, holds his ear to its chest, expecting it to speak. Hearing no heart, he reluctantly pulls away, leaves. He stumbles over a fallen tombstone, broken in half. The break is not clean. Lots of small fragments litter the ground. He places the pieces together. He cannot read its face. Then it strikes him. Where the stone is broken—previously hidden, now exposed—carved with exquisite detail, an egret carrying a frog on its back. On frog's back, a tiny dragonfly, sewing. Shivering, he knows it's time. Crossing the Grand Avenue Bridge, he heads away from New Haven into East Haven along Quinnipiac Avenue. Past the Montowese Package Store next to the Momauguin Meat Market. Its deep, dangerous irony astounds him. Picking up speed, he heads toward Hamden, fearful and eager as he finds Route 10.

As he nears the base of the Giant, it is nearly dusk. As he cuts across the road that cuts across the ponds, words take visible shape in front of him, in back of him, atop him. "Trapped in a goddamned cartoon," he growls, hoping his foolish irony will ease his dread. Sitting under the trail legend, he waits for Mercy. She doesn't arrive.

A pigeon with a baby's face wings its way across the moon. Climbing out of a sewer near where the egret used to rise, a white frog, with red tongue, and black feet with human toes, carries a sign. THE TOMBSTONE OF THE ONE WHO WAS SAVED FROM LIFE. A dragonfly spins red thread, covers the words, then traces with its needled torso: SAVED FROM LIFE A SECOND TIME. AWAITS A THIRD RESURRECTION. Frog spits on the sign, its saliva slowly dissolving the words.

There's a barely perceptible shiver of a pond lily leaf. Underneath, hardly visible, a miniature human body with frog's eyes and needle teeth. Lying on its back, in its airy grave, breathing in the space above the water, it pokes the underside of pond lily's leaf, scribbling.

Daniel's hands ache. The pores of their skin tingle. Small, coarse hairs emerge. His fingers fall off, replaced by claws. His shoulders crack. Out of the cracks spread webbed bones. Thin black scales cover them. Yellow and green circles appear. His eyes redden. Winged words peck his head, unbuckle his belt. Daniel steps out of his falling pants, scattering paper clippings.

Naked except for his boots, Daniel whirls and twirls, spreading great wings. As he ascends, he covers the moon. Embracing his body, he tightens his wings. Whirling, he dives into the Giant, breaking him in two.

Huge stone feet emerge, words biting their ankles.

Huge stone feet emerge, their heavy echo receding.

Huge stone feet emerge, carving steps into the returning world.

Daniel Thunderbird Man watches the earth transform. Houses collapse. Towns explode. New Haven harbor is erased. As the roads disappear, the ponds at giant's feet are reunited. The strange tribe in giant's belly emerges. Grace Yellowbird Faith wraps Daniel in her now-finished blanket. The air is spicy sweet with hemlock. Turning, they return to giant's closing belly. Whole again, giant closes himself, a blightless blanket covering his body. Deep within, water rushing. Daniel and Mercy sit together under a mountain laurel whose veins do not bleed.

Emerging, far, far in the distance, the beginnings of a shadowy shape.

www.ingramcontent.com/pod-product-compliance
Lightning Source LLC
Chambersburg PA
CBHW020011140726
47904CB00018B/2215